THE SECRET OF ABNEY HALL

THE SECRET OF ABNEY HALL

SUSAN BROWNRIGG

Fox & Ink Books

The Secret of Abney Hall is a Fox & Ink Books book

First published in Great Britain in 2026 by
Fox & Ink Books
University of Lancashire
Preston, PR1 2HE, UK

978-1-917894-30-2

1 3 5 7 9 10 8 6 4 2

Set in Kingfisher by Becky Chilcott.

A CIP catalogue record for this book is available from the British Library.

Printed and bound in Great Britain by Clays Ltd, Elcograf S.p.A.

For Rachel

ONE

Wednesday 15th December, 1926

IT'S A DIFFERENT SET OF REPORTERS, A DIFFERENT NAME THEY'RE shouting, but it's all unbearably familiar. The Hydro hotel is mobbed. Flashlamps spark like fireworks. This is madness!

'Are you all right, Jane?' Dr Pearce asks, his brow as wrinkled as any bloodhound's. He tries to take my hand. I push it away.

'Yes,' I lie, head down as we force our way through the crowd. Trying to keep up with Jim and Madge Watts. My employers.

Concentrate on breathing. *One*... *Two*... *Three*... It's a method I've used many times with anxious patients. Fingers grasp at my shoulders trying to get my attention. They haven't a clue who I am. Or at least, who I'm claiming to be.

The rush of noise falls away as I reach the safety of the lobby. I sense green leafy palms and polished wood, gleaming glass and stiff postures. The guests are going about their business, but there's an artificiality to the scene. Like everyone's putting on an act. Though they are supposedly reading a book or talking to a friend, their eyes dart repeatedly over to one woman who's sitting on a leather settee next to a particularly vigorous aspidistra.

Agatha Christie.

She's as described in the newspapers. An attractive woman, mid-thirties, a fashionable shingled bob. But her hair's fairer, no longer red streaked with grey; I found my first a few weeks ago and yanked the bugger out.

The family resemblance is obvious. Madge Watts squeezes her younger sister's arm. 'I've been so worried about you.'

Agatha's face remains blank as she fusses with the strings of pearls around her neck. Does she really not recognise her?

'It's me. Punkie.' Madge glances anxiously at Dr Pearce.

But Agatha is focused on the other side of the room.

I realise then that her husband, Colonel Christie, is here too, sunken in one of the armchairs.

Turning my head back, I frown. We're being watched by a man near the stairs. Shaggy hair, an ill-fitting crumpled suit. Pencil behind his ear. Notebook in one hand, cigarette in the other. His editor must've forked out for a room in the hope of an exclusive. He notices me looking and winks. You're not why he's here, I remind myself, but I angle my face away all the same.

Leaning closer to Agatha, the inspector says softly, 'Mrs Christie, your sister and brother-in-law have come to take you home.'

'To South Africa?' she asks.

'No, Agatha. To Abney Hall,' replies Jim.

She doesn't react.

Dr Pearce slides forwards; we are like chess pieces on a board. 'I don't know if you remember me. I'm your sister's family physician. And this is Miss Jane Goodbetter. She's a nurse.'

Agatha's tongue runs along her top lip, as though preparing to speak, then disappears. Silent again. Was she about to say she was one too? How much memory has she lost? Or could she really be faking her amnesia?

'I cared for your mother, in her final days.' This is true, but I mainly offer this information to provoke a response.

Her pupils dilate. A sign of stress? Clara Miller died after a nasty bout of bronchitis, and though Madge was at her bedside, Agatha couldn't make it in time. My duties were completed by the time she arrived, so I never met her.

'And for my father before his passing, too,' adds Jim. 'Nurse Goodbetter is a godsend.'

'A real comfort to us all,' his wife concurs. 'You couldn't be in better hands.'

Agatha raises her eyebrows slightly. I suspect she prefers to reach her own conclusion about me. But if she has any questions, she's keeping them bundled inside that brain of hers.

I wait while Madge speaks to Agatha and Archie in the corridor.

When they return, the police inspector crosses to us, checks his watch. 'Time to make a move.'

Agatha slips on her fur-trimmed coat. Tugging the brim of her cloche hat lower as though it can shield her from scrutiny. A decoy couple are sent out the front, while we all sneak from the side entrance like rats.

The planned quiet escape soon turns farcical. Reporters and photographers are on our trail all the way to Harrogate railway station, choking us like a cloud of dust.

'We'll give them the slip. Don't worry,' says the inspector, fancying himself a plotter as good as any mystery writer. He tells us he's planned a switch at Leeds which will see us divert to Manchester Victoria. 'They'll not be expecting that!'

I'm not convinced.

The press have been camped out at the estate gates for over a week and will be awaiting our arrival.

Agatha doesn't seem perturbed as Dr Pearce and I follow the others onto the platform. She shows no hesitation, even chatting merrily to her sister, though I can't make out what she's saying. A photographer catches the moment on film. I look back; the colonel and Jim haven't noticed. They struggle to keep up, lumbered with Agatha's suitcases. She has acquired a lot of luggage during her stay, it seems. The inspector has arranged for a private carriage for the four of them. We're in the next one along.

'So, Jane, what are your first impressions of Mrs Christie?' asks Dr Pearce.

'She seems quite bewildered.'

'Hmm. Yes, there's something quite owlish about those eyes of hers. A Tawny, perhaps.'

Our carriage door slides open before I can reply. Colonel Archibald 'Archie' Christie asks to address us. For a moment I think he's going to remain standing, but the rocking of the train makes that difficult. He sits next to me, facing Dr Pearce. I shunt myself nearer to the window.

'It is imperative that you make your assessment as quickly as possible, Doctor. When you confirm my wife's condition, we will finally get these hounds off our backs.'

'I understand, Colonel,' Dr Pearce replies. 'I am hopeful that

Mrs Christie will show signs of improvement once in a familiar setting.' His tone is, as always, measured; he rarely loses his head.

Archie grunts. 'Let's hope so.' He's back on his feet. A difficult, angry man, I think to myself. Has he always been that way?

Of course the state of the Christies' marriage has been exposed to all and sundry. His affair with Miss Nancy Neele was splashed over the national's front pages and savoured over tea at Lyons Corner Houses across the country. One of the most curious aspects of Mrs Christie's disappearance is that she signed into the Hydro under the same surname as her husband's mistress. Was that a sign of her disturbed mind? Or a cynical tactic to embarrass the pair?

I gaze out of the window as town gives way to fields of sheep. I'm guilty of having been just as fascinated with the Christie case as anyone else. It had all the elements of a good mystery: an abandoned motor car, her fur coat and old driving licence left on the seat.

Half the country had a theory as to what happened to Mrs Christie: accident, suicide or foul play – with most sizing the colonel for the noose.

When the police dredged the nearby Silent Pool many thought they'd find her body, but in a plot twist – Agatha's found safe and well in a Yorkshire spa town. Apparently, she's been there several days, dining, dancing and shopping.

I suppose it's no wonder the press and public are dubious about her illness. Could her disappearance have really been a hoax – a publicity stunt for her new book?

We alight at Manchester to hordes of press and bystanders. It's even worse than Harrogate.

At the platform barrier a male voice calls out, 'Why are you pretending, Mrs Christie?'

I turn as Archie shoves the reporter back. Could be the one from the Hydro? I'm not sure.

'My wife is very sick!'

He appears genuinely protective of her and yet his actions have been cruel and selfish. His apparent consideration for his wife now is not only too late, but risks confusing her further.

One of the photographers breaks free from the barrier. He lifts his camera and I automatically shield my face as the flash goes off. Was I quick enough? God, I hope so.

Outside, we separate again. The Wattses urge the Christies into their Wolseley, and I get into Dr Pearce's motor car for the ten-mile drive to Cheadle. I relax slightly as he manoeuvres us away from the station, but I am wrong to do so. Our little convoy is being pursued.

I grip my knees as we swerve along the roads of the city centre. Dr Pearce curses, then apologises, as an old blue motor car cuts between us and the green Wolseley. A photographer leans out of the passenger side, camera outstretched. It's the one who broke through the barrier. I slide down in my seat.

'Sorry, Jane,' Dr Pearce says, as he mangles the gears trying to stay in sight of the others.

This would almost be exciting if my stomach wasn't swilling about so. I hope I'm not going to vomit. I daren't open my mouth to reply.

The press are determined to get to the truth of Agatha's disappearance. I only pray in seeking answers they don't start to ask questions about me.

↔

At last, we've reached Abney. Dr Pearce brings his motor car to a temporary halt behind the Wattses' Wolseley while the lodge gates are opened. Someone's hung up a 'Trespassers Will Be Prosecuted' sign. Dozens more men lie in wait around the estate entrance. I cup my face so I can't be seen.

Padlocked in, we drive past the lake and swing right. There, at last, is the house itself . . . all mullioned windows and gothic grandeur. Sanctuary.

Pulling to a final stop, Dr Pearce hops out and unstraps my belongings. Agatha will be staying for a month at least, and I will be living in. I'm to ensure she takes her medicines as prescribed and must report any signs of her condition worsening to Mrs Watts. Short assignments suit me best, when I can be almost anonymous. I shouldn't risk returning to Abney, yet I feel a connection to Agatha. Her exposure in the press reminds me of my own plight. Besides, the Wattses are a good family and the pay is excellent. I just hope I don't come to regret my decision.

I watch as Madge hooks her arm through her sister's. Archie hovers, unsettled in someone else's realm, while Jim asks the hired chauffeur to bring in their luggage. It's quiet here, though the reporters' shouting still echoes in my mind. We traipse morosely through the arched stone entrance into the vestibule. Our heels pattering on the blue and terracotta tiled floor as we pass beyond the ornate wooden doors into the main entrance hall.

How church-like this family home is. Gargoyles outside, stained glass inside.

The Wattses' four dogs bark and sniff our shoes, their tails batting furiously against our legs. The smallest, a springer spaniel pup, tries to sneak past us but Jim catches it by the scruff.

Agatha pats one of the three terriers. 'Just like Peter,' she says, as the pets scurry away down the long corridor. The grandfather clock ticks softly as Patience, the parlourmaid, takes our coats, hats and gloves. She's the only domestic to insist on still wearing the lace trimmed mob cap from Jim's parents' heyday. No one knows her exact age, and they wouldn't dream of asking it. My best bet is she's nearing seventy.

Jim sweeps up the newspapers from the hallstand and hands them to Patience. 'Dispose of these, please.'

He won't want Agatha reading them.

Patience dips into a shallow curtsey, her knees cracking.

It's hard to pinpoint, but a subtle change has come over Abney since my previous stay. I suppose that's only to be expected. After Mr Watts senior's death in June, and his beloved wife, Anne, suddenly last month, the estate has passed down to Jim and Madge. There's a glass vase I don't recognise, and the umbrella stand is in a different position. I don't know how the younger Wattses will fit in all their possessions. Abney won't take easily to attempts to modernise her, she's too firmly Victorian with her shadowy corridors and gloomy tapestries. Beautiful fireplaces, though. I hope the one in my room has been lit; I am quite chilled.

'Let's go into my study,' says Jim, turning left. I get the impression there's serious business to discuss.

Archie looks even more uncomfortable. Madge and I reposition the chairs so they are in a subtle semi-circle facing Jim's desk. We sit, like children before the headmaster. The room smells of beeswax polish and hyacinths. There's a half-filled decanter and glasses on a side table. I could do with a tot to warm me up.

Agatha fiddles with her handbag, sliding the fashionable zip back and to. I open my rather scuffed black clutch bag, taking out my notebook and pencil.

Dr Pearce says, 'I understand you are having issues with your memory, Mrs Christie?'

'My wife has lost three years,' Archie cuts in.

I make a quick note of his reply, keeping my gaze on both men. A slight twitch at the corner of the doctor's mouth, but he switches tack and looks at him aslant.

'But she knows who you are?'

'Yes.'

'You said she thought you were Monty at first,' Madge amends, hands resting on her tweed skirt. 'Our brother. And of course she knows me.'

Agatha stares at the bookshelf behind her brother-in-law. She gives the impression of being completely oblivious to the conversation, but I suspect she's listening.

'But she has forgotten Rosalind.' Archie's eyes remain locked on the doctor. 'Our daughter.'

'I see,' says Dr Pearce, tapping two fingers against his collar bone. 'Is your daughter at Abney?'

Archie flushes. 'No. I thought it best that Teddy – that's our nickname for her – stay with my mother until . . .'

'Quite.'

I study Agatha's face for some kind of reaction. Still nothing.

'Well, I am happy to sign a brief statement about your wife's condition for now.' Dr Pearce lifts his leather bag and places it on the desk.

'Yes. Yes. As soon as possible, please, or we will never get rid of the press.'

'A most distressing situation for everyone.' He turns to Agatha. 'I advise complete bed rest for the next few days.'

'I can't be cooped up in my room,' her tone agitated.

'You must have peace and quiet,' he insists.

'Yes, Doctor,' replies Madge.

Agatha's eyes drop to her lap.

'Now,' continues Dr Pearce. 'Your sister tells me you have been suffering from neuralgia causing headaches and insomnia. I have a sedative here that will help.' He unclips the bag and takes out a bottle of Mellotal sleeping powder. I recommend half a teaspoon in water, Nurse.'

'No,' Agatha blurts. 'I don't want to be lost in a fog. I need to have my wits about me.'

'You have been under considerable mental tension. This will ease your nerves,' he replies, passing me the medicine.

I smile to reassure her.

'Doctor knows best,' agrees Madge.

From my experience that is not always the case, but I know better than to say so, even to Dr Pearce.

TWO

GETTING TO KNOW A PATIENT IS LIKE TRYING TO work out a puzzle – a mystery, even. Placing my suitcase onto my bed, I start to unpack. Buried at the bottom are Dr Pearce's binoculars. He's an avid birdwatcher and suggested I may find them useful during my stay at Abney.

By good fortune I have a corner room; raising the lenses I trace the driveway. Reporters and photographers are clustered on the other side of the gates. I frown and close the heavy curtains. Next, I take out Dr Pearce's copy of *The Murder of Roger Ackroyd*. There was mischief twinkling in his eyes when he loaned it to me. 'Discussing her writing might be another way to break down any barriers I suspect she'll put up.' It's a good suggestion. Agatha will require some gentle coaxing to start talking, especially to a stranger. But there's something about a uniform that makes people obedient.

I strip to my girdle, hang up the suit I travelled in, and slip on my uniform. Automatically, my posture alters, shoulders back, head high. After securing my nurse's cap, I wind my fob watch, then put aside my worn blouse for handwashing later.

Agatha's room adjoins mine. I knock gently on her door.

No answer. Easing it open, I peer round. She's fast asleep. Slipping inside, I notice a framed photograph of her daughter on the bedside cabinet. Did she have it with her at Harrogate? Yet Archie said she doesn't know who Rosalind is.

The little drawer is partially open. I spy a bottle of laudanum. A painkiller but it is also prescribed as a sedative. I'd better tell Dr Pearce later, but for now I follow his instructions and leave the Mellotal sleeping powder beside the photograph.

I head downstairs, past the painting of the crusader on horseback. I've been invited to join the family for something to eat.

At the bottom I pat the stuffed lion on its head, as always. He looks more moth-eaten than on my last visit here. The hall still has a feel of an eccentric castle, with the suit of armour on the other side of the staircase. The long corridor is lined with paintings, tapestries, taxidermy and Italian marble busts.

An electric servants' bell indicator board on the wall opposite the main staircase is the only modern touch. It always reminds me of the one we used at the asylum.

'That man is a plague,' Archie says as I go to enter the drawing room. Hesitating from going further, I tell myself that I'm not eavesdropping but rather just being polite. 'Chap's lucky I didn't knock his block off. Pouncing on us like that at the station. I'd like to wring his scrawny neck.'

'That's not advisable,' says Jim.

'Well, do something! Get them all turfed off.'

'Sorry, Archie. The inspector said there's nothing they can do as long as they stay the other side of the gate. It's public land.'

Archie huffs.

'You know, you don't have to stay,' Madge adds. 'I can take care of Agatha, and we have Nurse Goodbetter now too.'

'I'm not going anywhere. Not until I have a proper explanation for my wife's behaviour. I want a specialist brought in.'

They all go quiet. I take a deep breath before going in. It's like stepping into a den of bad-tempered bears, only this cage has been decorated with green silk wallpaper complete with an inscription at almost ceiling height. I read some of the words. *Wouldst have a friend.* I imagine Agatha feels very alone right now. In need of a friend.

'Tea, Nurse?' Patience asks while I help myself to sandwiches and cake. I do not appreciate how famished I am until I take my first bite, then peer between the pieces of bread. Salmon. The proper stuff, not paste. The family is also tucking in with gusto, to my amazement. The stress of the last few days hasn't affected their appetites.

The drawing room always makes me think of Midas, as though the king has touched every door and ceiling pendant and turned it to gold. The room is cluttered with more dark furniture and ornately framed portraits – one so thick and gilded that I'm surprised the weight hasn't pulled it off the wall. There are candlesticks, porcelain vases and plants on every surface. A fire blazes in the hearth.

'Do you fancy a game of bridge?' Madge asks once we've all eaten in silence, smiling hopefully at me, as Patience clears away the tea things. 'I thought we could make a four?'

I haven't a clue how to play. Snap's more my level.

'I'm going outside for some air,' snorts Archie.

'What a marvellous idea.' I practically jump to my feet. This might be my main opportunity to speak to him alone. Given the suddenness of his temper, I worry he could flit from the house at any moment. I need to tease from him how he really feels about his wife's illness.

Annoyance flashes across his face. 'Very good.'

We collect our coats and follow the line of the house to the left. I expect him to go down the stone steps onto the lawn where there are iron benches dotted about, or to follow the path down to Ten Penny Bridge and the waterfall. Instead, Archie turns right heading down the slope to the hidden tunnel running under the driveway to the lake.

It's sheltered from the bitter wind and curious eyes. He leans against the stone wall and takes out a cigarette and puts it in his holder. Used to grumpy patients, I know better than to push too soon for conversation. I let the silence build while he pats his pocket for his lighter. Good manners will eventually prompt him to fill the void.

He strikes the flint.

'How long have you been a nurse?'

I give my stock answer. 'Six years.'

'My wife was a VAD during the war. She said you professional nurses always looked down your noses at the volunteers.'

I've no desire to talk about war hospitals. But I need to keep him talking. I run my hand over the mossy wall. 'Your wife must have had a strong stomach. My role is mainly emptying bedpans and mopping brows.'

'Agatha did her fair share of scrubbing floors too, at first.' He blows out a plume of smoke.

'She enjoyed the work?'

'For a while. The dispensary suited her better, but she liked working with the other nurses. She found the doctors . . . difficult.'

I nod. Push down memories. Switch direction. 'I imagine Christmas at Abney is rather special.'

He holds my gaze. I try to hide my discomfort. He's testing me. Does he suspect I know he usually spends Christmas with his mother while Agatha came here with her mother and Rosalind?

'Christmas is for children.'

The sound of rumbling tyres passes over our heads.

Archie looks vexed. 'Who is this, now?'

We exit the tunnel in time to see a large woman in a white polka dot dress with matching cape, getting out of a prewar red Packard. Clamping an oversized red hat to her jet-black bob with one hand, a carpet bag in the other, she stomps to the front door and marches on through.

'Oh God. It's that dreadful Cherry woman,' groans Archie as we move towards the house.

The Wattses come out into the corridor as we discard our coats in the vestibule.

Mrs Cherry hollers over the sound of the barking dogs. 'Madge, darling. I had a right tussle with your gardener trying to convince him to unlock the gates and let me in.'

'Delia, dear. Were we expecting you?' Madge looks flustered.

'Apparently not. How was Harrogate?'

Madge opens her mouth to reply.

'You can tell me all about it later,' interrupts Mrs Cherry. 'We have more pressing matters to discuss first.'

Archie huffs. 'Actually, Jim, could I have a private word with you?' They slope off into his study together. Can't say as I blame them.

I thrust out my hand. 'I don't believe we've been introduced. I'm Jane Goodbetter.'

Mrs Cherry lets it hang there. I squirm realising there's a green streak from the tunnel on my skin. She casts her eyes over my uniform. I've been found wanting.

She scowls at Madge. 'Well, are you going to offer me a sherry or leave me standing here like a lamppost?'

'Oh. Of course, Delia. Do please come through.' She ushers the woman into the drawing room.

I should let the two women have their privacy, but if they're going to discuss Agatha, I might learn something useful – and I must confess I'm curious what's brought this overbearing woman to Abney. Rubbing my hands together as though chilled, I hold my head high and cross to the fireplace. Fortunately, they are too caught up in their own conversation to notice me holding my palms over the flames.

'It's the church hall roof, darling.'

Puzzled, I pick up one of the Christmas cards from the white marble mantlepiece and pretend to read the message inside, but really, I'm watching their reflections in the tall, gilded mirror.

'Vicar says the rain's coming through in bucketfuls. Literally.' She drops the bag beside the settee and rearranges the cushions, before sitting.

'Again?'

'Mmm. He's trying to find a roofer.'

'Have you suggested Gil?'

'Of course. But I think Reverend Whittle is hoping to find someone cheaper.' She rolls her eyes. 'Anyway, we obviously can't continue rehearsals there until it's fixed.'

'Clearly.'

Rehearsals?

'I'm glad you agree. You are a dear.' She blows a kiss. 'I knew Abney would be perfect.'

'Oh. You mean have the rehearsals here?'

My expression changes from confusion to disapproval. Surely Madge will refuse.

'You have the space.' Mrs Cherry sweeps an arm out dramatically. 'And the show is creeping up on us. Just three weeks before dress!'

'Actually, Delia, we have Agatha and Archie staying with us at the moment.'

Exactly.

'But not for much longer, surely. Besides, we'll make a pleasant distraction for you from all that unfortunate business.'

'I don't know—'

'Nonsense.' She claps her hands together. 'It's decided.'

My eyes widen in horror.

'I should really speak to Jim.'

Yes, you should. I pick up a pretty Chinese vase in jade green with white embossed flowers on it.

'I'd be careful with that, Nurse,' calls Mrs Cherry sharply. 'Very valuable piece. Don't want it coming out of your wages.'

I wince and gently reposition it.

'You *do* want your play to go ahead, don't you, Madge?'

'Of course.'

I know the battle is lost.

'Good, because we've a lot of catching up to do. The script still needs work and I've no idea how we're going to make the end of Act One work.' She gets to her feet again. 'Now, show me to your telephone. No point wasting more time, we've already lost half a day. I'll get the gang to come over straight away.'

I wander over to the window and look out onto the grounds. A woman like that has no trouble getting through padlocked gates. I can picture her haranguing poor Thomas, the gardener, or even getting out some bolt cutters and doing it herself. I knew ward sisters just like her. They didn't care who they rubbed up the wrong way if it meant they got the job done.

A figure zigzags across the lawn. Their head is strangely dark, and imp-like. I strain to see better, then realise they are wearing something over it. A balaclava.

I dash into the corridor and burst into the study. 'Mr Watts. Quick. There's someone in the grounds.'

His brow furrows. 'Wait here.'

Naturally I do no such thing, even with Mrs Cherry and Madge calling after me wanting to know what all the fuss is about. There's no time to answer. Jim bounds across the grass as the intruder scrambles over the boundary wall. I dash down the entrance steps and round the corner towards the terrace.

Jim has given up the chase and is jogging back towards the house. Will he telephone the police? I chew the inside of my lip.

Heading back too, I see Mrs Cherry and Madge are now in the doorway clucking like hens, muttering about those damn reporters. Something catches my eye above. Movement. It's Agatha. She's standing at her bedroom window. I should go and speak to her.

When I reach her room, she is still at the window. Her gaze remains fixed outside.

'He got away,' she says.

'Yes, but there's no need for you to worry.' I start straightening her bed sheets. Hospital corners.

'You don't know that.' She turns and stares at me. 'What's your name, again?'

'Nurse Goodbetter. Jane.' I pick up a pillow and plump it up.

'Oh yes. I remember. I suppose they want you to spy on me?'

'Monitor you.'

'I know the difference.'

I put the pillow down. 'Of course you do.'

She nods. 'Where's my husband?'

'Talking to Mr Watts.'

'But you were with him, earlier.'

So, she's been looking out of the window for some time. 'You were spying on me.'

Agatha gives a sharp laugh. 'Not on you. I don't care about you.' She rubs at her temples.

'Do you have a headache?'

'All the time.'

'For how long?'

She shrugs. 'Months?'

'You should have something to drink. Food too.'

'I must watch my figure.'

I raise an eyebrow, wishing I had a figure as trim as hers. 'Diet is key to your recovery.'

'Is that what Dr Pearce says?'

'It's what I say.'

She wrinkles her nose. 'Are you really a nurse?'

'Yes.' Doesn't she believe me? I hope this isn't a sign of paranoia.

'What is there to eat?'

'We could go to the kitchen and see.'

'Dr Pearce says I must stay in my room.'

'Dr Pearce isn't here.'

Her face lights up. 'I could murder a chicken leg or a chunk of ham.'

Without discussion we both head for the backstairs. There's something secretive about our hunt for food. Below stairs is stark and workmanlike, brick walls and ceilings. The smell of carbolic soap lingers in the air, but sadly no aroma of cooking. Cook must be in her room working on menus or orders for Abney's suppliers.

A house like this would once have had a whole team of servants, all starched aprons and deference. Now, other than Patience and Mrs Worcester who live in, Mr and Mrs Watts make do with dailies, though there's plenty of evidence of their past presence in the kitchen. Copper pans and jelly moulds. Welsh dressers stacked with blue and white. We go into the adjoining larder. It is brimming with jars and tins.

'When I came here as a little girl, at Christmas the storeroom was always open. We could help ourselves to chocolates and salted almonds whenever we liked,' says Agatha, peering under a dish on the cold slab. A wedge of crumbly Cheshire cheese. She pairs it with a jar of homemade pickled walnuts from the windowsill. I find the remnants of a loaf, the freshly baked smell lingering on its crust. We carry her loot to the long wooden table in the servant's hall. After fetching her a knife and plate, I watch Agatha work her way through the bread and cheese; she pulls out a soft brown walnut, popping it into her mouth like Little Jack Horner.

'You were right,' she says once her hunger is sated. 'I feel better for having eaten.'

'Good.'

'Goodbetter. Is that a real name? It sounds made up. Like in a book.'

'Like Mrs Cherry,' I prompt.

'Oh her. Yes, she does seem terribly phoney . . . doesn't she? But Punkie says she's exactly what she seems.'

'Which is?'

'A play producer. Only am-dram, for the MADS – that's the Manchester Amateur Dramatic Society. I don't mean to be a snob; I'm just stating a fact.'

'I didn't know your sister was a writer too.'

'Didn't you? Oh yes, the whole family has the disease. My father wrote bits and pieces, and my mother would make up brilliant stories for me when I was little.' She picks at some crumbs of cheese. 'Even poor old Monty has given it a go. I'm astonished my sister hasn't told you she was published first. Short stories in *Vanity Fair*. She's usually quick to tell everyone she's the reason

I'm an author. That she challenged me to pen a detective novel. We are awfully competitive. I'd love to have one of my books adapted for the stage, or even a film!'

'Are you writing anything at the moment?'

She sniffs. 'Trying. Perhaps I should put a nurse in my next one.'

I ignore that. 'Your husband told me you were a nurse during the war.'

'So you *were* talking about me.' She raises her chin. 'What else did he say?'

'Does it matter?'

She looks at me like I'm stupid. 'I thought you were supposed to be looking after me. Doesn't that mean you should be on my side?'

'Are you and your husband on different sides?'

She scoffs. 'Talking to you is like playing a game of tennis. If I was to put you in my book the readers wouldn't like you.'

'Ouch.'

She grins. 'A point for me.'

The door flies open. 'You're supposed to be in bed!' exclaims Madge. 'I've been all over the house trying to find you.'

'Poor Punkie, Abney is such a rabbit warren.'

'We didn't mean to worry you,' I add, hoping to mollify her.

Agatha offers the jar like a peace offering. 'Walnut?'

THREE

MADGE PICKS UP A CLOTH AND SWEEPS CRUMBS FROM THE table. 'Honestly, Agatha. Haven't we got enough on our plate?'

Agatha smiles as she looks down at hers, but she holds back from making a joke.

'Poor Jack's holding the fort with the vicar while I've been tearing up and down the stairs trying to find *you*.'

I ignore the disappointed look Madge is giving me.

'Why didn't you tell me Jack's home?' Agatha hurries out.

I must admit, I have a fondness for her nephew myself. His youth and energy always lift everyone's mood, and he has a diplomatic nature that is much welcome in a family with such conflicting personalities.

Madge drops onto Agatha's vacated chair. Her face looks drained. The ten years difference in age more evident than ever.

'I didn't mean to be sharp with Agatha. I've just been so worried about her.' She swallows. 'I always seem to fall back into the role of bossy older sister with her. I wish I could be calmer and patient, like you.'

I screw the lid onto the jar. 'I'm sure Agatha understands you want to protect her, perhaps . . .' I stop myself.

'Please, continue.'

'While I agree that Agatha needs seclusion, I think spending some time with her family and friends at Abney will aid her recovery. She could even take some gentle exercise in the grounds. I'd be with her, and you could concentrate on your play.'

'That sounds very sensible advice.' Madge looks relieved. 'Thank you, Nurse.'

We snake up the backstairs and catch up with Agatha near the drawing room. The vicar's sitting on the leather settee next to Jack as we enter. He's a thin, bald man with ginger eyebrows that give him a permanently outraged look.

'Ah, here's my mother,' says Jack, jumping up to greet us, his knees banging against the coffee table almost toppling Reverend Whittle's glass.

There's an aroma that reminds me of dried fruit.

Jack's face is still cherub-like, though he's now, what? Twenty-three? He brushes his hand through his blond hair, the colour and gesture reminding me of his father, as he makes swift introductions. I notice Reverend Whittle's cheeks are rosy as he stands, rather belatedly. How many sherries must Jack have plied him with?

Reverend Whittle clasps his hands around Agatha's as he babbles. 'St Mary's has remembered you in our prayers every day since we heard of your unfortunate accident.'

She twists her hand free, murmuring her thanks while glancing at the windows as though she'd like to climb out of them.

'Very kind,' says Madge.

She and Agatha perch together on the matching settee opposite. I sit next to them, but the springs seem to have gone at my end, and no matter how I position myself it's like being on a blancmange.

'Reverend Whittle has another matter he wishes to discuss,' says Jack as the men sit down again.

'Indeed?' Madge puts the stopper back in the decanter.

The vicar nods fervently. 'I imagine Mrs Cherry has told you that the church hall roof needs another repair. Your family has been such a great supporter of St Mary's over the years . . .' His eyebrows lift, waiting for her to take the bait.

Agatha whispers to me. 'Oh dear. It seems all those prayers come with a price tag.'

There's a sharp rap on the door and without waiting for a 'come in' Mrs Cherry strides into the room. 'That's that sorted. The MADS will be here within the hour. Oh! Vicar, I didn't notice you there,' she says as he and Jack stand. 'You'll be relieved to hear that I've found alternative arrangements for rehearsals.' She raises her arms to indicate Abney Hall. 'Isn't it wonderful news?' The man can't get so much as a breath in. 'We'll soon be back on track.'

The men sit down again.

Agatha looks surprised and mouths 'Here?' to her sister.

'What about using the annexe?' I whisper.

'Buckley Chapel?' Madge brightens at my suggestion. 'Yes, that would be better.' Her shoulders relax. 'I'll ask Patience to get it ready.' She bobs out.

The annexe is a bit of a curio. Made up of an ensemble of

old buildings. The most interesting part is the old chapel, an ancestral stone and lime building from Rochdale. Jim's father had it dismantled stone by stone and rebuilt in Abney's grounds.

Somehow, Mrs Cherry is close enough to pour herself a drink.

Mrs Cherry wafts a hand at me. I give up my seat. She addresses Agatha. 'Your sister tells me there hasn't been a stage adaptation made of any of your stories yet.' She takes a sip, grimaces, and immediately puts down the glass. 'I don't have any siblings. I was a late surprise to my parents, but I do understand rivalry. Did you see *The Claimant*? The reviews were quite kind, so disappointing for Madge that it barely survived the week. Still, that's the theatre for you! So many shows are a flash in the pan.'

I try to keep my face blank. Agatha's suggests she'd like to clout Mrs Cherry with the decanter. Heavy crystal would make a good dent in her skull, but I'm not sure it would stop her incessant opining.

'What's the play about?' I ask.

'It's a ghost story set in an antiquated mansion house,' Mrs Cherry enthuses.

Based on Abney, I bet. I've heard the servants say the place is haunted.

'The owner was an eccentric old widower who died leaving his estate to some distant relatives,' continues Mrs Cherry. 'They must spend the whole night there in order to inherit. You know the sort of thing . . . Furniture that moves in the night including a suit of armour; doors that were open suddenly locked. Hokum but the audience will love it.' She unclips her carpet bag and pulls out a wad of paper – the scripts, I presume – Jack divvies them out.

'Do you enjoy the theatre, Nurse?' asks Reverend Whittle.

'I haven't seen much.' I look down at mine. *When I Grow Rich.* A supernatural thriller in three acts. Only a small cast. Mrs Cherry has a part as well as being director/producer. Oh! and Madge is playing the ghost bride!

'I'll put you on the guest list for opening night,' says Mrs Cherry.

'Thank you, but my duties—'

'Nonsense. I'll square it with Madge.'

'Square what with me?' asks Madge, re-entering the room.

'Mrs Cherry was just inviting Nurse Goodbetter to our premiere,' explains Jack.

'Premiere! You make it sound very grand,' says Madge blushing. 'It's St Mary's Church Hall not the Shaftesbury.'

And I bet the Shaftesbury doesn't have a leaky roof.

'Now, Vicar,' Mrs Cherry swivels. 'I was hoping to persuade you to take over as the doctor.'

'Impossible at this time of year. Anyway, isn't that Paul's role?'

'That was the original plan, but—'

'I could do it,' Jack interjects.

Agatha's eyes widen.

'Excellent,' says Madge.

Mrs Cherry opens her mouth. Closes it again. I bet that doesn't happen often.

'Aren't you rather young for the part?' questions Reverend Whittle.

'We'll age him up. A bit of talcum powder in his hair. Easy,' says Madge.

Mrs Cherry frowns. 'I was hoping Jack would be our prompt. Agatha, do you fancy stepping in?'

'I'm supposed to stay in my room.'

Madge glances at me then says. 'If you'd like to help, Agatha, that would be lovely.'

Agatha beams – and Madge looks much happier too.

I suppose that means I'll have to watch rehearsals too.

'Time I was going,' says the vicar, picking up his jacket.

Madge walks him out.

When she returns, Mrs Cherry suggests a quick read-through of Act One. 'I want to see how those changes you made play out,' she tells her friend.

Madge nods her approval.

'Do you mind if I move about a bit?' asks Jack. 'I find it helps me get a feel for the character.'

Mrs Cherry's eyebrows rise. 'We don't normally—'

'What a good idea,' says Madge.

Jack moves the coffee table aside. I take his place on the settee.

'So Jack, you'll read Dr Tremayne, I'll be the housekeeper, of course, Madge you'll read the ghost bride and the solicitor, please. Which leaves Alice and Tom.' Mrs Cherry points at Agatha then me. 'Excellent.'

We race through the first scenes involving Alice and Tom arriving at a spooky mansion house. Then move onto a later one involving the doctor.

Fortunately we're not expected to act – just read the words plainly, though Jack hams up the role of the doctor, clearly enjoying himself. I must admit I'm finding it rather fun too.

'Good grief!' he bellows, hand to his forehead. 'You *gave* me an awful fright!' He takes three steps to the left, eyes on his shoes, as though counting. 'What are . . .' His head jerks up. 'What are you doing hiding *in* that cupboard?'

'I'm waiting for the ghost bride, of course,' reads Agatha. 'Haven't you noticed? She always makes an appearance at twelve exactly.'

'Dong!' says Madge. 'Dong, dong, dong, et cetera.'

'You can't say "et cetera". You have to do all twelve.'

Madge sighs. 'Really, Delia?' She dongs as instructed, just as the grandfather clock in the long corridor joins in. She pauses and is about to start again when another long case clock commences chiming. 'Oh! This is ridiculous.'

'We are rather overrun with clocks at Abney,' says Agatha, smiling at last. 'Well with everything, to be frank.'

Mrs Cherry taps her script.

Jack swivels on his heels. 'Did you feel that?' He flicks his head. 'Ow!' He rubs his neck. 'I'd better do that again . . . Did *you* feel that?'

'Feel what, Doctor?' Agatha reads.

'An icy draft.' He waves his hand back and to. 'How strange. It's gone now.'

More revisions are made. Jack's back on his tiptoes, pretending to creep along a corridor. 'You must know all the *nooks and crannies*, having been housekeeper here so long.'

Madge smiles encouragingly.

'Oh, yes, Doctor. Course it's been ever such a long time since anyone was allowed in the East Wing. Mr Tremayne had the door blocked up after his poor wife died.'

'Much better,' says Madge.

'Agreed,' says Mrs Cherry. 'Let's take a break. The other cast members must be due soon.'

'I'll go and see if there's any sign of them,' Jack says eagerly.

I should take a leaf out of his book and move about. I'm all stiff from being sat for so long.

Madge glances at her sister, but Agatha is watching the door while absently rubbing at the mark where her wedding ring should be.

The women sit together on the settee, making me think of the three wise monkeys.

Mrs Cherry puts a hand on Agatha's arm. 'You're worrying about your husband. Don't. In my experience, it never helps.' Her voice is unobtrusive for once. 'I imagine he told you he couldn't help himself, that he fell in love. Excusing away the pain and embarrassment he has caused you, making you think that he is the wounded party.'

'Delia. I was thinking of changing when the doctor enters,' Madge interrupts. 'I think the timing would be better if he appears after the ghost bride.'

'What? Oh, yes. Jane, pass me that pencil next to you.'

I fight the urge to tell her to get it herself, but a nurse must know when to pacify.

'Here you are.'

The cow doesn't even say thank you. I go back to the window and open it a touch, hoping the air will cool my temper too.

'I'm going to see Archie,' Agatha announces.

'Do you think that's wise?' asks Madge.

'He's my husband.'

'I just meant, well, won't that . . .' Madge looks to me for support, but Mrs Cherry butts in first.

'The more you go running after him, my dear, the more he'll want to get as far away from you as he can.'

I wince. She's right but she has no tact.

'And,' Madge continues, 'Archie's been under a lot of stress these last few—'

'*He's* been under stress? What about me?'

I twist my head slightly. Agatha's hands curl into fists. She holds them to her mouth.

'My mother dies and—'

'Our.'

'Yes, yes – I know you miss her dreadfully too – but you had Jim. I was alone.' Her fingers interlock, prayer like. 'Going through all her things at Ashfield, trying to decide what to keep and what to let go. It was awful, Punkie. Everything I discarded felt like a betrayal.'

My chest tightens. I too know the pain of losing your mother. Of being all alone.

'I did offer to help. You said you wanted to be on your own.'

Agatha flushes. 'You didn't have to listen to me. You could have come anyway.'

'For goodness' sake. There's no pleasing you.'

'Shall I order some tea?' I ask.

Madge looks at me gratefully.

'It's a bit late for tea and bloody sympathy,' Agatha hisses as she stands. 'Now, as I said, I'm going to see Archie.' She quits the room.

Madge and Mrs Cherry go back to discussing the script as if the row never happened.

'I'll leave you both to it,' I say, playing along.

Instead of going upstairs, I turn right into the terrace room. A huge hearth with a shiny copper fire dominates the back wall. I weave round an assortment of chairs to the adjoining door. I don't need to press my ear to the wood to hear Madge's scolding.

'. . . and I especially asked you to be careful in how you spoke to Agatha.'

'I was careful. You always pussyfoot around her. Anyway, I know what it's like to have a husband betray you. I thought she might appreciate the chance to open up about what went on.'

'To you? Really, Delia, she may as well do an exclusive interview with the *Daily Mail* as to take you into her confidence.'

'Nonsense. I understand the need for discretion. But I don't agree with bottling things up, because sooner or later the top blows and then there's a real mess to deal with.'

'Agatha's not bottling things up. She has amnesia.'

'So she claims.'

'It's true. Dr Pearce has verified it and now he's arranged for a specialist he knows to call here tomorrow. My sister will have professional help at some considerable expense to work through her issues.'

Mrs Cherry's laugh cuts off Madge's speech. 'Some quack who'll convince her that she's hysterical, no doubt. Agatha doesn't need a head shrink. She needs a good divorce lawyer. If you want to throw Jim's money at the problem that's what I'd suggest. What do you even know about this doctor, anyway?'

Madge's voice is quieter.

'. . . recommended him . . . neurologist . . . Dr Argyle . . .'

My heart flutters with anxiety. I press my palms against the cool wood to try and steady my breathing. The name so very familiar.

FOUR

I CLOSE MY EYES, SO I FOCUS ONLY ON THE WORDS COMING from the other side of the door.

'London?' Mrs Cherry sounds aghast. 'Couldn't Dr Pearce find you a decent quack in Manchester? This Argyle will charge you triple the going rate. Likely more when he sees this place.'

'Jim . . . happy to pay whatever it . . . ensure Agatha's well again.'

'I should've guessed Archie wasn't putting his hand in his pocket. Don't say I didn't warn you, Madge. You've always been as stubborn as a mule. That's one of the reasons I like you. Now, let's go over that dialogue once more. I think we can tighten the banter between the two of them.'

Stepping away from the door, I sink into one of the chairs and recall a memory of being in Matron's office. Her voice in my head is as clear as on the day. 'I don't like it any more than you do, Nurse, but it's going to happen and fast.'

I'd massaged my temples. A headache forming. Rumours had been swirling for the last month, ever since we'd been lumped together with the other county asylums: Lancashire, Cheshire, North Wales and Derbyshire were now Group 3. One in the cluster would be evacuated and the pin was stuck in us. All 2,160 of our inmates to be dispersed and Winwick Asylum to be renamed the Lord Derby War Hospital.

I looked down the list. 'Carlisle? York? This can't be right.'

'Inmates will go wherever there is space, but most will go to Lancaster,' said Matron.

That's still over fifty miles away.

'What about staff? Will we go too?'

'The new management haven't decided yet.'

I squeezed my thumb. I had to persuade them.

Madge's voice pulls me back to the present. I must stay focused. I move back to the door.

'. . . when Jim first proposed, Agatha was quite rude about him. Said he was too dull for me, that I was settling for a passionless marriage. You wouldn't know it to see how she dotes on him now. She always goes to him for advice, not me. Even with her writing sometimes. Perhaps she does it because she knows it frustrates me. Course, she was only a child then. She'd no concept of what makes for a strong relationship.'

'Money?' Mrs Cherry deadpans. 'Well Agatha's found out the hard way, hasn't she? I mean, we can all understand her being swept off her feet by a dashing pilot who declared his adoration. But when you're the wrong side of thirty, you soon realise he might be just as quick to sweep some other ingénue off her feet.'

'I don't think Nancy Neele was ever that.'

She snorts. 'Where is she now? Hiding away in some tawdry love nest, I suppose?'

'Middle of the ocean, actually. Jim said her parents have sent her away on a world cruise.'

'That will only make Archie and her more determined to be together once they're reunited.'

She's probably right.

'You ever met her, Madge?'

'God, no. Poor Agatha. You know what makes it worse? That she tried to be nice to Nancy. They were on some committee together planning a pirate children's play area for the British Empire Exhibition. And all that stuff in the newspapers about Nancy and Archie teeing off together. Agatha played with them too. I don't know where this rubbish has come from that she doesn't like the game. When she was on that Empire trip she won the women's cup. The papers will print anything. Jim's even hidden his clubs in a cupboard in case seeing them upsets her.'

'Or she sets about Archie with them,' Mrs Cherry offers.

'Don't joke. I didn't tell you, did I? She threw the teapot at Archie that last morning. That's why he stormed out.'

A bucket clangs behind me. A young parlourmaid with a constellation of freckles frowns at me. . . 'Were you wanting to go into the drawing room?' Something akin to a smile forms on her lips. 'The door shouldn't be locked. Here, let me try.'

'That isn't necessary. Thank you . . .'

'Kitty, Madam.'

Kitty. Yes, that suits her very well, for she makes me feel like a fledgling pinned under a cat's paw. I'm about to offer some excuse but catch myself. Why waste energy on another white lie? I must remember my position. She's what, seventeen? Bottom of the rung. Poor thing will have housemaid's knees within the year.

I'm surprised to find Agatha not with her husband, but sitting on the front steps stroking the young spaniel's ears.

'He likes that,' I say. 'What's his name?'

'Titch – and she's a her.' Agatha ruffles her brown and white coat. 'I think it's relaxing you as much as me, isn't it, girl?'

I sit on the other side of Titch. She licks my hand in greeting.

'Do you think it's true that dogs are a good judge of character?' Agatha asks.

'Clearly.' I grin.

'Ha. In my books I like to trick my readers. Have them trust the wrong characters. Play with their expectations.'

'Like a doctor,' I say, thinking of Argyle.

'Or a nurse.' She raises her eyebrows.

I press a hand to my chest in mock indignation.

'A doctor's the narrator in your new one, isn't he? I've just started it. You dedicated it to your sister.'

'Mmm, though Jim gave me the idea for it. They both like a good murder. It's one of the few things they have in common. A real chalk and cheese couple. You're not married, are you?'

'No.' Titch nudges me with her cold wet nose. I massage the back of her neck and my own shoulders soften.

'I had lots of offers.' Agatha looks wistful for a moment. 'Course if you were to get married you'd have to give up your job, wouldn't you? Different in the war. I was allowed to carry on nursing after Archie and I wed.

'Though I often thought if Archie had asked me to give up writing, I would've done. Moot point. We could never afford for me to stop.'

'You think if you did, he'd give your marriage another try?'

Agatha shakes her head. 'He's been quite clear. There's nothing I can do to change his mind. He was only pretending last time. All that talk of a holiday.' Closing her mouth, she breathes heavily through her nose. 'The joke is I can't write any more. Haven't been able to for weeks. Months.'

'That's understandable.'

'How would you know? Do you write?'

'No, but I know what it's like to be gripped by grief. And you aren't just dealing with your mother's death.'

'No. My marriage is dead too.'

We say nothing for a while, focusing only on petting Titch.

'Maybe you could try writing something non-fiction,' I eventually say.

She groans. 'Not a diary. Oh God, you're not one of those who wants their patients to write down their dreams, are you?'

I wrinkle my nose. 'Do you dream a lot?'

'What's a lot?' She shrugs. 'Mine are never very interesting.'

I'm not sure I believe her.

A car horn beeps down by the lodge gates.

'They're here!' calls Jack somewhere from the driveway.

Titch barks in reply.

Heels sound on the tiles behind us. Madge and Mrs Cherry come to greet the other am-drammers.

Agatha and I stand. The spaniel's tail frantic.

'Inside, Titch,' Madge orders.

The pup whines but does as she's told.

'Darling!'

Charles Trent is sadly all too familiar to me. He would regularly pop by to call on his Aunt Anne and Uncle James last spring. He likes to treat the family like he's one of them. I suspect he was hoping to be remembered in their wills. He's dressed in a taupe British Warm, no doubt 'borrowed' from S & J Watts.

'Ladies.' He gives a theatrical bow, then kisses Madge's cheek. 'You look wonderful.' He steps back. 'A little tired perhaps, but still gorgeous.'

'On your own?' Mrs Cherry accepts a cheek kiss too while looking over his shoulder.

'Sadly not. She'll be along in a minute.' He picks a minuscule amount of fluff from his double-breasted coat. 'Iris insisted on hopping out at the gates so the press could get a photograph of her. I left her there, boring them all silly about her debut in your magnificent play. Still, you can't help but admire her ambition. Manchester Amateur Dramatics Society may be a long, long way from Hollywood, but I wouldn't bet against Iris making the leap.'

Madge pales. 'You don't think she'll say anything about—'

'Me?' says Agatha. 'Hello, Charles.'

'Aggie. I was so sorry to hear about Clara's passing. As I told Madge, Christmas at Abney won't quite be the same without the oldies.' He pulls her into a hug. 'And don't worry about madam. She might not be the brightest bulb on the tree but she's perfectly discreet.' He looks me up and down. 'Jane! What a lovely surprise.'

'Mr Trent.' I nod in acknowledgement.

'When will I convince you to call me Charles?'

Not a chance. He'd see a switch to first names as a green light.

God help Kitty if she hasn't been warned about his wandering hands.

'Have you spoken to Humphrey about our flats?' says Mrs Cherry.

'Yes. He says we'll have them in time. Just been busy with setting up Fitups.'

'Flats?' I whisper to Agatha.

'Theatre backdrops.'

'Ah. And Fitups?'

'Theatrical Contractors. My brother-in-law's new business,' says Madge proudly. 'Scenery and props have always been a special interest of Humphrey's. He's confident he can make a go of it, outside of S & J's.'

That's where the Wattses' money comes from. A cotton manufacturer turned wholesalers now run by the three Watts brothers from a vast warehouse in the centre of Manchester. Charles is head of one of the departments, can't recall which, and I suspect he can't either.

A green Crossley speeds into view. Despite the cold, the soft top's rolled back to best show off the platinum blonde driver. Iris . . . I try to remember her surname from the script earlier . . . Caldwell, that was it.

A moment later, the young actress glides towards us as though the gravel is a red carpet. She's wearing an expensive drop-waist navy blue wool coat with fur trim. Iris dips her fashionable sunglasses, revealing striking blue eyes. *Can't see where she's bloody going*, I think, stifling a grin.

Jack's like an eager schoolboy as he lifts her vanity case from the back seat.

Iris speaks rapidly, like a 120-wpm typist. 'Oh dear. Are you all waiting for me? I was just telling those poor boys at the gate all about your terrific play, Madge. And how utterly thrilled I am to be starring in it, of course.'

'Starring's rather a stretch. You're bumped off in the middle of Act Two,' says Mrs Cherry.

Iris's laugh reminds me of rising soap bubbles, but her eyes show no amusement.

A third motor car, blue this time, winds its way up the drive, as battered as Iris's was polished. A short man with oiled-back hair gets out.

'Could you fetch my cardigan, Jane?' Agatha asks, rubbing her arms.

'Of course.'

'Why didn't you say you were cold?' scolds Madge. 'Charles, would you mind staying to show Richard the way?'

I hurry into the house and trot upstairs. The cardigan is on the bed. Grabbing it and turning to leave, I spot a photograph of Agatha and Archie on the mantlepiece, which I pick up. They look younger. Agatha, standing in a too-big, belted coat and hat, smiles genuinely. Archie seated, serious on the verge of miserable. On the back someone has written 'wedding day, 1914'. My hand knocks against a vase of spills as I go to put it back. It falls, smashing against the stone hearth. *Darn.* Dropping the fragments into the wastepaper bin, I realise the spills are still useable. The words '*The Advertiser*' in small print catches my eye. I untwist the newspaper strip. It's been torn from this morning's Stockport edition. I straighten then piece together the rest of the spills, reconstructing the article.

'AUTHOR'S DRAMATIC DASH TO ABNEY HALL – exclusive.' Below the headline is a photograph of Agatha and Madge taken at Victoria Station. They both look rather matronly, Madge especially so. Dr Pearce is captured behind them, but I'm relieved to see I haven't made it into the shot or have been cropped out.

I scan the story quickly, not wanting to be caught if someone comes into the room. For all its titled exclusive, there's nothing fresh here other than the photograph. Please let Agatha's disappearance be a nine-day wonder. Let the papers fill their pages with carol concerts and recipes for gingerbread.

Scrunching the spills into a ball, I go downstairs. At the bottom I pause by a suit of armour, open the visor and drop the paper inside.

FIVE

THE ANNEXE IS VERY ATTRACTIVE CONSIDERING IT'S SUCH A mishmash. The main part is a long hall with high diamond-paned windows. At the northern end, a smaller vestibule with a chimney which juts out at a right angle from the main building has been turned into a kitchen. Jim's father told me that they used to feed "the crowds at Christmas there".

Two old stone pillars flank the southern entrance. A church-like wooden door leads me into a light, airy space. A large stained-glass window on my right.

The MADS are at the far end of the hall, sitting on pews, by the only fire. Patience is holding a newspaper over it to draw the fire. Lit candles have been placed on all the windowsills but it's still rather gloomy.

'Another latecomer!' A man in a horizontal-striped pullover jumps up and shakes my hand. 'Paul Ramsbury.' He's handsome with a beard and curly brown hair. 'There appears to have been a miscommunication. I thought we were in the main house?'

'Me too. I'm Richard Buxton.' He smells of cigarette smoke and something else. Coconut? Must be the macassar oil he uses to sleek back his hair. 'I'm playing the family solicitor.'

He's a good fit, being a serious looking fellow with little round spectacles and a noticeable paunch. He turns to me and smiles. Opens a silver case and takes out a cigarette then offers me one.

I shake my head.

'Are you new too?' He lights up using a box of matches.

'Oh, I'm not part of MADS, I was fetching . . .' I hold up the cardigan.

'Nurse Goodbetter's looking after me,' says Agatha, taking it from me. 'I'm part of the scenery too, so to speak.'

'Don't mind, do you?' Paul holds out his hand for Richard's cigarette case. 'I seem to have forgotten mine.'

'Course not.' He passes the case and matches over.

'So you're the newcomer Delia's been raving about.'

Mrs Cherry on hearing her name comes closer. 'Richard, glad to have you on board.' She waves a hand as he offers her a cigarette.

'The cast for this play has been like a carousel, hasn't it, Delia,' adds Paul, taking a drag. 'Always someone new jumping on or off. But as I was just saying, I'm a permanent fixture.' He slaps Jack on the shoulder. 'Sorry, you won't get your chance to kiss Iris after all.'

Jack flushes.

'Actually, we've cut the kiss,' says Mrs Cherry.

'What?' Paul's eyes dart to Iris. 'I suppose that was your request.'

'Actually, it was mine,' says Madge.

That shuts him up.

Jack pushes the pews back to make more room for the performers, while his mother readies her pencil to mark up any changes. Paul, who isn't in the scene, sits front and centre, legs spread wide. Agatha and I sit behind him, a script open between us.

Charles sits next to Paul. 'Good to see you, pal.'

'I'm glad someone thinks so.'

'Iris still giving you the cold shoulder?'

She's checking her appearance in a gold compact with the Eye of Horus motif in emeralds.

'She'll come around.'

'Easy for you to say. It's me she blames and I don't have your easy charm.'

Charles slaps his back. Gets up and strolls over to Iris. 'Another present from Daddy?' He plucks the compact from her palm. 'Cartier.' He whistles. Passes it back.

She drops it into her clutch handbag, then smooths her green dress. The hemline fashionably cut just below the knee.

Patience straightens her white mob cap and picks up the ash bucket. 'If that's all, Mrs Watts.'

'It is. Thank you.'

'If we're all ready!' Mrs Cherry looks down at her script. 'Act One. Scene One. The House. Alice and Tom enter through the garden gate.'

'Fancy us having an Uncle Hector we never knew about,' says Iris.

'Great Uncle Hector,' prompts Agatha.

'Sorry! . . . Fancy us having a Great Uncle Hector we never knew about.'

'I suppose every family has a black sheep,' says Charles. 'Quite fitting given he made all his money in the wool trade.'

'Like in that nursery rhyme,' continues Iris. 'I've never understood why we teach children those creepy little ditties.'

'Oh, that one's all right, not like "Ring a Ring O'Roses" or "Three Blind Mice," says Charles. '"Humpty Dumpty", "Jack and Jill", aren't they all about someone dying?'

'Like poor Great Uncle Hector.'

'Hardly poor! And he was eighty-seven, Alice.' He pretends to knock. 'And some of them start off all right, like "Oranges and Lemons" – but then turn grisly at the end.'

Paul turns to me. 'Had a Nursie when I was a boy. Used to scrub behind my ears and feed me dippy eggs with soldiers. Goodbetter's such a mouthful, I might call you Nursie, too.'

I smile indulgently while fantasising about force feeding him boiled eggs with the shells on. 'Jane is fine.'

Mrs Cherry shushes us.

Great, she hates me even more now.

She doesn't miss a beat, getting up as she picks up her role as Hector's housekeeper. 'The house was extended in 1873. We don't use the old East Wing any longer. Not since the bridal night.' Mrs Cherry is convincing as the sinister old servant.

'Bridal night?' repeats Charles. 'Was Great Uncle Hector married?'

'Only for a few short hours. So tragic,' says Mrs Cherry, clasping a hand to her bosom.

'Perhaps the place is haunted,' stage whispers Iris to Charles.

They carry on for another half hour, Madge tweaking lines every so often. The doctor doesn't appear for a few more pages. Paul makes his impatience clear, fiddling with his script, wandering up and down, and being generally annoying. Richard, though, is very focused. Hoping to make a good impression, I imagine.

'Paul, make yourself useful and fill the kettle.' Mrs Cherry points to the vestibule.

'Yes, do,' says Agatha. 'Before you wear a hole in the Turkey carpet.'

'Coffee for me, old chap,' calls Charles.

'And me, please,' says Iris.

He grunts and goes to the kitchen, pushing a wedge under the door to keep it open, no doubt so he can still hear as the other MADS confab over the script.

Richard's practising his lines over by the window. He occasionally tugs his collar away from his neck as scarlet flashes up his skin.

'Agatha,' I whisper. 'Why is Iris giving Paul the cold shoulder?'

But she seems lost in her thoughts again. Is this part of the memory loss? Some kind of transient amnesia?

'Agatha,' I repeat.

'I heard you the first time . . . Maybe they're just pretending to hate each other but they're actually a secret couple.' She taps a finger against her cheek. 'That's an idea. Mmm. They could plot the murder together.'

'Iris and Paul?'

'No, silly. I was thinking it would work as a twist in a book. My readers like a bit of romance, even if you don't.'

'Tea's up,' Paul calls as he passes out the drinks from a tray. Charles opens a tin of Huntley and Palmers' Tivoli and we take turns picking out a chocolate biscuit.

'Right,' announces Mrs Cherry, after we've finished munching. 'Let's jump ahead to the middle of Act Two.'

'At last,' grunts Paul.

Jack and Richard pull a round table into the centre and reposition the pew. The cast take their positions. Charles pretends to pour Champagne, and then he, Iris and Paul raise an imaginary glass to toast Great Uncle Hector.

I quietly start scooping up the discarded tea things onto the tray. I'm surprised when Agatha starts to help.

'What? I'm not above scrubbing a few dishes. It's often when I do my best plotting.'

I jolt, as Iris suddenly wails, almost dropping the tray of crockery. She collapses to the floor, thrashing violently

Paul leans over her. 'She's been poisoned.'

'Strychnine,' says Agatha. 'Known for causing violent convulsions. Very bitter and fast acting. There's a clue to the killer there.'

'Right.' I have no idea. I'm too focused on Agatha. I'm loathe to admit it, but Mrs Cherry was right the play does seem to be a positive distraction.

'Oh, for goodness' sake. You're dead, Iris. Can't you keep still?' moans Mrs Cherry.

'It's not my fault. He's got bad breath.'

'I have not.'

'Here. Have a mint.' Mrs Cherry reaches into her carpet bag and pulls out a paper bag. 'In fact, everyone take one.'

I notice Charles takes two.

'That reminds me of my brother, Monty,' says Agatha. 'He's

terrible with money. Has been since he was a child. He'd spend all his pocket money then drag Madge into the sweet shop. He'd gaily order three pennyworth of pear drops, or whatever, then stare at her until she coughed up. She was always too embarrassed not to do so. Course nowadays it's Jim who bails him out.'

Was it the mints that prompted the memory? Or Charles? I must encourage her to keep talking.

I follow her into the kitchen.

'I have very few memories from when I was little.' I say, picking up a tea towel as Agatha pours water from the kettle into the sink. 'The ones I have always seem to be when I was upset or scared.'

'It's interesting how memory works, isn't it?' she replies. 'I've all these scenes from when I was a girl stored, just flashes of things. Being in the garden. Playing at trains. We don't get to choose what we remember.

'But you're right, they are often linked to strong emotions.' She plunges her hands into the water. 'That's why it's so strange that these last few days are a blur. Some of the guests at the Hydro were intrigued by Agatha Christie's disappearance, but I had no interest in her; and swear I did not realise she was me. How's that possible?'

'I don't know.'

'Do you think this doctor can really unlock my missing memories?'

'Dr Pearce must think so.'

'But do you?'

'I hope so.'

She nods, satisfied. 'Madge says there was a lot of rubbish

printed in the newspapers while I was missing. A series of photographs of me "in disguise". Stories that I was dancing the Charleston and singing "Yes, We Have No Bananas" at the Hydro. It's almost laughable.'

'What about the extravagant shopping trips?'

She groans. 'I needed some new things. I'd found myself in Harrogate with no luggage. My clothes muddy and torn . . .'

'But where did the money come from? The newspapers said you didn't draw from your bank account.'

'I had some with me.'

'Some?'

'Enough.'

But how much does she consider enough? A lot more than I would, I expect.

'Only in one article, a guest was quoted as saying you wore a money belt around your waist.'

She holds my gaze. 'When I had a perfectly good handbag?'

'Perhaps that was a red herring.'

She chuckles.

We return to the pew.

Now it's Iris's turn to sit on the sidelines. 'Madge . . .' she draws out the name in a way that reminds me of one of the younger nurses when she wanted something from a doctor. 'What if I wasn't dead. What if I could be revived somehow. Couldn't the doctor give me something?'

'You could pretend to drink a glass of tepid water with a couple of spoonfuls of mustard in it,' says Madge. 'Though there would also be the problem of faking your vomiting.'

Iris grimaces.

'No?' Madge's eyes twinkle.

This is the Madge I know, she's usually so full of fun. Naturally witty. Outgoing where her sister is shy. I can see the play will be a tonic for both her and Agatha.

'Let's jump back to the reading of Great Uncle Hector's will,' Madge continues.

Iris sulks while she, Charles, Paul and Mrs Cherry take their places at the table.

'Ready, Richard?'

He stubs out his cigarette and puts down his script. 'Yes, I think so.'

'We did say you'd need to be off book by rehearsal.'

'Oh, I am. I am.' He yanks at his collar again and finds his mark. Clears his throat. 'As executor of Mr Tremayne's estate, I asked you all to gather here today . . .'

I let my gaze drift towards the window. The sky is darkening. My eyes water, as I succumb to a yawn. It's been a long day, with tomorrow likely to be the same. I can't wait to take my shoes off and give my feet a good rub.

'. . . and therefore, in accordance with his wishes, the beneficiaries will be entitled to their share of the estate after having proved their worth by staying . . .'

Thud. Thud. Thud.

I look to the door. No one else appears to have heard it. I walk the length of the hall, but when I open the door there's nobody there, nor in my periphery. I was sure it had been a knock, but perhaps it was someone's idea of a joke? Playing into the haunted house theme. I shrug and go back to my seat.

Eventually, Madge brings the rehearsal to a close. Jack locks up as the MADS disappear into the night. Madge hooks her arm through Agatha's as they tramp back along the track towards the house. I follow behind, looking for any movement, listening for any unusual sound. I've never had a fear of the dark, but I still feel a sense of relief as we near Abney with her windows all aglow. Why, she looks almost festive.

It's too damn cold for the press to be at the lodge gates now, yet I can't shake the feeling someone is watching us.

SIX

Thursday 16th December, 1926

AN ABNEY BREAKFAST COULD FEED A FAMILY OF SIX FOR A week. The sideboard is laid out with assorted dishes. Eggs: boiled, poached and scrambled. Bacon. Sausages – beef and pork. Devilled kidneys. Racks of toast. Creamy yellow butter. Tea. Coffee. Juice.

No newspapers, I notice.

Agatha fills her plate, a positive change from her reported hotel diet of split toast and half a grapefruit, then sits next to her sister. I'm trying to read *The Murder of Roger Ackroyd.* It's really good, but I'm finding it hard to focus.

Archie walks into the room, bringing an awkwardness with him.

'Good morning,' says Madge rather stiffly.

'Morning.' He bypasses the stack of plates, reaching straight for the teapot.

'Lovely sausages,' I say, trying to distract Agatha, who is watching her husband's every move.

The Breakfast Room is just as cluttered as the others; the walls lined with gilt-framed portraits of men in ruffs or powdered wigs. I fancy they're the Wattses' ancestors?

'Titch! Come back here. Titch! Blast that dog.'

The spaniel bounds into the room, tail bashing against legs and furniture, followed by a slightly out of breath Jim.

Madge snatches the rest of my sausage off my plate. 'Here, Titch.'

The dog brakes and U-turns, bouncing over to her mistress, sniffing hopefully. Madge gently grabs her by the scruff and whips away the sausage.

'Thanks,' says Jim, slipping the lead over Titch's head. 'Jack and I'll take the dogs for a long one. Tire them out. Might as well go down to the lodge gates, tell the pack there'll be a final statement at one o'clock.' He departs with the spaniel.

Madge winces. 'Let's hope that satisfies them.' She offers me back the sausage. I shake my head.

'Peter's favourite,' Agatha says quietly. 'I normally sneak him pieces under the table.'

I can smell Archie's milky tea as he sits down next to me.

'Aren't you hungry?' Agatha asks him.

'You can always get something later,' butts in Madge. 'Just ask Cook.'

'Thank you. Actually, I think I'll take this up to my room. I have some letters to write.'

'If you think that best,' says Madge. She looks rather relieved. 'Now eat up,' she orders me and Agatha once he's gone, like we are irritating children. 'We've a full day ahead. Dr Argyle will be here at ten and then there's another rehearsal at two.'

I expect Agatha to make some kind of retort. But instead, she places her hand on her sister's. 'I really do appreciate you looking after me, Punkie. I don't know what I'd have done if I couldn't have come to Abney.'

Knowing what it's like to be without a home, I understand you never forget those who come to your rescue.

After breakfast, I crave time alone. I try reading some more *Roger Ackroyd* back in my room but keep going over the same paragraph. The words won't stick, so I decide to go for a walk around the grounds. A wheelbarrow filled with holly and ivy is at the bottom of the central stairwell. Someone has wrapped twine around the two central pillars of the archway.

An image flashes in my head. Colourful paper chains made by the patients spiralled around the clinical pillars of the ward and dangling from the ceiling. I still have a few links, faded now, like my memories.

''ere, let me move it out your way, Jane.' It's Thomas, the head gardener, in his dog-eared flat cap. 'I 'eard 'ow you were back with us. Nice it is an' all.' He grabs the wheelbarrow's handle with ever mucky hands.

'Busy as always, I see.'

'I'm a bit be'ind to tell the truth, love, but at least I got this lot gathered before the snow comes.'

His predictions about the weather are never wrong. I'm not a fan of the snow. Pretty when it first falls but soon enough it becomes churned up sludge, as grey as old knickers. If we get a good drift, it should shift those vultures at the lodge gates though.

'You plannin' on stayin' a while, Jane? Only I could 'ave a nice amaryllis put in your room, if you like? Might bloom in time for the New Year.'

'That's very thoughtful of you.'

He bows his head. 'No trouble at all.'

After grabbing my rather worn camel coat, I meander round the rhododendron bushes to the lake. There's a heron out on the water, should've brought Dr Pearce's binoculars with me. It was generous of him to lend them to me, I must make sure I make use of them.

It will be strange spending Christmas at Abney. I suppose there'll be plenty of benefits, and there's bound to be feasting from morning till night. I'll probably have to let my uniform out, if I am still here come New Year. But how long will I be needed? What if Dr Argyle's methods fail? What for Agatha then – somewhere like Winwick? Surely that's not an option. Yet we had all kinds of families signing over their loved ones to our care. Some seemed kind and caring, some not. They were all the same in my eyes. I can't let that happen to Agatha.

'You don't have a family of your own, do you, Nurse?' Matron asked me, during my induction.

Later, I think she thought the reason for my judgment lay there. And while my understanding of relatives' motives grew with experience, it never prompted forgiveness for the desertion.

I stride out, deciding to do a full circuit – beginning anticlockwise towards the boathouse. Even Abney's boathouse is church-like: the gable ends with thin short spires and its huge arched timber doors which open onto the lake. The walled garden's gothic ventilation shaft towers faintly in the winter gloom behind.

It's hard to recall spring with its blue cloudless skies. When I strolled here the ground was carpeted with fallen pink and purple rhody petals. The seasons are often interlinked with flowers, I think. Is it the same in other countries? Daffodils and bluebells in spring, sunflowers and roses in summer. Poppies . . .

The heron spreads its wings, startled by something perhaps. I pause, looking around.

It's Agatha. She's by the rhododendrons. Talking to herself in a scolding manner. Chin sat in her palm.

I swallow a lump in my throat. Try to make my voice light and breezy. 'What are you doing out here, Agatha?' My teeth chatter from the cold.

'Don't look so worried. Punkie gave me permission.'

'I'm meant to accompany you.'

She grins. 'I need to be alone when I'm writing.'

'Out here?'

'Looking for my typewriter?' She laughs. 'Saying my words aloud on a walk helps me work out my characters' dialogue and how they move.'

Thank goodness. My body untenses.

'Mind you,' she continues. 'I need to get moving myself.'

'You make it sound like blocking out a play,' I say as we walk on.

'I suppose it is. Though plays are easier to write. You can see the stage in your mind's eye, and you don't have to have all that dreadful description which clogs up a novel. If only I could find a manager to take mine on. I really hoped one would see some merit in *The Clutching Hand*.

'I could be another pair of ears for your story. I'd love to hear it.'

'Oh no. My ideas always sound unbearably dull when I try to explain them. Kills them stone dead.'

'I'm sure that's not true.'

'Oh, it is. My plots rarely make sense until I'm near the end.' Agatha groans. 'I jot these scenarios down in notebooks thinking how brilliantly they'll work. A kills B but B is really D. D is actually A's sister. But when I come to use them, suddenly they're absolute gobbledygook. I was hoping inspiration would strike if I got out of the house, but all I've got is mild frostbite. I'd better go in.'

I watch her head back to the hall. Then I carry on. As I near the boathouse I notice a trail of shoeprints going up to the door. They look fresh. It'll be one of the estate workers doing their daily grounds checks. But then I recall the mysterious door knocks yesterday. Instead of walking on, I go down the steps to the water's edge. Curious. Did Agatha come this way earlier?

The grass is crushed where someone has walked from the main path to the smaller rear door. It's probably locked. But I decide to check.

The ground is wetter here; I slide awkwardly, colliding with the wooden door. My cheeks burn, even though no one has seen me. Rubbing my bruised wrist, I glance round to make sure. The handle is one of those brass ring-pulls. Feeling the mechanism release as I twist and push it, the door gives.

I brace myself for bats, pigeons, rats and crazed madmen. Reading mystery novels isn't good for the heart. But poking my head inside, all is still. Thank God. There's a foul damp smell like stagnant water, then the lingering aroma of wood smoke. Moving into the boathouse proper, it's pretty dark, save for a streak of light from the small window above each door. I can just make out the slipway, an old rowing boat, coils of rope. There. I step closer, wary of the slimy ground. Yes. The remnants of a campfire. A ring of stones. Wood ash. Hovering my hand over to check for residual heat, it's barely detectable.

An old blanket lies close by, and a solitary apple core.

Enough. I retreat, stumbling back along the path, before scrambling up the steps. You'd have to be pretty desperate to doss in there. I'm not going to take their sanctuary away.

There's an almighty splash. A high-pitched whistle. 'Titch! You fool,' Jim hollers. 'Get out of there.'

SEVEN

'DIDN'T SEE YOU THERE, NURSE,' SAYS JIM, AS I APPROACH. 'Don't get too close, she's— *Titch*!'

The spaniel shakes herself, spraying me with pond water. I jerk back too late.

'Sorry. Foolish dog's always trying to retrieve live ducks!'

'I hope she didn't catch one.' I peel away a long strand of weed from my leg.

He laughs. 'She'd have a job. Not unless she learns to fly.'

'You all right?' Jack calls from over the way. The three other dogs are at his side, covered in mud.

Jim waves to confirm, then swoops with the lead again. 'We're finishing the loop, then heading in. Join us?'

I nod.

The three of us follow the rest of the pathway, gabbing about dogs, boots, and the weather. Typical country chat. A couple of times I almost mention the boathouse. But don't.

After crossing the roadway, we head towards Ten Penny Bridge. The dogs race ahead, Titch whining to be let loose.

'Not a chance,' says Jim, stopping to fix an undone bootlace.

'You're not too disappointed at not being in the play after all,

I hope?' I ask Jack, as we walk on.

'Takes the pressure off, to be honest. I was only doing it as a favour to Mother, really. I've got so much studying to do. I'd like to stay on at Oxford and do my master's while I make up my mind about my future.'

Ah. To be young and, better still, rich. 'Your mother said something about you taking up a position at S & J's.'

'I imagine she did. She'd like to see me married off too. Every time she drops some hint about Lady such-and-such or one of her friend's daughters. Last time I told her I'm thinking of entering the clergy. That shut her up.' He whistles for the dogs to come back. 'Did you notice her practically twitching when I was stuck with the vicar? She and Aunt Agatha say I've been obsessed with churches since I was a kid, but actually I'm debating going into politics. I suppose you know all about my great-grandfather being Mayor of Manchester.'

'Mmm.' I nod, hoping he's not going to start on family history. 'What about Iris?' I ask with mock innocence.

'That's just Charles amusing himself at my expense. It'll be someone else's turn tomorrow. That Richard looks a likely target. "I think you'll find it's pronounced *ton-teen*".'

Jack's imitation of Richard Buxton is spot on, but I'm less convinced by his denials over Iris. Mind you, I can imagine Madge's face at her son getting involved with an actress. The family may love all things theatrical, but she'd bring the curtain down on that.

I drag the soles of my muddy shoes over the scraper by the side entrance.

'You need a pair of galoshes,' says Jim, passing Titch's lead to Jack so he can head in with the dogs. 'I'll get Patience to see if there's an old pair of my wife's knocking about.'

'Thanks.'

I remove my shoes and pad inside. I love this part of the house with its minstrel gallery-like landing, and bright floral-inspired stained-glass sunroof. Next door is the huge council chamber for grand meetings, decorated in mock Tudor style; going from room to room at Abney is like travelling through time.

Leaving my shoes on the rack, I follow Jim down the wood-panelled cross corridor. We turn right. Ahead, the main staircase, where Thomas has festooned the pillars with greenery and berries. It all smells amazing. Ready to ascend, I pat the lion again. Habit is becoming superstition.

'Another of Father's finds,' says Jim. 'Story goes it killed a missionary. Course nearly everything in the house has a tale attached. No pun intended. There's a buffalo skin rug upstairs which he used to brag was "one of the last really wild ones killed". And that mounted bullock's head, further down the corridor, is one of the famous Chartley wild white cattle.'

I suppose every house as grand as Abney needs to have a good taxidermy collection, though the lion's too shabby to be classed as good. I don't mind the stuffed birds so much, but the case with the fox crouched over a nest of baby rabbits is grim.

'Your father clearly loved collecting.'

'Oh, yes. He was always at some auction or house sale, as you can tell.' He waves his hand at the cabinets, paintings and objet d'art. 'I'm afraid I'm as bad. Though my real weakness is photography. I even have my own darkroom.'

'I think your father said something to me once about a project of yours – old Cheshire houses?'

He smiles. 'That's right. We all need a passion. Agatha has her books, Madge her plays. You like birdwatching, don't you? Sorry, I'm blathering on, keeping you from your work.' He strokes the lion's head.

This much attention and it'll be leaking sawdust – or worse, woodworm.

But Jim isn't quite ready for the conversation to end, it seems.

'How is Agatha? Really.'

'It's early days, sir, but she appears better for being here at Abney. Don't you agree?'

His face lights up. 'Excellent. Thank you, Jane.'

⟷

'He's here,' says Agatha, entering my room at ten on the dot.

I put down *Ackroyd* and grab my notebook and pencil, then lead her downstairs.

'It's going to be all right.'

Which of us am I trying to convince?

Jim and Madge's voices are full of optimism – and then I hear that familiar Edinburgh brogue. My stomach flips.

'It's Nurse Goodbetter, isn't it?'

The Wattses slip away leaving me with the two doctors.

'I was just singing your praises,' says Dr Pearce.

Dr Argyle's brushed back hair is a touch greyer at the temples, but it is definitely the same man. His pupils dilate as he holds my gaze longer than necessary. My heart thuds like a dolly peg against a tin tub, but to my relief there is no flicker of recognition. He doesn't remember me. And why would he? A doctor of his status only sees the uniform. Nurses are there to do his bidding.

God, I hate him.

'Mrs Christie is ready when you are, Doctor,' I say, determined to remain professional, though my tone comes out rather curt.

'Mr and Mrs Watts suggest we use the library, Callum. It's this way.'

I start to follow.

Dr Argyle halts immediately. 'No need for you to join us, Nurse.'

'Actually, I think Mrs Christie would find Nurse Goodbetter's presence reassuring,' Dr Pearce differs, smiling at me. 'And I would find it helpful to have notes to refer to, when we make our joint assessment.'

'As you wish.'

We walk on, passing Kitty, who's hovering with a feather duster.

The library is sandwiched between the dining and drawing rooms and is much the same in appearance: damask wallpaper, fancy ceiling, chandelier, plus the usual furniture – chairs and another longcase clock. A three-quarter height bookcase fills one wall, but there's still room for more paintings. One of those globe cocktail cabinets. The octagonal table by the window has been cleared of its usual newspapers. I'll have to go hunting later.

Dr Pearce and I stand near the carved wooden fireplace while Agatha stands like a sentry by the door. In, but only just. I open my notebook.

Dr Argyle moves about as though quite at home, picking up a book to examine the spine before his attention is drawn to a painting of a train on a railway bridge. 'I believe the line cuts through the parkland here,' he says by way of an opening gambit. 'I imagine the estate grounds are extensive.'

No one answers. The only sound crackles and pops from the fire.

Now Dr Argyle crosses to the window and opens it. Rubs his chest. 'Beautiful gardens too. A lot of work, though.'

His commentary isn't relaxing Agatha, if that's his intention.

'Please have a seat, Mrs Christie,' he says at last, repositioning a couple of upholstered chairs. 'I hope you don't mind being so far from the fire. The heat affects my chest.' He slides one of the panes up, letting in the crisp winter air.

She does as instructed.

Dr Argyle sits opposite her. 'So, down to business.' He claps his hands on his thighs. 'Shall we begin with your medical history? I understand from your sister that you first developed neuritis while holidaying in Hawaii. A sports injury – from surfing?' His voice goes up a little at the last word.

I'm surprised too. I make a note.

'I can see you're holding your right shoulder rather awkwardly.'

Damn. I should have spotted that.

'Try not to hunch. It will only make it worse.'

Something softens in her as she takes his advice.

'Is the pain always on that side?' Dr Argyle's hand goes to his chest again. He gives a little cough.

'The first time it began as pain in my left arm, as though I'd strained it. The surfboards were very heavy – later it moved to my right neck and shoulder. The pain was unbearable and woke me early every morning.'

'You continued to surf?'

She nods. 'I wanted to make the most of the opportunity, knowing my husband and I would likely never get the chance to return there.'

'Aye, I see.'

The fire's making my calves prickle through my stockings.

'And did you seek any treatment for the pain?'

'A doctor prescribed an ointment. Nasty stuff. Practically burnt a hole in my skin. I assume it was capsaicin. Whatever it was, it didn't work.'

Dr Argyle nods. 'So what did?'

'We'd moved on to Canada. A lot of people had recommended the Hot Springs at Banff. I let the water run on my neck and shoulder for several days. It smelt powerfully of sulphur. Finally did the trick, thank goodness.'

'But now it has returned.'

'Yes.'

'Now that wasn't so hard, was it?' He gives her one of his smiles.

She's stony-faced. I try not to smirk. Bet he's not used to his charm failing.

He continues asking questions about her medical history, none of it especially interesting. The heat from the fire causes me to stifle a yawn. A moment later, I can't help closing my eyes. Dr Argyle's sonorous voice with a memory of when he first came to

Winwick to carry out a precursory inspection. I was about to go into Matron's office . . .

'You are a marvel, Matron. You and the superintendent clearly run a tight ship.'

She giggled like a schoolgirl. 'I just do my duty, Dr Argyle.'

'I only wish all staff members were as efficient as you. Last week I caught one nurse putting clean dressings in a kidney dish. I gave her quite a scolding.'

I imagined her pink cheeks suddenly paling. 'I can assure you that sort of mistake won't happen here, Doctor.'

'Then we shall get along very well. Now, there is a lot to be done before we take over in May. Shall we discuss the finer details?'

'Of course, Doctor.'

Yes, Doctor. No, Doctor. Three bags full, Doctor. Another sheep.

Warm fingers on my hand bring me back to the room. Dr Pearce looks concerned. I shift away from the fire. He smiles at me, then addresses his colleague.

'Mrs Christie has also been suffering from neuralgia.'

'Her headaches have been persistent for some months,' I add. At least I can contribute that.

'Do you have one now?' Dr Argyle asks.

She shakes her head.

'May I examine your neck and head, please?'

She does not object, so he stands and moves closer.

Agatha turns so he can gently press along her spine from the base of her skull to the first thoracic vertebrae. I waft myself with the notebook as he gets her to turn this way and that, all the time asking if there's any discomfort. Next, he holds up his index finger and instructs her to follow it as he moves it from side to side, up and down, watching her eyes.

'All satisfactory.' He leans in. 'What's this?'

He brushes her fringe aside. There's a faint yellowing to her skin. I frown. An old bruise?

EIGHT

'I HIT MY HEAD,' AGATHA SAYS QUICKLY. 'ON THE STEERING WHEEL when I crashed.'

'Which could easily explain the amnesia,' says Dr Pearce. 'Please, be reassured, Mrs Christie. Cases of memory loss are fairly common.'

'Though seldom alike,' Dr Argyle interjects. 'That's what makes amnesia both fascinating and challenging. As your symptoms are neurological, Mrs Christie, I'd be happy to take on your case. I'd need more time to explore your symptoms, but if your husband and brother-in-law concur, I will keep a daily appointment here with you. They may, of course, prefer to consider treatment at the Cheadle Royal.'

I recoil. It may sound benign, but its former names reveal its true nature: hospital for the insane, lunatic hospital, asylum. It has a terrible reputation for overcrowding and inhumane conditions. How can I warn Agatha?

'I don't think that likely,' says Dr Pearce.

My shoulders relax in relief.

'And unnecessary, as my interest in psychiatry means I'm amply qualified to treat you, Mrs Christie,' adds Dr Argyle.

'What do you think, Nurse?'

I'm surprised and flattered at Agatha asking my opinion. 'I think you'll recover best here at Abney.'

She smiles at me.

I don't like the idea of Dr Argyle probing inside Agatha's mind, but it's better than her being carted off to some god-awful institution.

'Excellent. Then we shall tell your brother-in-law the news.'

He takes Agatha's hand, and I think for a moment he's about to kiss it. But he just holds it for a moment.

'I'll see you again. Soon.'

Very gallant. Really, he does overdo it.

Dr Argyle turns to Dr Pearce. 'No need for you to stay, Robert – unless you want a lift home? We could discuss that other case more?'

My notebook thuds on the floor. Dr Pearce scoops it up and passes it back to me. He gives no sign that he has read the note I've quickly scribbled for him.

'Another time. I enjoy the walk,' he replies. 'Besides, Colonel Christie has requested I accompany him when he makes his statement to the press at eleven.'

The doctors don't ask if Agatha wants her husband to speak on her behalf. I can't say I'm surprised at their presumption. They never considered keeping their diagnosis confidential, either.

They go off to Jim's study while Agatha closes the window. 'Dr Argyle's very attractive, isn't he?' she says, her eyes twinkling with devilment. 'A pity it's the other doctor that's smitten with you.'

Panic fills my chest. 'Don't be silly. Dr Pearce is married.'

Agatha holds my gaze.

'Yes, OK. I get your point. But you're wrong. Dr Pearce doesn't think of me in that way.'

'Doesn't he?'

'Of course not. He's practically old enough to be my father.'

'That makes it even more likely. I watch people, Jane. I watched you both. His eyes flit to you constantly.'

'I don't believe you.'

Agatha shrugs. 'You'll soon see.'

I don't answer.

'Ah, you've already noticed. You've been trying to ignore it. He hasn't confessed yet, then?'

I squeeze my thumb. 'You don't think he will? No. You're mistaken, Agatha. People don't do things like that in real life. They squish down their feelings.'

'But you can't do that forever. Eventually it all comes bursting out.'

I want to retreat upstairs, but Archie's gruff voice stops me in my tracks. I linger behind the library door.

'So, what did this Argyle fellow say? Jim is playing silly buggers and said I'd have to wait till you and he have discussed the matter.'

'If that's what he said . . .' Madge's voice is steady.

I purposely don't look at Agatha, embarrassed.

'You've never liked me, have you, Madge? Always thought I wasn't good enough for your sister – just like your mother.'

'And we were proven right.'

He sighs. 'We married too young, too quickly. Then the bloody war. Months and months apart. And afterwards stuck in a tiny flat, and never enough money.' I hear the strike of his lighter's flint. 'I just wanted quiet . . . calm – but Agatha wouldn't leave me be, chattering incessantly. What was I thinking? How was I feeling? Fussing over me, wanting my opinion. It made me sick. Sick to my stomach. I've had enough!'

And with that, he stomps off.

I retreat to my room whilst Archie does his press conference. Agatha's hiding too. I almost suggest we go up onto the secret tiny roof terrace to see if we can hear anything but decided against it. Whenever there's a noise I peer out of the window to check if the journalists are leaving.

I can't believe how long it goes on. My curiosity builds like an itch. When I finally see the press depart, I know exactly where to go to scratch it.

I track Patience down at the side entrance. She and Thomas are dragging something huge and wrapped in hessian into the house. As I near, the scent of pine hits me. It must be a Christmas tree.

'Let me help?' I call, rushing to assist.

Patience is too old for this kind of caper. I'm a nurse, not a servant, so I shouldn't really be mucking in, but I want her on side. And neither protest when I grab the rope fastened around the heavy end and help them to heave it inside.

'Where's it going?' I ask, my breath catching with the effort.

'The drawing room, love,' he replies. 'Got another one to do yet for the terrace room.'

I shake my head, but I know Thomas wouldn't dream of complaining.

'You've both worked here a long time, haven't you?' I ask as we drag the bundle along the cross corridor past the glass taxidermy cases. I glimpse a magpie on its nest; something shiny in its beak. A pheasant on a bed of bracken.

'Since I were a pot boy,' says Thomas. 'Us lads would sleep in the bothy back then. Never imagined one day I'd be 'ead gardener meself.'

'You work harder than any man I've met,' I say. 'You've earnt your position.' I know he'd wave my praise away if only he had a hand free.

'It's the same for me,' says Patience, as we stop for a moment. 'Course things aren't as they were. When I came here at nineteen, I were one of a dozen maids. Back then there were a proper distinction between the rank of housemaid and parlourmaid. You worked your way up. Still, I've always felt this was a happy home.' She frowns. 'Everything's so unsettled now, what with the Wattses dying so close together and then all this trouble with Mrs Christie.'

'I know what you mean,' says Thomas. 'But bad times always pass.'

Patience nods sagely. 'Yes, we've both lived through terrible times, but I've always thought of Abney as a sanctuary from the evil in the world. Now, I feel like its crept in, somehow. I don't mean Mr and Mrs Watts, of course. No, it's their friends. These MUDs—'

Thomas laughs. 'MADS not MUDS.'

We lug the tree once more. We've reached the drawing room at last. The three of us hoist the tree into its stand, needles scattering everywhere.

'Whatever they call themselves, they're a bad bunch,' Patience continues, adjusting her grip. 'Always sniping and stirring things behind each other's backs but thick as thieves together. I overheard that Mrs Cherry on the teleph–'

Thomas shoots her a look.

'Well never mind what I heard. You know I'm not one to gossip, but what I will say is it wasn't a little white lie – it was a whopper.'

'Better not let Mrs Watts catch you eavesdropping,' Thomas admonishes, gathering up the hessian.

'Says you,' snorts Patience. 'I wasn't the one who suddenly decided the topiary needed a trim while Colonel Christie was making his statement.'

Thomas's expression is as innocent as a newborn babe.

'How did that go?' I ask, not fooled for a minute.

'Cocked it right up.' He shakes his head. 'Came off like a right stuffed shirt, as usual.'

'The colonel does seem rather tetchy,' I prompt.

'Tetchy! 'e's like a baby with a red raw bottom. The reporters gave 'im a proper heckling. Silly sod 'ad gone out in 'is carpet slippers an' all. 'e was fuming when 'e cottoned on.'

I bet.

'Well at least the reporters should clear off now,' I say, rubbing my sticky hands on my apron. Reckon the colonel's bags will be packed before nightfall.

Thomas scoffs again. 'The colonel's only gone and agreed

to an exclusive interview with one of them at five o'clock. Chap from *The Stockport Advertiser.* Reckons that'll get the others off 'is back. Fool. They'll all want an exclusive now. I caught one in the grounds this morning, y'know?'

'By the boathouse?' I ask. Anxiety making my chest tighten.

'No, what made you think that? This blighter was strolling through the parkland like 'e were master of the estate! Must 'ave come in via Newlands Road. 'e were lucky I didn't 'ave the shotgun with me, I can tell you. Mind you, I sent 'im away with a flea in 'is ear.'

'Good for you, Thomas,' says Patience. 'Let's hope the rest of them clear off too, now as Colonel Christie's made his statement.'

'Was he definitely a reporter?' I ask.

'Who else would 'e be? Weedy looking with scruffy hair.'

That sounds like the one who winked at me in the Hydro.

Patience tuts. 'And I've got to serve this one afternoon tea in the terrace room. Mrs Watts insisted they make this reporter feel welcome. Thinks a bit of cream cake will persuade him to write nice things.'

'Would be terrible if you overheard what Colonel Christie tells him,' I say, raising my eyebrows.

'Happen I might hear something,' she says with a wink.

The mantle clock chimes.

'Gosh, is that the time?' I check my fob watch, make my excuses and leave.

Cutting down the backstairs, I let myself out through the servants' entrance door. Running towards the walled garden, I dash past the ventilation tower, the chill air hurting my lungs.

As I near the boathouse, I slow and brush my hair with my hands checking for stray pine needles. I wipe my hands on my apron again, as I switch left, back to the boathouse. I should have picked somewhere else, but this was the first place that came to mind. Twisting the handle, I open the door for the second time and slip inside. Light streaks in for a moment as I close it behind me.

He pulls me close, smothering my neck in kisses.

'God, I've missed you.' Dr Pearce's breathing is heavy with anticipation, as it was on the train from Harrogate.

His hands slide over my hips.

'Oh, Jane,' he moans.

This is madness.

NINE

DR PEARCE STROKES A FINGER UP AND DOWN MY ARM. 'WHEN can I see you next?'

I'm repulsed. By his touch; by my omissions and the lies. I have a dozen excuses but none of them will wash.

'I don't know.' I keep my face turned away. 'They're getting ready for Christmas – and there's the rehearsals . . . It makes meeting you difficult.'

'That was clever, dropping your notebook to tell me to meet you here.'

'I wanted to suggest my being a conduit between Mrs Christie and Dr Argyle.'

'Interesting.' He tries to kiss me again. I turn my head. I suppose he finds it doubly exciting being in a forbidden place with me. I find it sordid. 'If someone sees us . . .' I don't need to spell it out.

Our affair began while I was caring for Jim's parents. First Mr Watts, then Mrs Watts. I had to spend long, drawn-out hours sitting at their bedside knowing all I could do was try and make them comfortable – and often not even that. It was almost as exhausting as being on the wards in its own way. A lonely, sombre job.

When at the conclusion of one of his visits Dr Pearce suggested we take a walk around the grounds, I was only too glad to escape into the sunshine. It seemed harmless enough. I only saw him as a doctor. Rather dull, but well-meaning.

Neither of us wanted to chat about work as we trailed around the estate.

'Look, there's a pied wagtail by that ash,' he said, breaking the rather awkward silence.

I hadn't a clue what he was on about. From then on, he'd point out the different birds, plants and trees enjoying my growing interest.

Brought up in the back streets of Wigan I only knew weeds from rubbing dock leaves on nettled shins or blowing on dandelion clocks to tell the time. It impressed me how Dr Pearce could look at a leaf and name the tree, often the Latin too. He could tell lime from elm, plucking a heart-shaped leaf from each.

'The lime is smooth, the elm rough or fuzzy.'

He taught me to tell hawthorn from blackthorn, distinguishable by their red and purple berries. Soon it became a habit; strolling round the lake or through the orchard with its three straight rows of apple trees, windfall gnawed and rotting on the ground.

I snuck out one morning in search of Thomas, keen to have a fact of my own to impress Dr Pearce with. Wanting to feel equal with him.

'I know just the thing, Jane. You ever noticed them two big trees by the ventilation shaft? The ones with the barrel-shaped cones.'

I nodded.

'Cedar of Lebanon – tell 'im the Egyptians used the resin and sawdust in the embalming process. That'll appeal to a doctor.'

It was between those cedars that he first held my hand. I should have put a stop to it then.

Dogs bark in the distance.

'I've got to go,' I say, straightening my clothing. 'Quickly, tell me what Dr Argyle said to Mr and Mrs Watts.'

'He said she has had a bad nervous breakdown, brought on by grief and exasperated by her marital difficulties. Much as I thought, she shows lapses of memory and severe nervous exhaustion. But he feels he can get her right in time.'

He starts in with the kisses again.

'No,' I say, sounding like Matron.

He holds up his hands and lets me go at last.

'I need to go too,' he sighs. 'Said I'd call at Mrs Griffiths if I was in the vicinity.'

As I reach the door I spot a second apple core by the old blanket. Looks fresh, which makes me feel a bit sick. 'Wait a few more minutes before you come out. We mustn't take any more chances.'

I press my fingers to my cheeks; they feel flushed as I hurry to the old chapel for the second rehearsal.

'You're late,' says Mrs Cherry. 'I can't stand tardiness.' She's dressed in royal blue with a matching velvet turban complete with peacock plume. She thrusts a script at me. My initials are marked on the top. 'Agatha can't make it. You'll have to be our prompt.'

'Shouldn't I check on her?'

'She's fine,' says Madge. 'The consultation with Dr Argyle left her a little tired, that's all.'

The pews are in a triangle. I sit next to Madge, wafting myself with the script. Agatha must still be smarting over what Archie said to Madge about her.

Charles is on the second, next to Iris. Paul on the third, opposite them.

Richard has a tray of drinks. 'That's the last of the coffee,' he says. He passes Paul a mug. 'Yours was black, right?'

He nods.

'I hope you put plenty of sugar in mine,' says Charles.

'And none in mine. I'm sweet enough,' adds Iris.

'And then the teas. There's some still in the pot, Jane.'

'Thanks.'

Mrs Cherry tuts and I decide not to bother.

'I'd love for someone to leave me a fortune like Great Uncle Hector,' says Iris, wistfully.

'You'd only blow the lot quicker than you apply lipstick,' says Charles.

'Says the man who is always up to his neck in debt,' throws back Iris.

Ouch.

He narrows his eyebrows. 'I'm not in debt, actually, darling. Just having a few cash flow issues.'

'Yes. It's all flowing in the one direction.' She waves her hand away and laughs.

'Oh, dear Charles,' says Madge. 'You feel the pinch more often that the barmaid at The George and Dragon.'

'More dry spells than a desert,' adds Mrs Cherry.

'On the breadline without any dough?' I offer.

'There's so many idioms and sayings about money, aren't there?' says Richard.

'Ooh, get you. *Idioms*,' Charles snipes. 'Watch out, Madge. I think we've another potential playwright in our midst.'

'We're a right mixture of princes and paupers when you think about it,' says Paul, taking a cigarette. 'Well, princesses.'

'I'd like a rich wife myself,' says Charles. 'How about it, Madge? Can I lure you away?'

She laughs. 'You're incorrigible!'

'Don't you mean encourageable?'

She bats her hand at his nonsense.

'No divorce? Oh well.' He cozies up to Mrs Cherry. 'I'll just have to settle for a nice rich widow instead. A little digitalis in her bedtime cocoa and all my money worries would be over.'

'Charles! That's horrid,' Iris scolds.

'I was joking. Anyway, you prefer hot milk as a nightcap. Don't you, Delia?'

'You cheeky monkey!' She beckons Madge closer. 'You must make sure Agatha updates her will. Though I assume there won't be much money from the sale of the house. They haven't been in it long, have they?'

Madge puts a finger to her lips and shakes her head. Not that it stops Mrs Cherry.

'There's income from her books to consider, though. Tell her to set up a trust for Rosalind.'

'I have nothing to leave anyone,' says Richard. 'Except for my motor car, and even that is on its last legs. It's a nightmare in winter.'

Mrs Cherry claps her hands. 'Right. Enough chitchat. Let's get back to it. Places, everyone. And from the top.'

I fold back the title page.

'Fancy us having a Great Uncle Hector we never knew about,' begins Iris.

I follow each word carefully. Every so often Mrs Cherry suggests a slightly different approach to a line or discusses the staging with Madge.

After about an hour, Madge suggests they work on the poisoning scene. 'Charles, we need the table.'

'Of course, darling.'

While he and Paul drag the furniture into position, Mrs Cherry, Madge and Iris go through a box of props, selecting tableware.

Richard sits next to me. Lights another cigarette. 'Look at me sweating like a pig.' He takes off his jacket, drops the case and matches into his pocket. 'I hope I'm not so nervous when it comes to the real thing. They're just all so good.'

'I'm sure you'll be fine.'

He smiles. 'Iris is quite wonderful, isn't she? And so young. I didn't have her confidence when I was nineteen.'

'I still don't.'

'I heard her father wasn't keen on her becoming an actress at first, but she must have won him round. He has a reputation for being your typical gruff mill owner, but apparently he's putty in his daughter's hands.'

'Oh, Caldwell's Cottons.'

'That's right. Sorry, I thought you knew everyone.'

'No. I nursed Mrs Watts's mother and Mr Watts's father in the spring. So I only know the family and Charles.'

'Oh, I see. Is he related?'

I shake my head. 'He works for S & J's.'

'Have you been a nurse for long?'

'Six years.'

'You must enjoy it, then. Or perhaps it depends on the patient? Imagine looking after Paul or . . .' He glances quickly at Mrs Cherry.

I pull a face.

He laughs. 'Still, that's the difference between being a hospital nurse and a private one. You get to choose whose bedside you attend.'

'You do.'

'Bet you never thought you'd be nursing a celebrity, though.' He lowers his voice. 'I'd never heard of Agatha Christie before her disappearance. Don't tell Madge, but I've been intrigued by it all. Though I do wonder . . .'

'What do you mean?'

'Well, her story doesn't quite add up. Does it? Did Mrs Christie take a train to Waterloo early Saturday morning, as it says in the newspapers, or did she actually travel the previous night. I can't imagine her spending all night in her motor car. Can you?'

That's a good point.

'She's arrives in London, suffering from loss of memory. But instead of going to a police station to ask for help, she goes to the Army and Navy stores to buy a coat. Yet she left an expensive fur behind in her motor car. Why? Then, there's that business with her ring. Telling Harrods to send it on to Mrs Neele at the Hydro once it was mended—'

Charles slaps his hands on Richard's shoulders bringing him to a halt. 'Stop chatting up, Jane. We're waiting for you.'

'Sorry.' Richard grabs his jacket.

Is Richard right to be cynical of Agatha's account?

The MADS take their places around the table. Charles, Iris, Paul and Richard are seated. Mrs Cherry looms over them as they work their way through the will reading scene.

Half a page in, there's a knock on the door.

Everyone turns.

'Who's that now?' complains Mrs Cherry. 'Jane, go see.'

I haven't the energy to argue. I get up and cross to the door.

'Oh! Reverend Whittle. Do come in.'

Kitty's behind him, leaning on one hip in an uninterested manner. They're both holding a cardboard box.

'Can I put this down now, Vicar?' she moans.

I usher them inside.

'Let me help you,' says Charles, eyes on Kitty.

'You're all right,' she replies, dropping the box onto the floor by the pews.

Reverend Whittle nods his head to acknowledge everyone. 'I hope I'm not disturbing you all.'

'Of course not,' says Madge, though her brow furrows. 'What have you got there?'

The others gather closer.

'Donations for the church jumble sale. Obviously with the roof, it has also had to be postponed. But then I had an epiphany! The MADS might be able to make use of some of the clothing as costumes.'

'How very thoughtful, Vicar,' says Mrs Cherry.

'The second box is poorer quality items, not suitable for resale; stained and whatnot. Perhaps you could pass those onto your gardener for scarecrows. There are some newspapers too.'

'Indeed. Thank you,' adds Madge. 'I'm sure Thomas will be very grateful.'

Charles is still hovering round Kitty. She pays him no attention, which unfortunately only seems to enthuse him.

'Shall we have a look?' he asks, shifting aside the newspapers from the box at her feet. The top one is this morning's *Advertiser* folded back to the Cheadle news page. The vicar as guilty of following the Christie case as everyone.

Luckily everyone is distracted by Charles grimacing as he holds up a pair of tatty men's striped pyjama bottoms. 'I don't think S & J's will be stocking these any time soon.'

The headline reads 'SPECIALIST TO ASSESS MRS CHRISTIE' but my eyes jump to the smaller headline below. 'Nurse hired to care for author'.

Picking up the pile, I race over the remaining words while pushing the newspapers back into the box. Thank God, I am not named. But how much longer before I go from anonymous footnote to headline news?

'This one's the costumes,' says Reverend Whittle putting down his own box and crossing to the window. 'Looks like there's snow on the way.'

Charles opens the lid. Pulls out a long piece of white lace. 'What's this? Net curtains?'

'I thought it would be perfect for the ghost bride,' the vicar replies. 'I always think it rather a pity that modern brides don't care for the more traditional Victorian veils. They are very pretty. Don't you think so, ladies?'

'Oh yes,' says Mrs Cherry. 'I wore something very similar myself. Major Cherry was in his uniform of course. Very dashing.'

'Mine was a quieter affair,' says Madge. 'We were still in mourning for my father, so we didn't have a reception. He'd been rather against my marrying Jim, but I don't think it was personal. Fathers never think anyone is good enough for their daughters.'

'No, they don't,' says Iris, her face serious.

'I suppose that's why so many elope to Scotland,' says Richard, offering the vicar a cigarette, who passes, before lighting his own.

'So romantic,' says Mrs Cherry.

'I must say I think a family's approval is vital.' Reverend Whittle frowns.

'But what if their family won't give it?' asks Iris.

'Well, I have no intention of getting married,' says Paul. 'Spend the rest of your life being henpecked. No thank you.'

The vicar rubs his hands together. 'Couldn't trouble you for a cup of coffee before I set off again, could I, Mrs Watts? Rather bitter out.'

'Oh sorry, we've run out. Will tea do?' she asks.

'Of course.' He smiles at Richard. 'We've met before, I think.'

'I don't think so . . .' He coughs. 'Excuse me, Vicar. I think I'd better get a drink myself.'

'I hope you're not coming down with something,' says Mrs Cherry.

'No, no.' He waves his cigarette. 'Should really give these up.'

'Richard is a clerk in the village,' Madge says, as he goes into the kitchen, where Kitty is clattering about with cups and saucers.

'A bank clerk?' asks Reverend Whittle, paling.

'I'm not sure,' Madge replies.

I go to help Kitty before she breaks something.

'I like my tea strong, Nursie,' says Paul, following me. 'Last time I went to the bank there was a girl working behind the counter.' He examines one of the cups, grunts, and puts it into the sink for rewashing. 'Bad enough women taking our jobs during the war, but there's no excuse for it now. Did you serve?' He points to Richard's thick-lensed spectacles. 'Or were you classified unfit?'

'I was in Serbia.' Richard picks up the kettle and tops up the teapot.

I glance back at Madge.

'Jesus! Watch what you're doing!' cries Paul.

TEN

'ARE YOU HURT?' I CHECK.

'He could've bloody scalded me.' Paul cries, as Kitty mops up the spilt hot water with a tea towel.

'I'm sorry. It was an accident.'

Richard puts down the steaming kettle.

'You want to get some new glasses, mate. Them jam jars obviously aren't strong enough,' Paul snarls before stomping away.

Richard's hands are shaking.

'Are you all right?' I ask.

'I'm fine.' He takes another drag on his cigarette. 'That type always wind me up. Wanting to know how your war was.'

I give a sympathetic smile. 'Go sit down. I'll finish the tea.'

Madge comes over and gathers up the milk jug and sugar bowl, placing them on a tray. 'The war provokes strong reactions, even now. Jim has always had mixed feelings about not serving. We lost eighty-five S & J employees.'

I've seen the memorial in the entrance to the warehouse. A granite tablet bearing the names of the staff lost and 'The Sentry'. A bronze serviceman in battledress clasping his rifle with bayonet, but it was his mud-clagged puttees that most struck me.

I fill the cups with tea, placing them carefully on their saucers. Pretty, delicate bone china with tiny pink roses around the rim.

'I was a VAD at Cheadle House Auxiliary Hospital on the high street,' Madge continues, quietly. 'Agatha was in the thick of it, down in Torquay, though she started off rolling bandages and preparing swabs, until the injured arrived. We received patients from other bigger hospitals to recuperate. Men suffering from trench fever, disordered action of the heart, shrapnel injuries. I remember one unusual case – a gunner who'd received a kick to the head from a mule.' She takes teaspoons from a drawer and adds them to the tray. 'But mostly it was cleaning and scrubbing, fetching bed pans and urinals, cleaning up vomit. One time Agatha had to help a young probationer clean up the blood after an amputation and together they carried the limb down to the furnace. Is it any wonder many of us would rather forget the war?' Her eyes follow Paul. 'I often suspect those most keen to reminisce were far from the front. If they saw action at all.'

Kitty and I dole out the tea. Iris has her compact out again. She snaps it shut and accepts a cup and saucer. At least she says thank you, not like Mrs Cherry.

'Want a hand with that lot?' I ask Kitty, cocking my head towards the donations. 'Save you two trips.'

Kitty glances at Madge.

'They won't even notice we've gone.'

I'm probably overstepping, but this is an opportunity to return to the hall and look in on Agatha. I'm not sure what's worse, her being alone and left to brood, or that she might seek out a confrontation with Archie.

Kitty nods and opens the door. I slide my hands under the box of good stuff and lift. It's not heavy, just awkward.

She folds down the lid on hers. 'We'll drop this one at the greenhouse,' she says. 'I can manage from there.'

Darn. Oh well, I can still find an excuse to nip inside.

'How long have you been working here?' I ask as we lumber along the track.

'Five weeks. I'm Ellen's replacement.'

'And you enjoy it?'

Kitty gives me a look. 'I clean grates and scrub floors.'

'But the Wattses are a good family?'

'S'pose.'

We pass Gardener's Cottage off to our right. I change tack.

'Thomas will be glad of these.' I give my box a little jerk.

'S'pose.'

I give up. Entering the walled garden through the wrought iron gate, I note again how it's always a few degrees warmer inside. More so when the heating between the bricks is on. In spring, the insides of the walls are covered with flowering fruit trees, traditional English apples and pears, but also quince.

All the neat rows of flowers and vegetables have died back for the winter, and it's hard to imagine everything in bloom. The roses' perfume a distant memory.

Ahead of us is the greenhouse; it stretches almost as long as the garden itself. Here there are a few signs of life: tiny sprouting seedlings, a spider crawling across a web on one of the panes of glass, a wood mouse that whips across the path and hides inside a terracotta plant pot.

Thomas is further along, hanging a brown sticky fly trap. 'This is a nice surprise,' he calls, beckoning us nearer. 'What've you got there?'

'Clothes from the vicar,' says Kitty. 'That one's for your scarecrows. This one's for costumes for Mrs Watts's play.'

I put the box down next to a sack of soil. She rests hers on the slatted shelving.

'Sent me 'is old frock coats and dog collars, 'as 'e? That'll frighten the birds.'

Kitty sniggers. 'You're wicked, Mr Budworth.'

'Let's see then.' He rummages through the contents, pulling out an assortment of torn and well-worn garments. Thomas picks out a faded blue cotton shirt. 'Nowt wrong with this one.' He holds it to his chest. 'Plenty o' wear left in it.'

Kitty giggles again.

He drops the shirt into the box.

'Now for the posh stuff.' He winks at her.

She opens the box, pulls out a bowler hat.

'The 'ead gardener before me used to wear one of these.' He tugs on the brim of his flat cap. 'Prefer this, meself.'

Kitty puts on the bowler hat; it drops over her eyes. 'You'd have to have a big head to wear this – like that Iris Caldwell,' she mutters. 'Thinks she's a blooming Clara Bow – she's not even Betty Balfour.' She swans up and down the greenhouse, pretending to wave to an appreciative crowd. 'Why, thank you. Thank you.'

I saw Betty in *Love, Life and Laughter*. She played a would-be actress who lives in a run-down tenement. The Caldwell's newly-built mansion is hardly that.

Kitty takes out the wedding veil and drapes it over her head. 'Wish I had a fancy compact mirror like her, though.'

'You look very pretty,' says Thomas. 'Now, this is fancy.' He pulls out a mink stole. 'Finest ferret,' he says, draping it round his neck.

We all laugh.

'Right, leave that box there.' He stuffs the stole back inside. 'We'll take that scarecrow stuff over to the bothy and I'll make you a brew. Could do with topping up my flask.'

It's only a short walk to the small brick building. I imagine it was cramped when half a dozen potboys used to sleep in it. Nowadays it's only used for Thomas's tea breaks. It's lovely and cozy, if a bit makeshift. There's a small range, freshly blackened.

Thomas puts the box by one of the old armchairs and sets about laying a new fire. I grab today's *Advertiser* from it and quickly scan the rest of the main story.

'Mystery writer Agatha Christie is being treated by a psychiatrist who specialises in treating insane patients at the Cheadle Royal. Among Dr Argyle's cases at the asylum are patients suffering from drug dependency, alcohol addiction, kleptomania, somnambulism and other sleep disorders. Dr Argyle was unavailable for comment.'

The reporter's inference is obvious. I curse and toss it onto the tinder pile. Rubbish like that's fit only for the fire. Thomas hangs his iron kettle over the flames, then opens a round tin.

'Is that Cook's fruit cake?' I ask, eyes widening. It's been months since I've had some. My mouth waters in anticipation.

'Sultana,' he replies, wiping a knife on a tea towel before slicing the chunk into three.

Kitty holds up three mismatched plates in turn for each piece.

I pinch a chunk of my portion and pop it into my mouth. It's deliciously buttery and sweet.

'So the vicar's back again, is 'e? Brought 'is begging bowl too, no doubt,' Thomas says while we wait for the kettle to boil. 'I 'ope 'e's not thinking a few clothes for my scarecrows will persuade me onto the church 'all roof. If 'e had got a proper company in the first time, like Mr Watts said, 'e wouldn't be 'aving to pay out for further repairs.'

'It's leaked before?' I ask.

'Oh, yes. Must be two years ago. There were a big fundraiser. 'alf of Cheadle contributed, with old Mr James giving a big donation. Only some folk are saying maybe 'e only got it patched.' He raises his eyebrows. 'To save a bob or two.'

If that's true, it would explain why Reverend Whittle looked worried when he thought Richard was a bank clerk.

Thomas swills the brown teapot with hot water, then spoons in the tea. Kitty nibbles at her piece of cake.

'Did you get the other tree in all right?' I ask.

Thomas shakes his head. 'Been told to wait till tomorrow, now. Wish they'd make their minds up. I don't know what's wrong with Christmas Eve. That's traditional.'

'Still, it'll brighten up the house.'

'Mmm.' He doesn't sound convinced.

'Patience and I can decorate them after the reporter's gone,' says Kitty, happily. 'Mrs Watts has got some new electric lights, especially.'

Thomas scoffs. 'And what's wrong with candles?'

'They're so old-fashioned, Mr Budworth.'

'Well I suppose that makes me an old fogey.' He adds more hot water to the pot and turns back to me. ''ow's rehearsals coming along?'

'Fine, I think. Mrs Cherry appears to keep a tight ship.'

'A bossy boots, you mean.'

'She said she'd had a . . . tussle . . . with you, trying to get in, yesterday.' I grin.

'Thought she were going to swipe at me with that ridiculous floppy 'at of 'ers. Waving at me like I was an irritating fly. No wonder 'er 'usband upped and died. Anything for a quiet life.'

Kitty snorts. 'My mam knows the woman who used to live next door. Used to hear *everything*. Said the walls were very thin.'

'I thought Mrs Cherry lived in one of them cottages opposite the war memorial.'

'Manor Cottage, that's right,' says Kitty, her eyes twinkling.

Thin walls, my foot. Still, there's worse sins than eavesdropping.

'Bet she were forever on at 'im. Poor chap.'

'Oh no,' says Kitty. 'Apparently, it were the Major that were always bawling at her.'

That reminds me of a patient I had at a cottage hospital I worked at for a short time. He was always finding fault, losing his temper if things weren't just so. Us nurses used to moan that he seemed to think he was staying at The Ritz: the sheets were too thin, we were too slow bringing the bed pans, the window was open too much or not enough. Never a please or thank you. The chaps either side of him had it as bad. Their snoring kept him awake. He was supposed to have the newspaper they were reading first. On and on the complaints went, and always so the whole ward had to earwig what he was griping on about.

Then, about three weeks after his admission, we got word he'd family coming to visit. I thought at first the woman was his mother; she was a tiny thing about four foot eight and bony with it; I remember her collar bone jutted out like a coat hanger. Spoke in a whisper when she asked to see her husband. But soon as she hit the ward, she bellowed his name and didn't let up for an hour. He sunk down into those too-thin sheets and didn't make so much as a peep.

'You were miles away,' says Thomas, touching my hand gently. 'I 'ope looking after Mrs Christie isn't bringing back any of your old trouble sleeping.'

Kitty watches me.

'I'm fine. Just ready for that cuppa.' I nod my head to indicate the teapot he's now tipping to fill my cup. I smile as Kitty transfers some of hers into her saucer, so she can sup from it.

'Magic stuff, tea,' says Thomas, unscrewing his Thermos. 'But you will say if you—'

'Of course. Promise.'

He fills up the flask, then his own cup. 'What's this new doctor like? 'ave you met 'im yet?'

'Yes, he seemed very professional.'

Kitty splutters her tea. 'Do you have a pulse?'

'Argyle's 'andsome, is 'e?'

'Gorgeous, Mr Budworth. I wanted to tell him: "You can take my temperature anytime."'

'Kitty!' Thomas laughs.

I bring the cup to my lips to stop myself from warning her to stay away from him.

'And will Dr Pearce be visiting again?' Thomas adds sugar to his drink.

This time I'm the one who splutters. 'Sorry, it's still a bit hot.' I blow over the surface. 'He didn't say either way.'

'Good man, Dr Pearce. Very attentive to old Mr and Mrs Watts in their final days. And always asked 'ow my knee was when 'e saw me in the garden or in the village – even if that salve 'e prescribed didn't really 'elp. I told 'im, it's just old age, nothing you can do for that.'

⟷

After finishing our tea and cake, we return to the greenhouse. Kitty goes to pick up the other box. I can see straight away that it's been moved, the bowler hat is on the floor.

'How did that get there?' Kitty scoops up the hat and gives it a quick waft with her hand to knock off the muck.

The flaps are open. It looks like the contents have been yanked out. They are no longer folded neatly.

'Where's the stole?' I ask.

It was on top when we left it. Pulling everything out, it's soon clear it's gone.

'Maybe a rabbit took it, Mr Budworth,' says Kitty.

'It 'opped up onto my shelving like Peter Rabbit, did it?' teases Thomas. 'I should know better than to leave the greenhouse unlocked. Lucky, there were nowt else worth nicking. No need to tell the vicar though.'

We shake our heads.

'You had stuff go missing before?' I ask Thomas while helping Kitty refold the clothing.

'In the garden? A trowel once, but that's going back a good while. There were a saddle and bridle taken from the stables in the summer. And scrumping's always a problem.'

'Maybe someone thought the stole was Mrs Christie's and has taken it as a souvenir?' suggests Kitty.

That's the daftest thing she's said yet. 'More likely someone took it to pawn it,' I say firmly, picking up the box.

Her eyes widen. 'Bet you one of them reporters took it. They were going mad for anything to use in their stories as a clue to her disappearance. I heard how one even got a barmaid to help him fake Mrs Christie's shoeprint on the doorstep of a deserted cabin. I'm going down to the lodge gates to have it out with them.'

'I don't think that's wise, love. Mr and Mrs Watts wouldn't like it.'

Kitty's bottom lip protrudes, but she nods her head.

But perhaps her idea's not that daft after all. Now one of the reporters has been granted an exclusive – the others will be even more desperate for a scoop.

ELEVEN

KITTY MUTTERS UNDER HER BREATH AS WE RETRACE OUR STEPS to the iron gate. Abney's frontage is spread before us. The billiard room juts out on my left; it's shape and the fact there's a cruciform in the brick above the window makes me think of the asylum's Roman Catholic chapel.

I was never one for praise and prayers. I'd seen too much suffering and poverty to believe in all that. I'd gone to church as a child, of course, though we were C of E, and for my parents' funerals. I squeeze my thumb. There was an Anglican chapel too at the asylum, but I never went inside. Not even for the service of remembrance. I knew I wouldn't be welcome despite all my excuses and apologies.

Instead, I hid behind a yew tree and imagined them filing into the pews in ranks: doctors first, then matrons, male nurses, female nurses, and finally the cleaners and porters. Listening attentively to the eulogy. Anger rises inside me.

The servants' entrance door clangs, bringing me back to the present.

Kitty's gone.

I decide to use the side entrance by the boys' room instead.

As I pass the billiard room windows on my right, I see two shadowy figures moving about. Muffled shouting. I'm pretty sure it's Agatha and Archie, though I can hardly press my nose against the leaded glass to be sure.

I turn the corner and mount the steps. Inside, I follow the passageway to the billiard room door then brazenly enter.

'Oh, sorry, I didn't realise there was someone in here,' I lie. 'The vicar dropped off this box of donated clothing for costumes.'

Agatha and Archie's faces are mottled pink.

'Punkie's still rehearsing,' says Agatha.

'Any idea where your sister would want this stored?'

'None,' says Archie, giving me a hard stare.

I glance round; there are more books in here than in the library. There are shelves of them all along the walls.

'Not in here,' he sounds exasperated. 'I'm using this room for the interview.'

'Wouldn't the terrace room be more . . .' I clam up. My opinion is not welcome.

'Suitable?' adds Agatha. 'See, Archie. Jane feels the same way. A games room could give completely the wrong impression.'

Archie snorts like a bull. 'You could always do the interview yourself if you have such strong feelings on the matter.'

'I don't think that's a good idea – with my memory loss I can get awfully muddled about things. I might get mixed up and say the wrong thing.'

'You wouldn't dare—'

Now he stops abruptly, perhaps unwilling to say more in my presence. He pats his pocket for his cigarettes and lighter, a sure sign of his stress.

'Jim doesn't even want the press in the house,' says Agatha, adding fuel to the fire.

'Fine! I'll do it on the bloody terrace then. See what impression that makes.'

He storms out.

Agatha collapses into a chair. 'Why does he have to be so horrid?'

I put the box down on the billiard table and kneel at her feet. Making myself smaller will make me less of a threat.

'I had a patient once, used to bawl at me day and night—'

She jumps up and steps around me, cutting me off. I guess she doesn't like me comparing my experiences to hers.

'You married during the war, didn't you?' I ask, as I stand.

She's by the billiards table now. She spins and points at me. 'You broke the spills vase in my room! I knew my wedding day photograph had been moved, and to think I accused poor Patience.'

'I— It was an accident.'

'Hah! You were snooping. Admit it.'

'It was the spills I was interested in. Mr Watts told Patience to dispose of any newspapers, so you won't see them by accident.' I move closer to her, trying to physically and emotionally shorten the distance between us. 'When I realised Patience had torn them into strips to make spills, I was curious what the local press had written about you, and about your coming to Abney, only the vase slipped from my fingers . . .'

'And where are the spills now? Not in the wastepaper basket.'

'I threw them away.' I bite my bottom lip. 'I admit I looked at your photograph too when I moved it to fill the gap, but I did it without thinking. I didn't realise it was taken on your wedding day until I saw the writing on the back.'

'No. I suppose we don't look like a typical bridal couple.' Agatha cups a yellow billiard ball. 'Archie and I debated back and forth about getting married; one then the other changing our minds, calling it off. We hadn't the money. He might be killed. My mother's failing eyesight. Head versus heart.' She absently rolls the ball round and round on the baize. 'Then just as suddenly, on Christmas Eve, Archie decided we had to be wed that very day. The scramble to get a licence, find a venue. Our determination grew with our giddiness. I imagine there were lots of couples like us. The uncertainty of war and the romance of eloping. We were in love. I wanted passion not security.'

Is she thinking of Madge?

'Being Archie's wife was like another of my imaginary games at first. I took cookery lessons, found us places to live . . . I've always loved houses. I had a beautiful dolls' house as a girl, later I put it in a cupboard so I could extend . . .' She spins the ball hard towards a pocket. Turns round. 'I don't see that my marriage is any of your business.'

The door swings open.

I groan inwardly as Dr Pearce enters. What's he doing back?

'Ah, Nurse Goodbetter. Found you at last. Could I have a word, in private?'

Agatha picks up the box and stalks out.

Dr Pearce makes sure the door is shut firmly behind her.

He gestures to a settee by the window.

We sit.

'I've been mulling over what you said in the boathouse, Jane. About it being useful for Dr Argyle to have a . . . what was the word you used?'

'Conduit?'

'Exactly. Between him and Agatha. So, I came back and raised it with Mr Watts and he thinks it's a good idea too.'

'You didn't say it was my suggestion?'

'No. Anyway, he's going to put it to Callum when he returns tomorrow.'

'Good.'

'I thought you'd be pleased.' He goes to stroke my arm.

I pull away. I need to go after Agatha. 'I'd better check Mrs Christie is resting.' I force myself to give him a quick peck on the cheek. I still need him onside. For now.

↔

It feels like I'm entering a party not a rehearsal when I step back into the old chapel. Iris and Paul are gathered around the table while Charles pretends to uncork the Champagne bottle again.

'Pop!' calls Madge.

Agatha is sitting with Jack and Richard on one of the pews. I sit on the end next to her. She blanks me.

This time there's actual liquid in the bottle, though it looks distinctly flat when Charles pours it into three Champagne coupes.

'To Great Uncle Hector,' he declares as they raise their glasses and drink.

'Urgh, it's rather bitter,' says Charles, coughing.

Paul screws up his nose. 'Lemonade. Couldn't we have actual bubbly?'

Mrs Cherry rolls her eyes.

'I've never understood why people drink the stuff,' whispers Agatha. 'I've never liked the taste of alcohol, and Champagne's the worst.'

Charles knocks back the rest of his drink. Then goes white as a sheet. Beads of sweat forming at his temples. He groans, clenching his stomach. Cries out.

'Oh God!'

TWELVE

'A STENCH FILLS THE ROOM. 'JEEZ,' SAYS PAUL, WAFTING THE air. 'What've you been eating?'

Charles's arms are still wrapped around his stomach. 'Sorry. I'd better . . .' he thumbs towards the door. Groans again.

'Hurry, dear,' says Madge.

'Your face, Jane!' sniggers Agatha. 'Did you think he'd been poisoned?'

I'm glad Charles's flatulence has broken her huff.

Mrs Cherry flushes. 'Yes. Well, it is getting late. Perhaps we should call today's rehearsal to an end while Mr Trent is inconvenienced. We'll pick up where we left off at eleven o'clock tomorrow.'

Everyone starts to gather up their coats.

'Will you stay for dinner, Delia?' asks Madge. 'We can discuss how today's gone.'

'That would be lovely, but I'll have to leave by eight-thirty. I'll see the others off then come back to the house.'

'Jack, would you lock up? Then ask Patience to make up a bed for Charles. I think he'd better spend the night here. And could you lend him a pair of your pyjamas?'

'Yes, Mother.'

The rest of us follow Newlands Road back to the front of the hall. Thomas has lit the lanterns that line the driveway ready for the MADS departure. Oh no. Kitty's marching towards the lodge gates. The silly girl must have decided to challenge the reporters after all.

Damn.

While the MADS are wishing each other goodnight, I hurry after Kitty. The fine rain is starting to turn to sleet. I look skyward, apparently the vicar was right. When the temperature drops overnight that'll turn to snow. It's already starting to stick on the ground. At least my nurse's cap will stop my hair from getting too wet.

Kitty's pulling back the bolt. The rumble of motor car engines firing up makes me instinctively turn. My foot stumbles on the gravel, and I go down, heavily, crushing my already bruised left wrist. I curse as pain surges from it. God, I hope it's not broken. What an idiot.

'Nurse Goodbetter!' Kitty abandons the gates and bends to help me up. 'What are you doing out here?'

'I . . .' I clasp my other hand to my wrist. Acid rises up my throat into my mouth. I swallow, grimacing. As I turn towards the house, I realise my knees are stinging. I lift the hem of my uniform; my stockings are laddered. Tears well.

'You'll have a lovely couple of bruises, come morning,' says Kitty, surprisingly sympathetic. 'You should get that wrist looked at properly. I think Dr Pearce's still here. Come on, take my arm.'

I might be pleased at having diverted her if I wasn't in agony.

Every step radiates pain in my ankle as she guides me back to the hall and it's even worse when I climb the steps to the entrance. I'm done in by the time we reach the library, wincing as I flop into one of the leather chairs. I prop up my arm to keep my wrist aloft while Kitty gathers an assortment of cushions. She eases off my shoe and places my foot onto the pile. She is unexpectedly gentle, and it feels nice to be the one being nursed for once.

'Won't be a minute,' she says.

In fact, by the longcase clock by the window she is more like four. To my relief when Kitty returns, she's accompanied by Madge who tells me Dr Pearce has left.

'But I'm sure I can manage. Kitty, would you help Patience set up the afternoon tea in the terrace room.'

'Yes, ma'm.'

I glance out of the window. The snow is falling heavier now. Hopefully the reporters will retreat to their motor cars and Kitty will forget her plans to interrogate them about that stole.

Madge puts the jar she's holding onto the fancy green malachite table next to me.

'Can you move your fingers for me?'

I wriggle them.

'Good.'

'Can you flex your wrist?'

I rotate it left and right, down and up, trying not to cry out again. 'Lucky I'm right-handed,' I say with fake brightness.

'Hmm. Fortunate too that Agatha doesn't require any physical nursing.'

Madge unscrews the lid; the pungent smell of comfrey fills

the air. She tuts. 'What were you doing on the driveway, anyway?'

I still haven't prepared an excuse, so I moan as a diversion.

She reaches into her pocket, retrieving a bandage and a small butter knife. She unrolls the crepe then slathers one side with the green leafy paste. I suck in my breath as she straps up my wrist, then repeats the treatment for my ankle. She works with confidence and a firm touch.

'Dr Argyle would like you to pass on any observations you have about Agatha's behaviour.' She clamps my bandaged wrist. 'I can't say I like the idea of you being what my father would call a snoop.'

I don't know the word, but her squeezing my wrist makes her point only too well.

'Agatha is not the only one who values her privacy. I don't suppose you know who told *The Advertiser* about your being employed to look after her?'

The increase in pain makes my eyes smart. 'Please. You're hurting me. It wasn't me, if that's what you think.'

She holds my gaze but releases my wrist. 'Good. There, all done.'

↔

I must have dozed off. When I wake, it's to the sound of the longcase clock striking the half hour. 7.30 p.m. I can hear the family dining in the room next door.

Colonel Christie must have long since finished his interview. The mood he was in earlier, I dread to think what he might have said about Agatha to the journalist. He must know talking to the press again only distresses his wife further. How can he be so cruel? Does he hate her that much?

As I close the shutters, voices make me start. I try to see who it is, but it's pitch black.

A female voice. Too faint to identify. The words indistinct until her voice raises. 'Where've you been? I've been hanging about like a stray cat waiting for you.'

'Sorry . . . I'm here now, aren't I?' A man.

More whispering.

'Really?' Her again. Pleased. No, more than that. Excited.

'I told you it would work . . .'

I strain to hear, but it's hopeless.

Her voice rises again. 'I'd better go. We don't want to be seen . . .'

It goes quiet. They must have moved away from the window. I peer out again but still can't see who it was.

My wrist is stiff but the pain's eased. I massage it gently as I retreat to my room.

I press the electric servants' bell then sit on the bed. I kick off my shoes then peel off my ruined stockings. The bruises on my knees are purplish and tender.

'Ah, Patience,' I say a few minutes later. 'I'd like some hot water, please, to bathe my knees.'

'Oh, you have been in the wars!' she exclaims. 'Kitty said as you'd taken a tumble on the driveway. You poor thing. Does no good to be racing about. Seems we're all at sixes and sevens. Colonel Christie's only gone and cancelled the interview last minute. I thought Cook was about to flip her lid,' she says, picking up the ewer from the washstand. 'Been baking all morning for nowt. Kitty and I had only just laid it all out when we had to take it away again. So we're not best pleased either. Not that we said a dicky bird. Get it?'

I shake my head in confusion. Funny, Archie doesn't strike me as the type to change his mind about things. Still Agatha will be relieved. I know I am.

'Still his loss is our gain,' she continues.

'Is it?' I'm even more befuddled.

'Oh yes, Nurse. Mrs Watts won't stand for any wastage, so the family will have the sandwiches with a consommé later and Cook's to save the Victoria for the MADS tomorrow.' She grins. 'But the scones won't keep so we can have them as a treat for all the inconvenience.'

I rub my ankle.

'Oh, galoshes, miss!'

'Galoshes?'

'I'd forget my head if it wasn't screwed on. Mr Watts asked me to find you a spare pair. I'll do it at once.'

'It's not urgent. After the water, will be fine.'

'If you say so, miss.' She's still nursing the ewer like a baby. 'I could fetch you one with the galoshes. A scone, I mean.'

'I think you'll have enough to carry.'

'Oh! Ha. Yes.' She waves the ewer like a beer stein and leaves.

I lie back on the bed.

Oh! There's me amused by Patience's scattiness when I haven't told Dr Pearce about finding the bottle of laudanum in Agatha's bedside drawer when I put the Mellotal sleeping powder in her room. I suppose now she's being treated by Dr Argyle, it's him I should tell, yet I'm reluctant to do so. Laudanum's a reliable enough pain killer but it's also a strong sedative. I'm worried Agatha could take both, by accident or worse. Perhaps I should hide it.

Where is Patience? My knees are still throbbing. I think I've some arnica in my nurse's kit. It's on the dresser by the window. Should close the curtains too.

The lanterns flicker on the driveway. I jerk with shock at the shadow of an impish figure running pell-mell. The mink stole held aloft like some kind of strange tribute to the gods.

THIRTEEN

I HOBBLE SHOELESS TO THE DOOR. THE TELEPHONE'S RINGING downstairs, in the long corridor, as I reach the landing.

It stops, then Jack's voice. *'Gatley 2827. Abney Hall . . .'*

Patience ambles up the stairs, singing 'One named Peter, one named Paul,' and somehow clutching the ewer and a pair of short rubber boots.

'Quick, give me those galoshes.' I reach out my arms.

'Oh, hello, Iris. It's Jack . . . Did you want my mother?'

'Is something the matter, Nurse?' asks Patience, pushing back her white mob cap.

Too breathless to reply, I sit on the steps.

Jack sounds concerned. *'Slow down. I can't make out what you're saying.'*

I pull on the boots, my wrist complaining at the effort.

'Tell me where you are . . .'

Back to my feet I almost trip in my rush. Idiot.

'Now, Iris, promise you'll stay there . . .'

Hurrying on, I stumble to the front door, desperately scrambling at the handle. Am I going to be too late?

The darkness works in my favour as I creep towards the lawn, my borrowed boots tread cushioned by the newly fallen snow. The back of the house is illuminated by a couple of garden lanterns, highlighting a trail of footprints, no bigger than my own. My left ankle throbs, but I limp on, adding my own to the terrace and down the steps. The figure has their back to me. The mink is alive, snaking over the snow. I squint, trying to work out how this can be. Then I realise it has been attached to a piece of string and is being dragged along.

Like a toy.

Relief rushes over me. It's not a man at all but a boy. Eleven. Maybe twelve. My heart jolts. Not much younger than David was when I last saw him.

'Hey, you!' I call out.

The boy spins round. His eyes panicked in the hand-knitted balaclava slot.

'This is private property,' I call.

He drops the string and runs, sliding over the snow.

I have no chance of following.

Bet that's who knocked on the door during rehearsals. Just the sort of prank a kid would play. Probably local. I bet Thomas knows him.

Cautiously, I crunch over the crisp snow to retrieve the mink. The stole is grubby and damp. Its weaselly face, slightly squished, seems almost perturbed from its short time back in the wild. Cutting diagonally back to the entrance, I'm in time to see Jack hurrying down the steps.

'Oh, Jane! Just the person. I need you to come with me into the village.'

'What's the matter?'

'Iris rang . . . I'll explain on the way. I'm going to borrow the Wolseley.' He brushes his fringe from his eyes.

Once we're in the car, Jack tells me about the phone call as we drive the back way along Newlands Road skirting the corner of Buckley Chapel.

I'm only half-listening, focused instead on looking for that scamp from earlier. I keep expecting him to dart out from behind a tree at any moment.

'She was so upset; I couldn't make out most of what she was trying to say,' he explains.

'Mmm,' I reply. His jumping to Iris's rescue makes me think he does have a pash on her. Strange she should call on Jack to be her knight in shining armour.

We pass under the railway bridge. Jack brakes. A motor car abandoned in a strange position.

'Isn't that Mr Buxton's?' I ask.

'I think you're right.' Jack pulls to a stop so his headlights shine onto the battered blue Morris.

We hop out.

'Richard must have lost control. Skidded on an ice patch, I expect,' says Jack. 'Damage isn't too bad. Some of these dings and dents look old. He was lucky, could have been a lot worse.'

There's a bad scrape above the wheel arch on the driver's side. 'Funny he didn't come back to the house for help.'

'Must have been closer to home.'

'There aren't any footsteps. It's like he's disappeared into thin air.'

'The snow covered them, that's all,' says Jack. 'Don't worry, this isn't like one of my aunt's books. Nobody got murdered.'

I laugh.

We get back into the Wolseley and continue towards The Green. As we pull up by the war memorial, I glance over to Cheadle Hall, where Jim and Madge used to live.

Jack goes round to open my car door.

The George and Dragon is over the road. A former coaching inn, it still has the original archway. That's where I spy Iris in an ankle length fur coat and beside her, slightly slumped, Paul.

Jack's unhappy expression tells me he's spotted them too.

'Let me do the talking,' he says.

That might not be the best approach, if Paul's had one too many as I suspect.

'Jack!' cries Paul when we reach them. 'Come to join the party?'

Iris's brow wrinkles on clocking me.

I realise I'm still clutching that damned mink.

'I didn't know you were bringing Jane too.'

He mouths something in reply to her, but Paul yanks my arm before I can work out what it was.

'Let you out the mad house, have they, Nursie?'

My heart contracts with fear. How could he know . . . but I realise he can't. He means Abney, surely.

'What'll you have?' Paul slaps his hand onto Jack's shoulder.

My father liked a drink, same as most of the fellows in my street save for a few that had taken the pledge. Most of them would go down the pub, laughing, singing songs. Some carried on when they got home. One or two got angry on it. The day after their wives would be pulling down their sleeves or be ready with another excuse for a new bruise. No doubt there's plenty there still who developed a taste for the hard stuff in the trenches. Dependent ever since their twice daily stand-to ration of rum.

'You've had enough, Paul,' says Jack. 'I've come to take you home.'

'Home? I'm not going bloody home.' He swings round, shouldering the door frame.

'Wrong approach,' I whisper in Jack's ear.

'No, Paul,' pleads Iris.

He spins again. 'No!' he shouts. 'No.' His nostrils flare. He jabs his finger at her. 'What right do you have—'

'I'd love a brandy,' I say, quickly, keeping the stole behind my back. 'It's freezing out here and some of us have forgotten to put on our fur.'

He stares as though trying to process. 'Didn't take you for a drinker, Nursie.' Then he roars in laughter. 'Don't usually agree with women in pubs, but in your case,' he waves a finger at me, 'I'll make an exception. You can have a double.' He starts patting his pocket, for his wallet, I assume.

'Course we could raid the drinks cabinet at Abney,' I say conspiratorially. 'I bet your mother and father keep it well-stocked, don't they, Jack?'

I hold his gaze, willing him to go along with my ruse.

'I'm not sure that's a good idea,' says Iris, her striking blue eyes furious.

I do love that posh people try to hold on to good manners no matter what.

Her interjection proves the decider. Paul lurches forwards.

'Start the engine, boy!' he calls. 'We're going for a drive!'

He staggers to the Wolseley. Iris, exasperated, totters after him in her ill-chosen heels.

I grab Jack's hand, to stop him from hurrying after them. 'Take the scenic route,' I whisper, before getting into the front.

Paul's snoring when we finally pull onto Abney's driveway, his head lolled against the window.

'Well done, Jane,' whispers Jack.

'I hoped the journey back would lull him to sleep, like putting a baby in a rocker.'

'What if he wakes, though?' asks Iris from the back seat. No chance of praise from her.

'With the amount he's put away, I think that very unlikely. We don't want him getting hypothermia though.'

'Your fur coat, Iris,' says Jack. 'Drape it over him like a blanket.'

She frowns but eases herself out of it. I don't suppose she wants it stinking of drink and sweat.

We get out and huddle together. The mink bundled in my hands keeps them toasty, unlike the rest of me.

'You'll have to stay the night, I'm afraid,' whispers Jack.

Iris looks up the driveway. Surely, she's not going to insist on walking back to the village in the dark.

'Fine.' Though her tone implies it's anything but.

We traipse inside, to be greeted by Titch, who sniffs excitedly at the mink stole.

'Leave,' I whisper.

What a good girl; her waggy tail even melts the ice queen a

little. She pats the pup's head rather tentatively.

'How about that brandy, Jack?' Maybe a nightcap will warm Iris up. I pull off my galoshes and pop them by the door.

'Oh. I think there's still some sherry in the drawing room?'

'Bet Cook has some left over from Stir-up Sunday,' I suggest. 'It can't have all gone in the pudding.'

We sneak downstairs like children on Christmas morning hoping to get a glimpse of Father Christmas. There's a different atmosphere in Abney after dark. Like the house isn't quite asleep. I remember it was the same at Winwick, moving through the wards you always had a feeling that the building was watching you. I wondered sometimes if the patients sensed it too.

The kitchen is still warm from all the baking Cook did earlier, though the room is spick and span; not a sprinkle of flour to be seen. I realise getting Jack to take a protracted route back, means I've missed out on one of Cook's scones. Even reheated consommé or a slightly soggy tomato sandwich would be welcome – though I draw the line at cucumber. Revolting stuff.

We check the cupboards for the brandy until Iris comes up trumps. Jack sloshes a generous amount into three glasses, brandy ones of course, while the high-pitched ding as we clink them together tells me they are quality crystal. Before I came to work at Abney, I never knew these things had any significance, all I was ever bothered about was that a drinking glass was clean, or clean enough – didn't even have to be a glass, for that matter. I sip, holding the amber liquid in my mouth to savour the taste, before swallowing, a satisfying warmth running down my throat.

'Thanks for coming to my rescue,' says Iris.

Evidently the brandy is working already, because she is looking at both of us.

'Has this happened before?' I ask.

She presses the glass to her lips.

Jack answers for her. 'Once or twice.'

'You won't tell your mother,' urges Iris. 'I don't want Mrs Cherry finding out.'

'Not if you don't want me to.' Jack reddens. 'Probably best she doesn't know about you staying over either. You can use one of the guest rooms. It'll be an early start, I'm afraid. Even with that fur coat it'll be pretty chilly in the motor and you'll both need to be fresh for rehearsals.'

Paul's going to have a hell of a hangover. I knock back the rest of the brandy.

'See you tomorrow, then.'

I leave them to deal with the glasses and head up to bed with my furry friend.

FOURTEEN

Friday 17th December, 1926

I WAKE SWEATING AND BEWILDERED. SCENES FROM MY NIGHTMARE still lingering. I was back at Winwick in a long white corridor. Someone was sobbing. But I couldn't work out who. I just knew I had to get to them. The corridor became a terrible labyrinth, twisting and turning. Only instead of finding dead ends it was people stopping me from continuing on. Dr Argyle, Matron, Dr Pearce. Even Agatha.

'You're confused,' they each said. 'No one's crying.'

Then, suddenly, I'd found him. When he lifted his head, he was wearing a balaclava. I tore it away and screamed in horror. His face now the mink's.

I get out of bed and put on my uniform. While buttoning up my cardigan, I check the dressing table again. Could have sworn that's where I left the binoculars.

Oh! There they are on top of my suitcase by the window. I look down to the driveway where Jack parked the Wattses' Wolseley. Can't see if Paul is still asleep inside. I hope not – it's snowing again.

There's a knock on my door. Kitty strides in holding a plant pot with a bulb in it.

'Mrs Christie's asking for you.' Her eyes are taking in everything. I see her gaze go from the washstand to the dressing table to the bed. 'Oh, and Thomas said this is for you. An ama-something or other.'

'Amaryllis.'

She jerks her head in agreement and puts it on the windowsill.

'Patience told me Colonel Christie cancelled his interview.'

She tuts. 'Nosey old bat left me to clear away the afternoon tea so she could earwig out on the terrace.'

'She had set it all up,' I say.

'With my help.'

I scoop up the mink stole. I'll ask Agatha where she put the rest of the donated clothing.

'It turned up, then?' Kitty asks.

'A boy was playing with it in the garden.'

She frowns. 'Let me guess, skinny? Wearing a balaclava?'

'You've seen him too?'

'Oh yes. I've seen him – and when I see him next time, I'll give him a hiding.'

My eyes widen.

'I've told our Colin he's not allowed to come into the estate, especially after dark.'

'Oh! He's your brother.'

She nods. 'He keeps going on about this place being haunted. And now he reckons he's seen faces in windows and a blood-soaked maid.'

'Sounds like he has a vivid imagination.'

She grunts. 'Gruesome, you mean. He's obsessed with that bloody dog's grave down by the orchard an' all. Always hanging round by it.'

I've seen it on my walks with Dr Pearce. A grey slab laid into the ground engraved with the words *Dandie Dinmont died May 1919*. Always thought it was funny having a big headstone for such a small terrier.

Kitty's still whinging. 'It were bad enough when he were pinching apples and making dens, but now he's stealing furs! Going to get me in trouble, he is.'

Apples? Ah! That's who's been using the boathouse. 'I'm sure he meant no harm,' I say.

'My mam says he's a delinquent.'

My heart freezes. 'You shouldn't use that word, Kitty. He's just having fun.'

'Well, he won't be having any more fun, I can tell you.'

No point arguing while she's so surly. I leave her to make my bed. I imagine Iris has made hers and snuck out first thing. I wonder just how foul a mood Paul was in when he woke all cramped and cold in the Wolseley. Will he remember anything of the night before?

My stomach grumbles. I'm ready for my breakfast. I bet Agatha is too.

As I enter her room, she points at the mink stole and laughs. 'That looks like a prime candidate for my F.O.R.'

'Your what?'

'The Faithless Order of Rats. Yesterday, I thought you were

one of them too, but I've decided to give you a chance to redeem yourself.'

'I'm glad.' I wiggle the mink's head. 'I was going to put this with the other donated clothes the vicar brought. It must have fallen out of the box. Where did you put it?'

'Oh. In the boys' room. Punkie keeps a lot of her fancy dress and theatrical stuff in there now. Jack and his cousins don't use it anymore now they're all grown up.'

That's the room opposite the billiard room.

'Actually, I suggested to Dr Argyle that we use the boys' room for our sessions,' adds Agatha. 'That end of the hall is quietest, and it's away from the terrace.'

'What time are you expecting him?'

'Nine o'clock.'

'Good. That gives us plenty of time for breakfast.'

↔

Patience is standing by the sideboard. Today there's porridge and kippers with freshly toasted muffins. I hope Kitty helped her fetch it all upstairs.

No sign of Charles Trent. I suppose that's no surprise. When I do see him, I'll advise he doesn't eat for the rest of the day. There were footsteps up and down the corridor all night. Between that, the flush going every few minutes and my nightmare it's no wonder I'm tired. He'll be having a lie-in. Wish I could. Never mind. Coffee first. I reach for a cup.

'Ooh! Good old Cook!' exclaims Agatha picking up a jug of cream. 'My favourite.' She pours out a glassful. I decide to give the porridge a miss. Kippers are a no too. I don't want fishy breath.

I pluck for muffins, adding butter and jam.

'Good morning, Agatha,' says Jim, seated opposite his wife. 'Looks like more snow on the way.'

'Mrs Cherry will have to use her bosom as a snow plough,' she replies. 'When I was young, I always wanted a bosom, and then when I finally got one the fashion changed, and women wanted to be as flat as a pancake.'

'Agatha!' scolds Punkie. 'Jim doesn't want to hear about your bosom.'

'Don't you, Jim?'

I stuff muffin into my mouth to stop myself from laughing.

'Don't be childish, Agatha.'

'It's fine,' says Jim.

'See, Punkie, Jim thinks my bosom is fine.'

I almost choke.

Jim roars with laughter.

'That's not what he meant.'

'It's what he said.'

'Oh, for goodness' sake.'

The door opens and Archie enters. The mood deflates like an old party balloon.

'Ah. I'm glad everyone's here. Wanted to tell you that I'm departing this morning. Gathered up my things. I've ordered a taxi, and I'll take the train back to London.'

'You can't leave.' Agatha's eyes flash to her brother-in-law. 'Jim, tell him he has to stay.'

'You are welcome to remain as long as you like, Archie. I hope we've made that clear.'

'Thank you. However, I have matters to attend to at home – and if this bad weather continues, I might end up stuck here for days.'

'I could come with you.'

'No, Agatha. Besides I'll be back in time for Christmas, to drop off Teddy.'

She turns her head. Pretends he isn't there. And when she turns it back again, he isn't.

I finish my muffins and polish off two cups of tea before I start to feel almost human. Just before nine, Agatha and I go to the boys' room. It's similar in size to the billiard room. There are some eye-catching pieces of scenery propped up against the far wall. Fake woodland, a window looking out onto a garden with hollyhocks and delphiniums, along with a fabric backdrop depicting what I think is a courtroom, a royal coat of arms in the centre.

There are also a couple of large chests and a wardrobe, for fancy dress and costumes I assume. The donated box of clothing on the floor next to them. I put the mink stole inside.

There's a water jug, and three glasses on a side table. I position two wicker chairs near to it.

'Drink?'

'Please.'

I take a sip from my own glass then sit on an old church pew just as Dr Argyle enters the room.

'Mrs Christie.' He nods in greeting. 'Nurse.'

I offer him water too, but he declines, so I take out my notebook and pencil.

'No need for that. I like to keep things relaxed in my sessions. Informal.'

'Of course, Doctor.'

'So, how will this work?' Agatha asks, abruptly.

'All in good time.' He dials his smile up to maximum charm. 'I've been reading one of your books, since I saw you last. *The Mysterious Affair at Styles.* I like that Hastings chap.'

'Did you work out who the murderer was?'

I take another sip, glad of something to do.

'No, you beat me, Mrs Christie. Very clever, all that business with the spills vase.'

I almost splutter.

'And how is your shoulder?'

'Much the same.'

'It's still affecting your sleep?'

She stares at him as though he's dense.

'Dr Pearce gave you some sleeping pills. Have you used them?'

'Only in my books, to poison characters or as their means of sui—'

Her cockiness withers at the word.

'Your guardedness is understandable, Mrs Christie, but unwarranted. We will discuss your feelings of melancholy only when we both feel you are ready.' He rubs the top of his chest, although I note the fire has not been lit. 'Yesterday you told me you weren't taking any medication. Do you stand by that statement?'

Her eyes flick to me. 'I do.'

'Honest communication is essential between patient and doctor if we are to succeed in your recovery.'

Between doctor and patient too? I want to ask.

'I am being honest.'

Oh, Agatha. For someone admired for her clever plotting she is blind to how this particular spider spins his web to set a trap.

'Because I have it on good authority that you also have a bottle of laudanum in your room which was not prescribed by Dr Pearce.'

Her eyes flick to me. Anger burning. 'What I have or don't have in my room is private.'

I shake my head at her, trying to tell her that I haven't peached.

'I have a headache. I'm going back to my room,' she declares, getting up.

'As you wish, Mrs Christie,' he says, trying to salvage some pretence of being in control. 'I have no other appointments today. So, I will see you when you are feeling better. Perhaps in an hour?'

The door bangs shut.

I feel like slamming doors myself. I must stay calm. 'Who told you about the laudanum?'

'Who told you about the laudanum, *Doctor*?'

I'm not the only one trying to suppress my fury. I wait for him to continue.

'That's confidential, Nurse Goodbetter. Besides, the real question is why you didn't inform me about it.'

'It was an oversight, Dr Argyle. It won't happen again.'

Why do I sound like a scolded child?

'I'm relying on you, Nurse, to make Mrs Christie see how vital these sessions are. Will you promise me that you will do your best to persuade her of the benefit?'

'Of course, Doctor.'

'Dr Pearce tells me you have been a nurse for six years. You came to the profession after the war?'

'That's right. I was caring for my family before that.'

He murmurs his understanding. 'And you have always worked in a private capacity?'

'Yes.' He's asking too many questions. What if I'm the fly, not Agatha? I take another swig of water, my mouth awfully dry.

He is a patient man. I can feel him glow at my discomfort. At making me reveal more of myself than I care to. I put down my glass. A month after the War Office took over at Winwick, the Germans used chlorine gas for the first time at Ypres, great clouds of yellow smothering the infantrymen, gunners, engineers – and medics like Dr Callum Argyle, of course. Those worse affected were evacuated to the Casualty Clearing Stations, then on to the war hospitals eventually. Those still in the trenches were given only cotton face pads soaked in baking soda to hold over their faces.

It is my turn to spin a web. 'My dad had miner's lung and my mum's chest was as bad. She was a weaver. One of them breathing in coal, the other cotton dust. After their deaths, I decided to train as a nurse.'

His hand goes to his chest again. 'I'd like you to fetch me that bottle of laudanum, Nurse Goodbetter. The Mellotal sleeping powder too. I don't like the idea of Mrs Christie having both within her reach, not while she is so fragile.'

'I quite agree, Doctor.'

Who told Dr Argyle about the laudanum? Madge is the most likely candidate; I can't imagine Jim or Jack poking through Agatha's personal belongings. It could be Kitty, I suppose, or even Patience.

FIFTEEN

I LEAVE THE BOYS' ROOM, STILL PUZZLING OVER WHO THE telltale could be, and almost collide with Patience.

'Are you all right?' I ask.

She looks confused again. 'Yes, miss . . . actually, no, miss. I was trying to find Thomas. He's meant to be bringing in the other Christmas tree. I was going to say to him he makes a good bird scarer. Get it?' She laughs. Holds up her index fingers. 'Fly away, Peter. Fly away, Paul.'

Crackers! I smile. 'I haven't seen Thomas. Sorry.'

'Ellen said he was up here.'

'Kitty, you mean. Ellen doesn't work here anymore. Well, I'm sure he'll come looking for you if he needs you. Is she still clearing the breakfast things?'

'Who?'

'Kitty.'

'Oh! I was meant to help her. I'm such a fool. Forget my head if it wasn't screwed on.' She trots off down the corridor. It isn't hard to keep up.

'See, here she is,' I say, brightly.

Kitty's coming from the opposite direction holding a tray

piled high with used plates and cutlery. She carries herself like a debutante. I can almost picture her with the tray on her head, rather than a book, practising her deportment.

'There you are!' she scolds. 'Where on earth have you been?'

'Patience got a bit mixed up and went looking for Thomas.'

'I'm sorry, Kitty. I'd forget my head if it wasn't screwed on.' She swivels towards the breakfast room door.

'There's no point going in there now. I've done it all.'

'Why don't you go on ahead to the drawing room?' I suggest.

'Yes, Nurse.'

Once Patience is out of earshot, I turn on Kitty. 'Did you have to be so sharp with her?'

'I'm not the one in the wrong. She's always wandering off. Never finishes a task properly.'

'I think she's struggling with her memory.'

'A proper Sherlock Holmes, aren't you? If you ask me, she's not half as bad as she makes out. It's just an excuse. She wants putting out to pasture. Honestly, if she says that line about forgetting her head one more time, I swear I'll scream.'

'Go easy on her. She's an old woman.'

'I don't care if she's as old as Methuselah.' The tray jerks, the dishes clatter together. 'There's plenty would happily take her place.'

'You're going to damage those plates.'

'What's it to you if I do? You're a nurse, not the housekeeper. So stop sticking your beak in where it's not wanted.'

I take a deep breath. 'Someone has to keep an eye on you. Running all over the estate on some . . . some wild mink chase!'

Her freckled face reddens. 'And *someone* has to look out for Mrs Christie, because you're doing a rubbish job.'

'What do you mean by that?'

'I mean that you haven't even noticed she's in her room crying her heart out, 'cause you're too busy having a go at me.'

My blood rises. 'Why didn't you say so!' I hurry up the stairs, fuming.

As I reach Agatha's door I can hear heavy sobbing from the other side. I go to turn the handle then stop. Kitty's words burn in my mind.

I've felt the sting of that accusation before.

Matron frowned at me. 'Sit down, Nurse.'

There was a manilla folder on her desk. She pulled out several sheets of paper from within and laid them out like a fan. Tapped them in turn. 'Several reports for tardiness. The same for inattentiveness. Last week you were reprimanded for dozing at a patient's bedside.'

'I haven't been sleeping well.'

She pulled a face. 'You should have told me sooner. I'll ask one of the doctors to prescribe you some Mellotal. I know our work here is nearly done, but we've still plenty to do in preparation for the patients leaving. This is not the time for you to slack off. We work with dangerous, unpredictable boys and men. One lapse of concentration can be deadly.'

I shake off the memory and go into Agatha's room. She's lying on the bed; her face turned to the wall. I go to her bedside cabinet but the Mellotal sleeping powder is not there. Agatha must have thrown the bottle away.

I open the drawer and take out the laudanum.

'Has he gone?' she asks.

'No.' I sit on the edge of the mattress. 'Mrs Christie, I know you're very unhappy, but you can't hide away forever.'

'Can't I?'

'Listen. I'm going to be blunt. If Dr Argyle believes you are showing symptoms of mental malady, hysteria, paranoia, or suicidal thoughts, then he could have you admitted to an institution.'

'Punkie wouldn't allow it.' But there's a slight wobble in her voice.

'Doctors can be very persuasive, believe me. If they say it's in your best interests, can you be so sure your sister wouldn't agree to it?'

She turns over. Her face is blotchy.

"You need to take back control, Agatha. If you want to get rid of these doctors – and the press, for that matter – you need to demonstrate that you are capable and moving on with your life. Now I'm going to take this to Dr Argyle. I hope you will follow my advice and come back downstairs.'

↔

I re-enter the boys' room not knowing if my words have had any influence on Agatha. Dr Argyle is still sitting in the same chair. I pass him the laudanum.

'What about the sleeping powder?'

'The Mellotal's gone. Mrs Christie must have disposed of it.'

He studies the label then puts it on the table beside him. 'Did Mrs Christie make any complaint about you taking it?'

'Of course not,' she says, appearing behind me.

Dr Argyle smiles but holds back on the wattage. 'A short-term prescription can aid sleep, but I believe that time away from the patient's usual environment is the best treatment for insomnia.'

'You're saying I shouldn't go home?'

'I wouldn't advise it. No, Mrs Christie.'

We agree on that at least.

He waves his hand, gesturing for her to sit.

'And what about Dr Pearce,' asks Agatha, casting a quick glance at me. 'Does he agree?'

'You'd have to ask him, Mrs Christie,' he replies.

'You both studied at the University of Edinburgh Medical School, didn't you?'

His eyebrows rise. 'We did. How—'

'I do my research, Doctor. Sir Arthur Conan Doyle studied there too.'

'Before my time, of course. Your Hastings is a bit of a Dr Watson.'

'Rather amateur of me. I don't think I'll use him in my next book. Oh, sorry. You like him, don't you?'

I stifle a giggle with a fake cough. 'Bit of a frog.' I press my fingers to my throat and clench my teeth together as I cross to the water jug on the side table and pour myself a glassful.

'I'm glad to hear you are thinking of your next book,' continues Dr Argyle. 'Something supernatural, perhaps, like *The Hound of the Baskervilles*?'

Sir Arthur is well known for his interest in spiritualism. I read somewhere that he wanted to help with the search for Agatha. He apparently gave a medium one of her old gloves for a reading.

Goodness knows where he got it, if it really was one of hers? I'd like to know, but I must try to be inobtrusive.

'What an excellent suggestion. You should try your hand, Doctor.'

'Oh. Ha! Fiction isn't my forte. Though I have had articles and letters in *The Lancet*, of course.'

Agatha frowns. 'I hope you don't intend to write about me.'

He holds her gaze. 'I could say the same to you.'

'Touché.' She massages her neck. 'There has been quite enough rubbish written about me already.'

'Of course, the press and public will speculate. It is only human nature.'

Agatha tenses.

This time Dr Argyle seems to realise his misstep. 'That must have been unpleasant.'

'It was,' she replies, still riled. 'I'm a puzzle to be worked out like the solution to one of my mysteries. Am I the unreliable narrator, the deceived wife, the cynical author desperate for more fame? And the journalists spur them on with their theories and exclusives.' She closes her eyes. 'Listen, Doctor. You can hear them swarming round the lodge gates like a cloud of bluebottles. I'd like to swat the lot of them.'

I could put my head in my hands. Talk like this makes her sounds paranoid.

'At times of extreme emotional strain, a person often feels an overriding desire to run away. To escape.'

At least she's listening.

'In some cases, the person bolts physically, in others their retreat is mental. And sometimes, both. Dr Pearce proposed that your amnesia was caused by the blow to your head when you lost control of your motor car. I disagree. I believe your mind is trying to protect you by blocking out painful memories, but blocking out those memories is mentally and physically exhausting. The memories may be deeply unpleasant but only by facing them square on will you be able to move on with your life.'

She fiddles with her bracelet, twisting it one way then the other. 'What if I don't want those memories back? What if they are too painful?'

And I know exactly how she feels.

'Ah. That is the crux of it, is it not, Mrs Christie?' replies Dr Argyle. 'You fear that if you give in to the pain these memories bring that you will break down completely. But it is the only way forwards.

'Through hypnosis we can unlock your memories, and you will gain an understanding of yourself. As a writer you will know the etymology of the word, no doubt. Hypnos – from the Greek god of sleep. Another Scot, Dr Braid, came up with the term, though he later considered the word inadequate. Actually, he set up practice in Manchester. He was fascinated with the possibilities of the art, after seeing a mesmerist perform hypnosis and was determined to see if he too could induce a test subject into a sleep-like state. Or as it is more accurately described monoideism – a trance.

'I have used the method myself with great success while treating amnesiac shell-shocked soldiers during my time at the Lord Derby War Hospital.'

My stomach clenches, but he continues without so much as a

glance at me. I am assured again that he does not remember me from there. I remember how I pleaded with him when he made his precursory visit. Trying to get him to see how upsetting it would be to send all the patients away. Begging him to at least consider letting the youngest stay. Those that would find the evacuation most distressing.

If only he had listened, everything would be so different. I blink back tears.

'But we must not run before we can walk, Mrs Christie. My initial treatment is a talking cure. Now make yourself comfortable.'

Agatha looks as stiff as when she came in.

He continues regardless. 'Excellent. Shall we begin with a time you remember with fondness. When would that be?'

Her expressions change as she thinks. At last, she answers. 'At the hospital.'

Dr Argyle waits.

'I'm wise to that little trick of yours, Dr Argyle. Hoping I'll fill in the gap you leave.'

He smiles. 'This was where?'

'Initially at Torquay Town Hall which had been commandeered to be used as a war hospital. I'd already, like many women, signed up to do first aid classes. This was in the eighteen months before war broke out. As part of the training, I spent two days a week helping on an outpatients' ward. I had to treat this poor child who had been badly scalded.' She glances at me. 'I can still remember the disapproving look from the staff nurse. The child was in agony as I soaked off the dressings from her leg. But I did it.

'When war broke out, I began my detachment as a VAD. I was

a ward-maid, so on basic cleaning duty. However, after five days I was moved up to the ward. Then I was emptying bed pans and urinals, cleaning up vomit, delousing or being a human handrail for the doctors.'

Dr Argyle's face hardens.

'God, the number of mackintoshes I scrubbed. I still sometimes dream about them now. That or I'm standing by the steaming crock, trying to tell if it's boiling. And some of the professional nurses were very tough on us.'

'Understandable as many volunteers were untrained beyond rolling bandages,' adds Dr Argyle.

'I felt I had a real vocation for nursing and would have been happy continuing to work in the hospital. But I got the flu and congestion of the lungs. So I had to take the best part of a month off. When I returned, they had opened a dispensary. I was offered the role of assistant. It sounded interesting and the hours were better. But it turned out to be monotonous work, and I didn't enjoy it as much as nursing. Though I did learn a lot about poisons.'

He nods. 'Thank you, Mrs Christie. Now, I'd like you to tell me about the time when you were unhappiest.'

She stiffens. 'Must I?'

'If you wish to get better.'

SIXTEEN

Agatha takes a deep breath. 'That would be when my mother died . . . and afterwards when I returned to Ashfield to see to her affairs. To pack up the house.'

'Your husband didn't accompany you?'

Agatha tightens her grip on the chair armrest. 'No. He had business in Spain. Then he was needed to help in the general strike, so he stayed at his club in London.'

'But you wanted him at Ashfield.'

'Of course.'

Dr Argyle waits.

'We were used to being separated. The war meant we were barely together. That was the reality for lots of couples. We missed each other terribly. It was all so romantic. Exciting. But the reality of married life kicked in. Money worries, of course. Archie working all hours. I suppose it's normal for a wife to feel lonely. I missed the hospital. I suppose at least then I had my writing. The characters are a kind of company. But I was determined to be a good wife.'

'Do you think you succeeded?'

'I tried. Perhaps I tried too hard.'

Agatha looks lost in thought.

'Sometimes I'd make one of my specialities for supper. Late one afternoon, I had this sudden craving for a cheese souffle. It turned out rather marvellously. Only when Archie got home, he turned up his nose and said he couldn't eat a thing. He suffers from nervous dyspepsia. He'd go to bed and I could hear him groaning. Then later he'd suddenly announce he felt better and asked me to get him treacle or golden syrup.'

I hardly think sugar would have helped.

Dr Argyle nods. 'Let's return to Ashfield . . .'

'Must we?'

He nods.

'There was just so much to sort. Room after room. Box after box. I ate less and less. I tried to be strong for my daughter's sake. Tried to keep my grief, my despair from her. I wasn't sleeping. I was so muddled. I couldn't think straight. I was crying all the time. And most of all I was tired. So very tired.

'Only one thing could make me feel better. Archie. I begged him to come, spend the weekend, but he said it would be foolish to spend so much money on what could only be a short stay – and besides, he had golf.'

I'm glad Archie's gone. If he was here, I'd want to thump him.

'Your husband did come to Ashfield, eventually.'

'Yes. For Rosalind. Not me. It was her birthday. I was so happy. But then he spoilt even that. He was like a stranger. Cold. Sharp. He told me he was in love with another woman. That he wanted a divorce.

'It was my fault for having not stayed in London. I should have just boarded up Ashfield. I'd made myself sick. "You know I hate it when people are ill or upset." But what he really meant was that he couldn't stand being unhappy and that was what I made him.'

Dr Argyle waits for a moment. 'You are doing very well, Mrs Christie. Now. Let's move forwards in time again. What do you remember about your time at the Hydro?'

Agatha shrugs. 'Don't you read the newspapers?'

'It is your perspective I am interested in. Your recollections. Your feelings.'

'Fine. But I really don't see how it's going to make me better.'

I pull a *please behave* face at Agatha.

She draws in her breath.

He tries again. 'You sign the register and are shown to your room. You take off your coat. Sit on the bed. How do you feel?'

Agatha closes her eyes. 'Safe. No, that's not the right word.'

He waits. 'You felt a sense of relief, perhaps?'

'Yes. I'd been so tired. Now I felt lighter. Everything was going to be all right. Like when I can't make a plot work and suddenly a simple solution pops into my head. I was unburdened. There was nothing to worry about other than which health treatment to book or which entrée to have at dinner.'

'You were all alone. That didn't trouble you?'

Agatha's eyes flash. 'I was anonymous.'

'You were Miss Teresa Neele of Cape Town.'

'I don't remember.'

'You visited there on the Empire Tour with your husband.'

'We went to lots of places.'

'But South Africa was special? You learnt to ride the waves there.'

'Yes.' Her eyelids flutter.

'You were happy there.'

'I thought I was. But what if my past was a lie? A deception.'

I want to reach out to her, but I know Dr Argyle wouldn't approve.

Dr Argyle places a hand on his chest. 'It is understandable that you question the veracity of your past experiences and emotions, Mrs Christie. We build memories like a house of cards. But it is all too easy for our version of the past to collapse.'

The clock strikes. The hour is up.

There is a knock on the door and Madge enters.

I go over and squeeze Agatha's hand. 'Well done.'

'Ah, Mrs Watts. I am very pleased with the progress your sister is making.'

We leave them to talk. Agatha is subdued as we head down the cross corridor. I'm worried that all this solitude and soul searching will plunge her back into depression.

On reaching the long corridor, I see that the drawing room door is open.

Kitty and Patience are sitting on the floor, easing glass baubles from tissue paper wrappings.

The smell of pine welcomes us.

'Oh, you're decorating the tree,' exclaims Agatha. 'Can we help?'

'The more the merrier, Mrs Christie. You can start by unpacking that one.' Kitty points to one of the many wicker baskets. There are tiny glints of colour from within.

Patience holds one shaped like an icicle to the light. 'Isn't it pretty, Mrs Christie.'

She smiles. 'Beautiful.'

Kitty passes me a pair of scissors. 'That ribbon needs making into bows.'

'Oh. Right.' I gather up a roll of red with gold trim and slice off a length. I'm mauled to death with my left wrist bandaged up, but I manage to twist it into shape.

'Not bad,' says Kitty.

Soon there's a nice pile of them at my side. Patience fixes baubles to the lower branches while Kitty drags a step ladder closer to the tree to hang more from the uppermost ones, then reaches out for a green bauble from Agatha.

I look to the window. The snow has started up again.

'I bet you love being at Abney, Mrs Christie,' says Kitty. 'You must get loads of ideas for your books when you stay here.'

'A big country house does make a good setting for a murder mystery. A defined number of suspects all in the same place.'

'Oh, yes. That's true. I were thinking of all the ways you could do someone in just using stuff lying about.'

Agatha smiles. 'There's certainly plenty of old and antique weaponry to choose from: pikes, halberds, axes, swords, blunderbusses, flintlock pistols and rifles. There's even a South Sea Islands war club. Oh yes, a murderer would be spoilt for choice. They could stab, shoot or cosh their victim.'

'You dunt need something fancy either,' adds Kitty. 'There's carving knives galore in the kitchen, all kept nice and sharp, or they could bash someone's brains out with that wooden meat tenderiser.'

'Very messy though,' says Patience. 'Much more discreet

to slip some rat poison into the person's dinner. That'd do the trick.'

'I like to use poison, in my books. I learnt all about them when I was working in the dispensary during the war. The greenhouse is also a good source for arsenic. The murderer could use soaked fly papers like the Black Widows of Liverpool, or use weed killer like Mary Ann Cotton.' She grins at me. 'She was a nurse.'

I roll my eyes at her.

'In your next book can you make it so the parlourmaid is the murderer. We'd love that, wouldn't we, Patience?'

'Oh, yes.' Patience giggles.

'Perhaps.'

That means no. Servants are rarely considered seriously as suspects in mystery stories by the detective or the reader. They're often portrayed as a bit dumb, even when they've spotted a clue they usually haven't twigged to it. Or they're the blackmailing type who've seen the murderer doing something which makes them guilty, only they end up getting killed themselves.

Agatha grins. 'You know when Archie and I were first married, money was tight. I told myself I simply had to find a job. He thought that rather ridiculous. After all, what on earth was I qualified for? Not to be a governess. Or a companion. And then I got it! I could be a parlourmaid. After all, there was a fashion for tall ones back then.'

'We'd be glad of an extra pair of hands, Mrs Christie,' says Patience.

'Yes, I suppose so few people work in service nowadays,' replies Agatha. 'You must have worked here a long time, Patience.'

'Oh, yes, ma'm.'

'I remember coming to Abney as a child at Christmas time and you were always there, behind old Mr Watts, waiting to take my wrap. You haven't changed a bit.'

Patience laughs. 'Well you have!'

Agatha laughs too.

'It was always a long journey,' she continues. 'But I always knew there'd be a splendid nursery tea waiting for me and the other children. Oh Jane, it was heavenly. Homemade bread and farm butter and the strawberry jam was the sweetest I'd ever tasted. And there were sponge cakes and those other ones that had a funny name.'

'Jumbles,' says Patience.

'Ha! Yes, jumbles! Oh and there was the most beautiful dolls' house – I've always loved dolls' houses – and an old rocking horse in the window.'

'That was Mr James's. Had a real horsehair mane and tail.'

We work for an hour or so before finally adding strands of silver tinsel to the tree. I look up to see Jack strolling across the now white-encrusted terrace towards the back steps with Titch and the other dogs. He's coming from the direction of the orchard. Perhaps he's been down Newlands Road.

'Won't be a minute. I just need the lavatory.'

Jack's taking off his snowy boots by the back door. The dogs are all sitting waiting for him, even Titch.

'Morning, Jane.' He pulls off his damp cap.

'Morning, Jack. Now I know why I didn't see you at breakfast.'

'Thought I'd get these brutes' walk out of the way nice and

early.' He ruffles the fur on the fox terrier's head. 'Made sure Iris got out all right too,' he says sotto voce. 'I'm afraid she and Paul made a sorry pair at six a.m. I'm going to put the Wolseley back in the garage in a minute. Oh! Which reminds me, Richard's motor is still parked up by the railway bridge. Perhaps he's had a job finding someone to come out to fix it.'

'Or maybe he can't afford a mechanic. He clearly hasn't paid for those dents to be repaired.'

'True. Quite the detective, aren't you.'

'Hardly. I didn't have a clue that Mr Ramsbury had a drink problem.'

'Why would you? He's very good at hiding it. He doesn't swig from a hip flask every five minutes. No, his problem is once he starts, he can't stop. You did well to distract him, last night.'

'Distracting patients is rather a forte of mine. It comes in handy when you have to administer an injection.'

'I'll remember that if I ever need to jab someone with a needle.' He checks his watch. 'I'd better get the dogs cleaned up. I'll see you at lunch, no doubt. Ah, that sounds like the rest of the MADS arriving.'

I twist round to see. He's correct. I move towards the long corridor curious to see what state Paul and Iris are in.

But it's not them. It's the vicar. Again. He must really want that donation and with haste. Jim is beside him, waiting while Reverend Whittle shrugs off a long black coat.

'Everything all right, Father?' Jack calls.

'Nurse Goodbetter, would you please fetch my wife. I think she's gone to speak with Cook in her room.'

'Of course, sir.'

Jack and I exchange a perturbed look.

'I wish Reverend Whittle would leave us in peace,' he grunts.

SEVENTEEN

COOK AND MADGE ARE SITTING CLOSELY TOGETHER studying Cook's handwritten recipe book. They look up on hearing me enter.

'Pardon me, Mrs Watts, but your husband is asking for you. The vicar's here.'

She grimaces. 'Sorry, Mrs Worcester, we'll have to continue our conversation later.'

'That's quite all right, ma'am.'

As soon as Madge is out the door, I slump into her vacated chair. The wood still warm.

'Would you be as quick in her grave?' asks Cook, grinning at me.

'It's been a long few days. I feel like I've been on that new scenic railway at Belle Vue.'

'You wouldn't get me on that thing, especially not after that poor lass fell out of it . . . Cup of tea?'

'Can a duck swim?'

She laughs and gets up.

'So, what's bothering you, love?' she asks while filling her electric kettle.

'Someone's been telling tales to Dr Argyle about Mrs Christie.'

'Oh dear.' She picks up a tin of biscuits. 'What've they been saying?'

'They told him that she had some laudanum in her drawer – on top of the sleeping pills Dr Pearce gave her. I don't suppose Mrs Watts said anything to you?'

'You think she's the one that told him.'

I nod.

Cook puts the tin on the table and sits down. 'That would make sense, happen she's looking out for her little sister.'

'Little? Mrs Christie's thirty-six.'

'A younger sibling is always little to the older child,' she replies prising off the tin's lid. 'I was the youngest of seven and all my brothers and sisters still treat me like the baby of the family when we're back together. Mind you, there's only three of us now.' She smiles sadly offering me the biscuits.

David's face flashes in my mind for just a moment. 'Mrs Christie thinks I tattled on her,' I reply, taking one. 'Every time I think I get closer to her, something scuppers my efforts. Now Dr Argyle's made me retrieve her medicine and give it to him.'

'This Argyle is worried that she might do something silly, is he?'

I squeeze my thumb. 'But Colonel Christie told the press she'd never take her own life.'

'What would he know? Where's he been all these months? Hiding at his club or playing golf,' she scoffs. 'Doesn't take a genius to work out where he really was.'

'He was with Nancy Neele, you mean.'

'With what she's been through it's no wonder Mrs Christie was at her lowest ebb. Keep a close eye on her, Jane.'

I get up. 'I'll have that tea another time.'

'Now before you go rushing off, maybe you can help with a mystery of my own. I think someone was pilfering from my pantry last night.'

'Oops. Sorry, Jack and I brought Iris Caldwell, one of the MADS, down here. We helped her collect Paul Ramsbury from the George and Dragon and poured him into the Wolseley. Then we brought him back here to sleep it off. The rest of us had a drop of your brandy as a nightcap.'

'You didn't help yourself to anything else?'

'No.'

Her brow furrows. 'I see. Well don't make a habit of it.'

'Promise.'

I give her a hug, sneakily snatching up another biscuit from behind her back.

I grin as I take a big bite.

'Cheeky monkey!'

Chomping on it, I head back into the long corridor, my ankle aching a little from the effort. There's a commotion at the front door. Jack's nearly knocked off his feet as Mrs Cherry blusters in. She shrugs off her coat, revealing a gold trouser suit which matches her beret.

'Madge!' she calls. 'Madge!' She wheezes with breathlessness, and not only from the cold it seems.

Though my ankle makes me wince, a sense of foreboding makes me pick up speed.

'Where's Madge?' she demands.

'With Father and Reverend Whittle,' replies Jack, casting his head towards the study.

'Damn it. He's brought the news before me. That man loves to spoil everyone's fun.'

'What news?' persists Jack.

She clutches her hands to her heart, but there's a glint of pleasure in her eyes. 'Dr Pearce has been attacked.'

My chest tightens. What? I stumble back, knocking into a marble bust on a pedestal.

Before I can ask any questions, the front door swings open and Iris and a bleary-eyed Paul walk in, gabbing feverishly as they peel off snowy coats, hats and scarves. All the noise brings Agatha and the parlourmaids out of the drawing room too.

'What's all the fuss?' asks Agatha, looking at me. 'Are you all right?'

Breathe, Jane. Breathe. I shake my head.

'Someone coshed Dr Pearce over the head,' says Paul. 'He was found sprawled on the consulting room floor first thing this morning.'

Patience gasps.

Agatha's eyes dart to me, then the MADS. 'Is he badly hurt?'

'There was a lot of blood, apparently,' says Iris, biting her lip. 'Everyone's talking about it in the village.'

'Everyone's talking about what?' asks Charles, appearing on the landing. He's still wearing a dressing gown. Jack's, I assume. He'll be lucky to get it back.

'Dr Pearce. He's been attacked.'

Jack ushers us all into the drawing room. 'Patience, could you bring some tea for our guests, please.'

'Yes, sir.' She bobs, then tugs at Kitty's elbow. 'Come with me,' she whispers.

My heart's still hammering as I wander to the window and look out at the falling snow. Poor Robert. I know ours is no great love affair, but I do care for him. I blink back tears then turn back to the room.

Agatha shifts Titch from one of the settees so she, Iris and Mrs Cherry can sit together. The others take the one opposite.

'How are you feeling?' Agatha asks Charles.

'Dreadful. But my stomach's finally settled.'

'Nurse Goodbetter thought you'd been poisoned.'

'That might have been preferable.' He places a hand on his stomach.

I force a smile.

Titch slopes over to me and nudges my leg. Funny how dogs know when you're upset. I lean down and stroke her head.

'His poor wife,' says Agatha. 'It must have been a shock finding him.'

'She didn't,' says Iris. 'Window cleaner raised the alarm.'

Mrs Cherry gives her a knowing look. 'Milkman told me Mrs Pearce hasn't been living there the last two months. He's dropped their order to a pint every other day. Gone to stay at her sister's.'

I can feel myself gawping. That can't be true. He'd have told me. Wouldn't he?

'Doesn't sound like she'll be rushing back to sit at his bedside and hold his hand any time soon,' adds Iris.

Agatha glances at me. Trying to read my reaction. Poker face, I tell myself.

Madge steps into the room, followed by Reverend Whittle. 'You've heard the news, then.'

Titch runs over to greet her.

'Isn't it sad, Mother,' says Jack, getting up so she can sit.

'Terribly.' She pets Titch who is now laid out at her feet.

'What time did it happen?' asks Agatha.

'No one's quite sure,' replies Reverend Whittle. 'Could have been last night or this morning.'

'That's not very helpful.'

'Real life isn't like your books, Mrs Christie, where everyone has to have an alibi for a five-minute window of opportunity,' scoffs Paul.

'Well, the motive seems obvious enough,' says Charles. 'Drugs. Some of these fiends will happily kill for a fix.'

I know only too well how addictive some drugs can be.

'Then why not break into Woodruffs?' asks Agatha. 'The pharmacy's right next door.'

'Because addicts aren't rational. They're opportunists,' replies Charles.

Madge sighs. 'The police believe Dr Pearce let his attacker in because there was no sign of a break-in.'

'They've taken away the surgery appointments book,' adds the vicar. 'They must suspect a patient.'

What about his personal diary? I crush the thick curtain material. I know he keeps a note of our meetings in it. I can't risk his wife – or anyone else – finding it.

'Listen to us all gossiping,' scolds Agatha. 'We must pray that Dr Pearce recovers, and soon.' She casts me a supportive smile.

I should be grateful, but I hate having everyone's attention now on me. Thankfully the door opens and Patience and Kitty enter with a samovar on a tea trolley.

'Ah, excellent, just what we all need,' says Madge.

'Lovely,' agrees Iris.

The vicar rubs his hands together. 'You'll be pleased to hear that I've arranged for that man you recommended, Mrs Cherry, to come and take a look at the church hall roof this afternoon. I fear the repairs will be costly, though.' He looks to Iris. 'I wonder if perhaps your father might be interested in sponsoring the works?'

'I don't think . . . that is, he doesn't care for the theatre.'

'I didn't realise, dear. Such a shame.'

'Delia,' says Madge, 'I'm not sure it's wise us traipsing over to Buckley in the cold and wet again. Let's do the rehearsal here, instead.'

'Good idea.'

'We're still waiting on Richard,' says Iris as Patience offers her a plate of mince pies.

'None for me,' says Charles, pulling a face.

'Are we? Oh yes,' replies Mrs Cherry, taking a cup of tea from Kitty. 'I hope he hasn't got your upset stomach too, Charles. Well, Agatha can read his lines until he arrives. Hopefully he won't be much longer.' She glances anxiously at the weather.

'Oh, Mother, I meant to tell you, he's had a bit of an accident with his motor car. Down by the railway bridge,' says Jack, his eyes flitting to Iris. 'I passed it when I was out walking the dogs.

Looks like it's been there since yesterday.'

'Oh dear. That'll be why he's late. Do we have a telephone number for him, Delia?'

Mrs Cherry delves into her carpet bag. Titch slinks over to try and help. 'I jotted it down somewhere,' she says, pushing the pup's muzzle away. 'Ah, here it is.' She passes a scrap of paper to Madge. 'It's his landlady's.'

'Oh and Jack, ask Thomas to get the driveway gritted too. We don't want anyone else having a mishap.'

'Yes, Mother.'

Tea finished, Madge sees the vicar out then goes to telephone Richard. Seeing the men start to push back the furniture, Iris gets out her compact and studies her reflection.

While they're all occupied, I slip out of the room and scoop up my coat and a scarf from the stand in the vestibule. Then I whip off my nurse's cap and stuff it into the pocket. I go to the side entrance door to switch into my galoshes and wrap the scarf around my head. Even so the cold is like a slap to the face when I step outside. Not sure if the press is still loitering at the lodge gates, I turn left and follow the track that becomes Newlands Road. I won't be visible from the drawing room. Doubt they'll even notice I'm not there.

My galoshes crunch satisfyingly into the newly fallen snow. There's been quite a flurry and there's no sign of it easing up. It will be a test of my ankle's strength walking the half a mile or so into the village.

Dr Pearce's surgery is within his house on the High Street. I'm presuming the receptionist will have locked everything up so

I'm not sure how I'm going to get inside. Running several ideas through my mind, I realise I'm now beside Richard's motor car again. There's a thick crust of snow on the Morris's canvas roof. I realise the driver's door isn't shut properly. As I go to close it, I spot the keys are still in the ignition.

He must have forgotten them in his panic at crashing. I lean in to retrieve them for safekeeping and spot a copy of the *Daily Mirror* on a cushion on the driver's side.

The paper's from the 10th of December. The headline blares "Intensified Search for Mrs Christie Fails" above four photographs from Newlands Corner, the area she went missing from. What a strange coincidence! Perhaps the name resonated with Agatha? Drew her there?

One shot is of an aeroplane, supposedly scouting the scene, another shows Archie driving a motor car, a woman and a fox terrier behind. Her beloved dog, Peter, I assume.

Turning the page to see if there's more about Agatha inside, I find a loose printed flyer.

MANCHESTER AMATEUR
DRAMATIC SOCIETY AUDITIONS

When I Grow Rich – A new play by M F Watts

Saturday 11th December, 10 a.m. to 5 p.m.
St Mary's Church Hall, All Welcome

Telephone: Gatley 2891 for further information

Someone – Richard, surely – has circled 'M F Watts' and written next to it in small block letters 'AGATHA'S SISTER'. I fold the flyer and put it in my coat pocket with the car keys then get out. I can ask him about it when I see him at the hall later.

EIGHTEEN

HIGH STREET IS BUSY WITH PEOPLE SHOPPING IN THE RUN UP to Christmas, despite the snow. I pause by the drinking fountain while I wait for a tram to pass before crossing over.

As I near Dr Pearce's, I spy a couple of old women in the doorway. I can just make out a notice pinned below the surgery's brass name plaque. Closed until further notice. I linger at the pharmacy, pretend to be interested in the window display. A poster taped to the glass advertises *When I Grow Rich.* Illustrations of oranges and lemons form a border and an executioner's chopper cuts through the title.

I remember playing the game as a child, holding up our arms to form an archway then bringing them down suddenly as an axe.

'It's true then,' says the woman in a headscarf to her friend.

'Must be. Come on, let's get some cough drops from next door. Mr Woodruff will tell us all about it.'

I keep my head down and cut round the back, startling a small flock of starlings. Their iridescent feathers glinting in the winter light. My dad called them sheppies. I remember asking Dr Pearce about the name. Said it came from their habit of landing on sheep's backs to feed off ticks. He told me they're ruthless, breaking eggs and killing chicks so they can take over nesting boxes.

A tall iron gate leads to the yard behind the surgery. I scan up and down the back alley, then dip inside. Urging myself on, I go to the back door. Try the handle. Unsurprisingly, it's locked. I spot a couple of marks in the mud where the window cleaner must have leant his ladder to do the back windows.

As I step back to look up, I stumble into something hard. Ouch. I rub my poor ankle again. It's an upturned terracotta plant pot. Surely not? I lift it, and yes, there's a spare key under it. How did the police miss that? The Winwick staff would never be so foolhardy. Getting into Matron's office in her absence took a lot more orchestration.

Quick as a flash, I'm in. They've probably already dusted for fingerprints, but just in case, I use my nurse's cap on the handles. Then I pull off my galoshes, so I won't leave mucky footprints. Unwrap the scarf. A telephone is ringing further down the hallway. My heart quickens.

There's something eerie about an empty waiting room. I circle the table in the centre. It's covered with magazines: *Country Life*, *Punch*. *British Birds Journal*. There's a half-drunk cup of coffee next to the telephone.

I could leave now. Should leave now. But I'm determined to locate his diary, so instead, I go into his consultation room. It's not clinical like the wards at Winwick, more gentleman's study: bookcases, leather chairs both sides of a tidy desk with only an inkstand and silver service bell on its surface. No photographs. But on closer inspection the room's purpose becomes clear: a framed certificate on the wall, a mahogany and leather examination bed, a privacy screen, a small glass cabinet containing medicine bottles, and a wash basin. I was expecting to find the room in disarray.

Course my eyes are drawn to the blood, dried and brown where it seeped into the carpet. Must be true about his wife – no woman would have left a stain like that untreated. The whole lot will have to be ripped out now.

His doctor's bag is beside the desk. Surely a drug addict would have at least snatched that. I use my nurse's cap again to open it and tip out the contents. Sedatives. Painkillers. Aspirin. Somnoform with inhaler. Antiseptic. Thermometer. Tongue depressor. Stethoscope. Syringe. Leather Surgical kit. Bandages. Sutures and needles. No diary. I shove everything back inside.

Sitting in Dr Pearce's chair, I pull open the desk drawer. Spare prescription pads, elastic bands and paperclips. A paper bag of pear drops. I'm almost tempted to take one to ease my dry mouth. Spare pens and ink.

His diary is under a false bottom. I let out a long breath.

My hand trembles as I flick through the pages looking for my name or initials, but they're not there. Have I been worrying about nothing? His appointments at Abney are marked through the year, most frequently between May and November. Sometimes he's jotted down a particular bird he's seen. A chaffinch. Nuthatch. Magpie. Woodpecker. One starts to appear with more regularity than the others. A jay. A shy, pink bird found in woodland. The dates match. Jay must be his code for me.

I close the diary. The bandage around my hand is looking a bit dishevelled. Should really have changed it this morning. I use a pair of scissors from the surgical kit to cut away the old wrappings. The comfrey has dried up. Carefully flexing my wrist, I decide it is mended enough.

As I'm putting the kit back, the sound of a key turning in the front door causes me to jolt. I look round for somewhere to hide. There's the privacy screen, but my feet would show below – and damn, I've left my galoshes by the back door. Braving it out, I put my nurse's cap back on and shove the bandage scraps into my coat pocket with Dr Pearce's diary.

Ellen is bending down to pick up a newspaper from behind the door as I step into the reception area. Does she work here now?

'Can I help you?' I try to channel Matron's natural command of a situation. The age gap between us naturally giving me an air of seniority. I hold my hand out for the paper.

She passes it to me. Today's *Advertiser.*

'Nurse Goodbetter . . . I wasn't expecting to find anyone here.' The former parlourmaid's eyelids flicker nervously. 'Did the police ask you to come?' Her neck flushes. 'I . . . I clean for Dr Pearce. Cover reception sometimes too, lunchtime, or when someone's off sick.'

I need to get rid of her before she starts to question what I'm doing there. 'Someone will contact you in due course.'

'My nain's not on the telephone, Nurse.'

'Then I'll send a wire. Leave me your address.'

She nods.

Reluctantly I let her into the waiting room proper. She goes over to the reception desk. Rummages for paper and a pen . . . God, she's taking an age.

At last, she hands over her note. Her handwriting lacks confidence.

'Four Cromer Road,' I say.

'Do you know where they've taken Dr Pearce . . . so I can send a card or summat.'

'I don't. Sorry.' I hold open the front door for her. 'Take care, Ellen.'

I lean against the wood once she's gone. What kind of a monster am I? More concerned about a diary than Robert. Even the cleaning girl's got more empathy than me. But the truth is I don't want to be at his bedside clutching his hand. Knowing he and his wife could be separated doesn't change anything for me. If I don't go to see him, he'll realise that. Won't he?

I sit in one of the waiting room chairs and open up the newspaper.

"DRAMATIC TWIST AT ABNEY – EXCLUSIVE."

'Plans for Mrs Christie to have quiet while she recuperates at Abney Hall have been thrown into disarray by the arrival of the Manchester Amateur Dramatics Society producer/director, Mrs Delia Cherry, yesterday (Thursday). The MADS had been rehearsing Mrs Watts's latest play – *When I Grow Rich* – at St Mary's Church Hall. However, a recurring roof leak means the cast, including audience favourite Miss Iris Caldwell who played Cinderella in last year's MADS pantomime, has decamped to the Wattses' home.

'A MADS spokesman told *The Advertiser*: "Rehearsals are going very well. We are confident the roof will be repaired in time for curtain up. We are thrilled with our cast and excited to be showcasing another marvellous play by M F Watts. We anticipate *When I Grow Rich* will be very popular with local theatre lovers, so we advise buying a ticket with alacrity so as not to risk disappointment. Tickets are on sale at Cheadle Post Office from today.'"

That'll be Mrs Cherry's doing. I leave the newspaper on the table with the magazines. Then put on my galoshes again before replacing the key under the plant pot. Taking a different route back, I follow the main road rather than cutting through the estate. I want to see if there are any reporters still there, but I'll keep to the other side of the road, so they hopefully won't notice me.

The snow is even thicker now, and it's still coming down. The sky is white with it, and I feel chilled to my core. There's no press at the entrance – the bad weather, and the lack of news since Archie's departure, must have seen them off at last. I cross over. The gates are still locked but one of the day gardeners is spreading sand and cinders on the driveway, so I call to him to let me enter.

'Is Thomas about?' I ask, while he undoes the bolt.

'Not sure, Nurse. He was on about taking another tree into the hall when I saw him this morning at catch-up.'

Winding my way through the trees I see a familiar balaclaved figure by the lake, chucking stones at the frozen surface. What did Kitty say his name was? Ah yes, Colin. Perhaps a word from me will convince him to stay away.

I veer off the path, treading cautiously so as not to fall again.

Colin, apparently bored of his throwing game, slides on to the edge of the iced-over pond. He skids left and right, arms out with enthusiasm if not much grace.

'I wouldn't do that, if I was you.'

His head flicks round. 'I'm only playing.'

'I know. But these are private grounds.'

'For the rich folk, you mean.' He jerks his chin in disgust.

'Yes – and they don't like it when boys set up camp in their boathouses. Fires can be dangerous. As can ice. It might not be as thick as it looks.'

Colin side-eyes me, before twizzling round. 'I know what I'm doing.'

'Well don't come crying to me if you fall through.'

'I'd have a job, wunt I. Cause I'd be drowned at the bottom.'

I laugh despite myself. 'That's true. Be terribly sad for your sister, mind you. Seeing you dragged out all blue and bulging eyes.'

'I'd be gruesome, wunt I?' His eyes shine with delight. 'You a parlourmaid like our Kitty, then?'

'No. I'm Nurse Goodbetter. But you can call me Jane.'

'Kitty said how there's only her and the old one.' He looks puzzled. 'Is that how you know what dead people look like? Cause you're a nurse?'

'Yes. Though I've never seen a drowned person, truth be told.'

'Me neither. I have seen a dead man though. Me grandad were laid out in our parlour, and I thought I'd found one, only I were mistaken.'

'Oh?'

'He were only sleeping in his motor car.'

'Ah, yes. Must have given you quite a shock.'

'Oh nowt frightens me. See.' He pushes further out.

My stomach churns. 'I can see that.' I try a different tack. 'Has your Kitty shown you where she works?'

'Not likely! She dunt want me coming anywhere near her. Says I'm a pain in the bum.'

I laugh again. 'Well how about we make a deal. If you come off that ice, I'll show you the kitchen where she works. We can ask Cook for a warm drink. Cause I'm freezing, don't know about you?'

'I dunt get cold,' replies Colin, but he slides off the ice anyway. 'Reckon she has any biscuits?'

'I expect so.'

'Oh wait. My bag.' He scoots over to a bush and pulls out a tatty leather satchel and slings it over his body.

NINETEEN

TURNS OUT COLIN AND I AREN'T THE ONLY ONES TAKING refuge in the kitchen. Thomas is here too, his hair damp from working outside.

'This is Kitty's brother,' I say, removing my coat and scarf. 'Colin.'

'Sit down, love,' says Cook. 'I'm Mrs Worcester and this is Thomas. Would you like a cup of hot chocolate?'

His pupils dilate. 'Ooh, yes please.' He pulls off his balaclava revealing even more freckles than his sister. He looks round at the room, taking it all in. 'Blimey! Look at that silver teapot.'

Thomas passes a plate of shortbread biscuits. I take one. Colin takes two, putting one in his pocket.

'What?' he says, catching my disapproving look. 'Them upstairs wunt miss 'em.'

'He's a growing lad,' says Cook. 'Have another.'

'Dunt mind if I do.'

Thomas smiles at me. 'Good news about Dr Pearce.'

My heart jumps. 'Good?'

'He's going to be OK, love,' says Cook. 'Didn't anyone tell you?'

'No . . . I went out for a walk.'

'He's not as badly hurt as first feared,' she continues. 'He's been discharged and sent home. A relief to us all.'

Home? I let out a breath, realising how easily I could have been caught snooping. Will I never learn?

Cook's still talking. I tune back in.

'Naturally, Mrs Watts has insisted that he stay here while he recovers. I suppose it makes sense with you being on hand to keep a professional eye on the doctor too.'

'He's coming to Abney?' I squeeze my thumb.

Her brows dip. 'I thought you'd be pleased.'

'I'm glad he's on the mend, it's just I'm so busy looking after Mrs Christie.'

'I'm sure Dr Pearce won't be any bother, love.'

My being at Robert's beck and call certainly won't help convince him I want to break things off.

Colin holds out his mug for filling. 'Is it ready yet?'

'Nearly.' Cook waves a spoon at him.

'You getting owt nice for Christmas, lad?' asks Thomas.

Colin sighs. 'I'd like a fishing rod. Dunt think I'll get one though. Mam says they're too expensive. Probably be gloves again. She's always knitting.'

'She make your balaclava? It's a cracker. I wouldn't mind one like that, keep me toasty when I'm working.' Thomas winks at Cook. 'What about you, Jane? What you 'oping for in your stocking?'

'Oh, nothing particular. Chocolates are always nice.'

'Ooh yes,' agrees Cook. 'I love a soft centre.'

Thomas slowly nods his head as though making note.

'I bet them upstairs will get some terrific presents,' says Colin. 'I bet it's all gold bracelets and diamond cufflings.'

'Cufflinks,' says Cook, sniggering, pouring out the hot chocolate.

'Oh, Thomas. Did Jack mention there's a motor car broken down in the grounds?'

He nods. 'Belongs to one of the MADS. Richard, is it?'

'That's right. No one been to see you about retrieving it?'

The door swings open and Kitty and Patience walk in.

'Nope, but they want to get a move on 'cause if this snow keeps up it'll soon be buried under a drift.'

'What'll be buried?' asks Kitty. 'Oh no! What are you doing here?'

'Hiya, sis,' Colin replies, mouth open showing half-chewed biscuit.

'He was playing on the frozen lake,' I explain.

'Should have left him out there. With any luck he'd have fallen through the ice,' she says rolling her eyes.

He sticks his tongue out at her. She returns the gesture.

'Like two peas in a pod,' says Patience.

'Urggh,' they say in unison. 'We're nowt like each other.'

Everyone else laughs.

'So what's been buried?' Kitty repeats. ''Ere, dunt be eating all them biscuits,' elbowing him aside so she can take one, before passing the plate on to Patience.

'A motor car,' says Thomas. 'Belongs to that new chap who's joined the MADS. Richard summat.'

'Ah! The one who's got Mrs Cherry stomping about like a bad-tempered elephant 'cause he hasn't shown up for rehearsals . . . "And not even had the courtesy to telephone,"' Kitty mimics.

'He's still not arrived?' I ask. 'I was going to give him his keys. He left them in the ignition.'

'I seen him in his motor,' says Colin. 'Thought he were dead. But he were only sleeping.'

'What you on about? I've told you to stop making stuff up.'

'I'm not. She knows.' He points at me.

'He's right, only that wasn't Richard. It was Paul,' I explain while checking the teapot, a plain brown one for the staff of course. 'Jack and I went out on a bit of a rescue mission in the Wattses' Wolseley. Iris rang in a bit of a state. Paul had had one too many. We left him to sleep it off in the back of the motor.'

'Urgh. Pity he weren't frozen to death,' says Patience. 'Rude, he is. I was behind him in the post office the other morning. Stinking of ale he was and only just gone nine o'clock. Told me to get out of his way – and the way he spoke to Ellen last time he was here.' She tuts.

Colin tugs at my sleeve.

'Just a minute . . . I found something else in his motor car, actually. Richard's, that is.' I unbutton my coat and place the audition flyer on the table. 'This was inside a copy of the *Daily Mirror*. Mrs Christie's disappearance on the cover. Looks like Richard worked out that Agatha is Mrs Watts's sister.'

'Hardly a secret round here,' says Kitty, tartly.

'I imagine not.' I don't know why it's bothering me still.

Colin tugs my sleeve again. 'Jane, it wurnt that one he were in.'

'Yes. I know.' I turn to Thomas. 'Did you get the second Christmas tree in?'

'Yes. It's in the dining room ready for decorating. Not sure I agree with doing it so early, but if it takes Mrs Christie's mind off her troubles, I suppose that's a good thing.'

'She were certainly enjoying herself during rehearsals,' says Kitty. 'You wouldn't think there were owt wrong with her.'

'Good for her,' says Cook. 'She deserves to have her fun after the way her husband's treated her.'

'What did her husband do?' asks Colin.

'Never you mind. Have another biscuit.' Cook slides the plate towards him.

'Ta, missus.'

I sip my tea while Colin slurps his hot chocolate.

Kitty nudges him. 'Stop that.'

'I wonder if Dr Pearce's wife is enjoying herself now, an' all,' says Patience. 'I suppose she was the one who coshed him.'

'What are you on about?' says Kitty, shaking her head.

'He's been carrying on behind her back, hasn't he.'

'Colonel Christie,' tuts Kitty. 'Not Dr Pearce.'

My cheeks flash with heat. Cook's eyes linger on me. 'Warm in here, isn't it,' I say, fanning myself.

'Always feel it more when you've been outside,' says Thomas.

The bell next to the indicator board rings. Boys' room.

'Come on,' says Kitty, pulling on Patience's arm. 'And I want you gone by the time I get back,' she adds, giving her brother a black look.

'Patience seems more muddled than ever,' says Thomas once they're both out of the room. 'I imagine all this change with the younger Watts moving in hasn't helped. And God knows she's getting on in years.'

'And how many in Patience's case is anybody's guess,' says

Cook, grinning, as she helps herself to a biscuit. 'I remember when old Mr Watts had to fill in the last census. Proper embarrassed he was, having to ask us servants how old we were. Patience said she was fifty.'

'Fifty!' I can't help laughing.

Colin looks confused. I suppose anyone over the age of fifteen is old to him.

'Well us women are sensitive about these things,' adds Cook. 'We don't like men knowing exactly how old we are when we're no longer on the sunny side of forty. You'll be just the same in another few years, Jane.'

'And the older you get the more you worry about your future,' says Thomas. 'If you're not fit enough to work, what 'appens to you then? This younger generation don't feel obliged to provide stipends and so on. She might have a little nest egg put away, but with costs going up like they are, that could be troubling 'er too. Maybe you could 'ave a word with Mrs Watts?'

'I'll see what I can do.'

'Good lass.'

I finish up my tea. 'I'd best be getting back to Mrs Christie. Now what are we going to do about you, Colin? I don't like the idea of you trying to get home alone in all that snow.'

'He can help me roll out some pastry,' says Cook. 'Kitty can see him safe home at the end of her shift.'

'Pastry? Int that for girls?'

'I was going to make jam tarts. I suppose you think them's for girls too?'

'What type of jam?'

'I've not decided yet. Maybe you could help me choose.'

'All right.'

'Make sure you wash your hands first,' I say.

He groans. 'Do I have to?'

'Yes,' Cook and Thomas reply in unison.

↔

I'm lost in my thoughts as I trek up the back stairs. Perhaps I can persuade Madge to let Kitty look after Dr Pearce instead. Something like a shadow catches my eye. Ahead of me, there's a shape draped in white. My heart thuds as I try to make sense of the image.

A door closes. I pick up my pace. Laughter erupts. It's coming from the boys' room. I inhale deeply and open the door. The figure – a bride, I now realise – is in the centre of the room; the MADS gathered around chuckling.

She turns. Madge's hair under the veil is whitened with talc or flour. Her face paled with greasepaint. Black smudged around her eyes.

'You look frighteningly good,' says Charles.

Iris clutches her stomach. 'You're giving me the collywobbles.'

Madge does a twirl. 'I did the makeup myself. Is it all right?'

'Perfectly grisly,' says Delia.

Agatha sidles up to me. 'Punkie loves dressing up. At school she used to prank the teachers by wearing disguises – and she's never grown out of it. The more outlandish the better. The nun was a favourite and one time she met a friend at the station dressed as a Greek priest! Can you imagine? It's where I got my idea for a fake beard from.'

'Oh, right.' I don't say that I've always thought such plot devices rather unconvincing.

'Get out of there, Titch,' scolds Madge.

The pup has her head plunged into one of the chests. She looks up. The mink stole dangling from her mouth.

'Drop!'

Titch runs off with her prize and starts to chew on it.

A camera has been set up on a tripod. Kitty and Patience are manoeuvring a backdrop showing a large window with a garden view, in front of it.

'Left a bit,' says Mrs Cherry. 'No, my left.'

Patience pauses to fix her mob cap, then shuffles back the other way.

'Punkie's roped Jim into taking some publicity photographs to advertise the play. She's dug out her old cuttings to give the MADS some ideas.' Agatha points to a scrapbook on one of the wicker chairs.

'Jack, why don't you put on the black and white pinstriped three-piece suit,' says Madge. 'We'll use you as a stand in for the solicitor. It's in that other chest.'

'Yes, Mother.'

Mrs Cherry scowls but Madge doesn't seem to notice. Or perhaps she's choosing not to.

Iris goes to the chest and tips back the lid. 'Urgh!' she cries. She lifts out a white apron. It's stained wet and red. 'Blood!'

Titch drops the now soggy mink and scampers over to see what the fuss is about. She sniffs the air with interest then starts pawing at Iris.

'Blood? Don't be silly,' says Charles.

'I'm not being silly. It's blood, I tell you. Titch knows.'

TWENTY

AGATHA ROLLS HER EYES. 'ANOTHER OF YOUR PRANKS, Punkie?'

'Honestly, Mother.' Jack swipes the apron from Iris. 'It's just fake blood. Patience, would you take it to be washed – and these shirts too.' He gathers up a bundle and passes it to her.

Titch slopes back to the mink.

'Yes, Master Jack.' Patience frowns, examining the apron.

'You can go too, Kitty,' Madge adds. 'Tell Cook we'd like soup and rolls in an hour. We'll have it in here, please.'

'Yes, Madam.'

I take off my coat and hang it over the back of the chair carefully so the diary, keys and flyer won't fall out of my pockets. I pick up the scrapbook, sit down and open it. Seeing all the cut-out newspaper columns makes me start for a moment. The headlines blur, words swimming as I remember how I snipped out every article I could find. I block the memory and focus. Most of the reviews are similar, praising the first act and the quality cast but harsher about the latter scenes. The critics and audience were reportedly intrigued by the new playwright's identity, and when it was revealed M F Watts was a woman the reviews became more disparaging. One declaring: 'Mrs Watts is a charming middle-aged married woman. She lives in Cheshire and is known in Paris and Riviera society,' while another describes her as the wife of a Cheshire squire. *The Manchester Despatch* shares that her husband has an estate where she 'indulges a practical interest in agriculture and writes on political economy – hardly a subject that one would expect to lead to play-writing.' Only one or two describe her as the sister of Agatha Christie.

'Ladies, you can get changed in the cloakroom,' says Madge. 'You know where that is, don't you, Delia?'

She nods.

'And Gentlemen, Jack will show you to the facilities.'

I continue scanning the scrapbook while Agatha and Madge tweak the position of the backdrop. I'm surprised to read that Madge was too shy to make a speech despite being loudly cheered by the audience, with the star Fay Compton saying a few words on her behalf. And that she went away immediately after the play to avoid publicity. It seems she is like her sister in that regard. A few small reports suggest that a new home will be found for the play at the end of its run – but Miss Compton is suddenly taken ill and undergoes an operation and the cuttings stop.

I look up at the sound of Madge moving the other wicker chair closer to mine. Agatha looks happy enough tidying away the unwanted costumes.

'I hope you're not finding it too dull a read?' Madge asks.

'Not at all.'

'I can still remember the thrill and terror of seeing my words brought to life. And the strangest part was that all the lines sounded quite new to me when spoken by professional actors. Under the glare of the limelight, I was aware of every laugh achieved or missed.' She reaches out to take the scrapbook, flicking past pages of staged photographs of key scenes. In one a man seated at a table points a revolver at a second who recoils dramatically. In fact, the cast adopt over the top poses in most of the photographs. Some scenes involve the characters attending a fancy-dress ball. One man in tails has a ridiculously large stuck-on moustache, another is dressed like an Elizabethan courtier, while a larger, older woman is garbed in a flag and helmet.

'My brother and I would go to the theatre every week,' Madge continues. 'And when Agatha was old enough, she came too. We Millers always got seats in the pit stalls. Jim's parents were great theatre lovers too – his brother's an actor, you know? And it's a Watts tradition to see the pantomime in Manchester on Boxing Day, though I don't suppose we'll go this year.'

'I don't see why not.'

She bites her bottom lip, her gaze on Agatha. 'Perhaps.'

'Routine can be reassuring to a patient. Regular meals. A good sleep pattern.' I must word this carefully. 'And taking medicines as prescribed. I hope you feel able to raise any concerns about Agatha's general care directly with me.'

She flushes. 'Of course, Nurse.'

'Thank you . . . about my looking after Dr Pearce–' But I'm cut short by the MADS return.

Madge gets up and starts fussing over them all, tweaking collars and adjusting hemlines with a packet of pins from a sideboard. Mrs Cherry looks almost unrecognisable as the intimidating housekeeper. Her high-necked ebony blouse is very Victorian, and her jet-black bob is now hidden under a grey wig in a French pleat.

'You don't look fat enough to be the solicitor,' says Paul. 'Here stick this inside your suit.' He chucks a cushion to Jack.

I close the scrapbook as Agatha takes the vacated wicker chair, just as Jim enters the room, several film rolls in his hand. He loads one into the camera.

'Right, who wants to go first?'

'Let's have Charles and Iris with Madge,' replies Delia. She directs the pair to sit on either side of the table, with the ghost bride looming ominously behind them. 'Hold her hand, Charles.'

Iris's cheeks pink.

'That's better . . .'

Don't tell me the poor thing has a crush on him.

'Now raise your arms, Madge.' Delia moves in, adjusts the veil. 'Perfect.'

Jim takes the photograph, then repositions the tripod. While the three wait, I notice Iris keeps glancing at Charles, although he appears oblivious. There's always banter between them, but he never flirts with her – and Charles flirts with everyone. What was it he said about Iris? Not the brightest bulb on the tree. That was it. Perhaps he's not as shallow as he makes out.

Nah.

'Jack, we'll have you in the next one,' says Madge.

While they swap over, I take the opportunity to nip to the lavatory. As I wander down the corridor, I spot Patience hovering by one of the glass taxidermy cases. She's still holding the bundle of laundry.

'Is something the matter?'

'Oh, Nurse. I'm tied up in knots.'

'Come, let's sit down and you can tell me all about it.' I reach for the terrace room door handle.

'Oh, I couldn't, Nurse, not in one of the family's rooms. It's not proper.'

'The kitchen?'

She shakes her head. 'Somewhere private.'

'We'll go to my room, then.'

Patience follows me upstairs, meek as a lamb, while I try to think what is troubling her. A falling out with Kitty, perhaps.

'Here we are,' I say.

She follows, still somewhat reluctant. I reposition the dressing table chair and perch on the end of my bed, indicating for her to sit.

Patience does, still gripping the laundry tight to her bosom. 'You won't say anything, will you, Nurse? To the Wattses, I mean.'

'That rather depends on what it is that's upset you so. We might feel, after we've discussed it, that telling Mrs or Mr Watts might be necessary.'

'But they've had such a difficult year with Mrs Miller dying in April, old Mr Watts in May, and then his wife just last month. Well, you know, of course you do. And now all this business with Miss Agatha.'

'Yes, yes . . .' I wish she'd get to the point. I suppose her mind is rambling again. 'It's something to do with the family, then?'

'Oh, no, Nurse. It's the apron.'

'The one from the dressing up?'

'I know I was meant to take it to the laundry to be cleaned, but I thought as maybe I shouldn't. You see, I recognised it as mine straight away. I had to fix the hem, and, well, my stitching's not what it was – my eyes have gone a bit foggy, especially for close up work. So it was only fit for wearing when scrubbing floors, really.'

'Well, that's to be expected at your . . . Let me see.' I hold out my hands so she can pass me the apron. The stitches are crooked as she said. I peer at the rusty-red stain.

'It is real blood, isn't it? Not theatrical stuff?'

'Yes.'

'I thought you'd know. Being a nurse. The police would know too, wouldn't they? They can tell between human and animal blood, can't they? Blood groups too. That's how they get murderers nowadays. That and fingerprints. No point trying to kill anyone anymore.'

I let out a breath. 'I'm pretty sure this is only raw meat juices.'

She laughs. 'Oh. Thank goodness. Gave me a right turn when Miss Caldwell pulled it out, I can tell you. "How'd it get there?" I thought.' Patience puts her hand to her mouth, rubs her finger over her top lip. 'Then I remembered how Ellen had scorched hers with the iron. She didn't have a fresh one, so I lent her one of my spares. A day or two later she left Abney. I thought she must've packed it up with her personal belongings, accidental like.'

'Well, it seems she ruined yours too and was too embarrassed to admit it. Don't worry. You haven't done anything wrong.'

She looks puzzled. 'Me? I know that. But you can't be right, Nurse. You see she was wearing it last night.'

I vaguely remember correcting Patience when I thought she'd

meant Kitty. 'But Ellen doesn't work here anymore. She works at Dr Pearce's surgery.'

Her face flashes with relief. 'You must think me a silly old woman. It's no wonder I'm muddled after all this trouble these last few days. Always someone disappearing or appearing. Like one of them funny foreign weather clocks I've seen on sale in Pauldens.' She holds up her index fingers. Draws one back. 'Mrs Christie disappears.' Brings the other finger forwards. 'Then she reappears.' She laughs at herself. 'Who'll be next?'

'Well, if Ellen has been given her job back, I'm sure Mrs Watts will tell us,' I reassure her, passing the apron back. 'And don't worry, a long soak in some cold salted water should lift the stain. My mother and I used to take laundry in all the time.'

'You don't need to teach your grandmother how to suck eggs,' says Patience.

I smile. Not wanting her to know anything's wrong.

So, Ellen was here last night when she had no right to be. And didn't Patience say she'd seen her when she was looking for Thomas to help him with the Christmas tree?

What is Ellen up to?

The MADS hardly notice me as I slip back inside the boys' room after a quick visit to the lavatory. Jim and Jack take out the photography equipment while Iris and Madge tidy away the costumes into the wardrobe and chests. Mrs Cherry stands talking to Charles and Paul. For once her voice is quiet. I sidestep subtly to try and hear what she's saying.

'I was worried he was out of his depth,' she says.

'He did seem rather nervous,' says Charles.

'Nervous? Chap was sweating like a coal miner,' says Paul. 'And I like a cigarette, but he was smoking like a chimney. We all get a bit of stage fright, but this is only the rehearsals. You should be glad he's bolted, Delia.'

'But who will I get to replace him at short notice? If I can't find someone soon, I'll be obliged to give the role to Jack. I don't know how much longer I can make excuses to Madge – especially now she's got him in the publicity stills.'

'Can't you twist the vicar's arm?' asks Charles.

'He's too busy.'

'Well, it is Christmas,' replies Paul.

She sighs. 'If only Dr Pearce wasn't too poorly. We could have asked him. He'd have been perfect.'

'How inconvenient of him,' says Paul.

Mrs Cherry shushes him. 'We'll have less of the malapert remarks from you, thank you very much. You're already on thin ice . . . Madge, dear,' she calls, as she wanders over to her friend.

'Looks like it'll have to be Bertie Wooster after all,' says Charles with a grin.

Paul scoffs. 'Can you imagine? Good gwief!' He clasps his hand to his forehead. 'You *gave* me an awful fwight!'

He sounds nothing like Jack, but Charles still laughs. Since when were these two so chummy?

'Still, Richard wouldn't be the first new MADS member to bolt,' replies Paul. 'Can't say I care for being bossed about by two women myself. Thank God the next play's written and directed by a fella.'

Urgh.

Madge checks her watch. 'Let's take a break. We're supposed to have soup about now.'

Everyone except Charles voices their approval. She pushes the electric servant's bell.

I slide back towards the chairs. My coat's been moved. My heart thuds. I look round, trying not to let my panic show. Where is it?

My chest rises rapidly. There's a bunch of coats all piled up on a pew in the corner. Dashing over, I start to search through them. Charles's British Warm is on top, then Iris's fur, Mrs Cherry's coat, Paul's trench coat – and then finally mine. I scoop it up and slide my hand into one pocket, the flyer and Richard's car keys are still there, then the other. Empty. I swallow. I start over, this time patting each coat in turn.

'Lost something?' asks Agatha, strolling over.

'A . . . book. It was in my pocket.' I look to Titch but she's still mauling the mink stole.

'This one?' She holds out the diary. Eyebrows raised.

Has she looked inside?

'Thank you.'

'I found it on the floor. Must have dropped out when I gathered up all the coats. I didn't know it was yours.'

Agatha holds my gaze. Does she know it's Dr Pearce's?

I try to keep my hand steady as I take the diary, but there is a question in Agatha's eyes.

Mrs Cherry walks to the centre of the room, distracting us both.

'Jack has kindly agreed to step in and read the part of the solicitor today,' Mrs Cherry begins. 'As I still haven't heard from Mr Buxton, I feel I've no option but to replace him. I've been in contact with a number of other amateur dramatic companies, and I hope to find someone suitable soon. Unfortunately, as you'll appreciate, they're all pretty busy with Christmas productions and rehearsals for pantomimes, so they're rather slow getting back to me. Still, I hope for good news soon, and the show must go on.'

'Hear, hear,' says Madge.

'While we wait for lunch, I'd like to spend some time working through some of the more technical parts of the play . . . Jim, would you please bring Arthur in.'

Jim grins. 'Sir Arthur.'

TWENTY-ONE

AGATHA LOOKS TO THE DOOR. 'CONAN DOYLE'S HERE?'

'Different Arthur,' says Mrs Cherry with a wink.

What is she up to?

Jim goes out. Doors open and close. There's a squeaking sound like something needs oiling.

Then there's a glint of metal as he wheels a suit of armour complete with lethal looking axe into the room on a sack trolley. Oh no, it's the one I dropped the spills into.

Titch drops the mink and runs forwards, barking furiously.

'Stop that!' commands Jim. 'Jack, take her out and throw that thing in the bin.'

Jack gingerly picks up the mink and uses it to lure the pup out of the room.

'Now, we need to work out how we're going to get Sir Arthur to move towards Dr Tremayne in Act One,' says Mrs Cherry. 'We could try a flat trolley, but we'd have to make sure he stays rigid and doesn't topple.'

'What about some kind of fishing wire,' suggests Iris.

'Really?' says Paul, rolling his eyes. 'I hardly think that would be strong enough.'

'Well, we certainly need whatever we use to be invisible,' replies Mrs Cherry, kindly.

'Wouldn't the easiest thing be to have somebody actually in the suit?' suggests Charles.

Mrs Cherry's eyes light up. 'I agree. That was my conclusion too.'

I can't believe I'm about to say this. 'Wouldn't it make sense to use someone not in the cast?'

'I'll do it,' says Agatha, before I can volunteer.

Damn. What if they find the scrunched-up spills?

'Are you sure?' checks Madge.

'It's only one line and it'll be funny.' She goes over to the suit of armour.

'And heavy,' I add, trying to put her off.

'Well, that's easily resolved,' says Charles. 'You mix real chest plates and the helmet with other pieces made out of fabric or cardboard.'

'Punkie, you're great with a sewing machine.'

'I could give it a go.'

'Marvellous!' Mrs Cherry beams.

Agatha lifts off the helmet and turns it over ready to try on.

'I wouldn't. Not without something to protect your face,' says Jim.

'I'll make a padded coif,' offers Madge.

Jim beckons Jack over so they can dismantle Sir Arthur's torso and arms. I rush forwards to help as father and son separate the breastplate from the backplate.

The paper has likely dropped right through. Could be in a leg or a foot.

'You were right, it is heavy,' says Agatha, passing me the helmet. I feel something else against my skin. I curl my hand. Newspaper.

'Don't worry, it'll feel lighter when you wear it,' says Jim.

I put the helmet on the costume chest and put the scrunched-up spills into my apron pocket. Then sit down. Relieved, I pick up a script from the chair next to me to remind myself when in the act the moving suit of armour happens while Jim and Jack fit the chest pieces to Agatha.

'Excellent,' calls Mrs Cherry, passing her the long-handled axe. 'Don't forget your chopper.'

'Poleaxe,' corrects Jim with a grin. 'Ideal for hacking and piercing.'

Strapped in place, Agatha moves cumbersomely back and to, swinging the weapon.

'I'm still not sure this is a good idea, Mrs Christie,' I say. 'What with your sore shoulder.'

Agatha laughs and tosses me the axe.

'Oh!' I exclaim, catching it. 'It's not real.'

'Of course not,' says Mrs Cherry. 'We switched the real one.'

'You should still be careful swinging it about. If you get any pain . . .'

'Yes, Nurse.' Agatha takes the axe back.

'Ready, Paul?' asks Madge.

'Always.'

Mrs Cherry scoffs. 'Jane, will you prompt, seeing as you've got the script open? Just in case *anyone* forgets their line.'

A flash of annoyance crosses Paul's face.

Mrs Cherry narrows her eyes then steamrollers on. 'Paul,

I need your reaction to be big so that the audience can really feel your terror. Agatha, you have to imagine there's a backdrop here. Wood-panelling and a pair of antlers, that kind of thing. You stand against it. We want to give the audience a jump scare when you first move.'

Agatha moves into position.

'Paul, you enter stage left.' Mrs Cherry wafts her hands impatiently. 'That's it. Good.' She nods her head as a cue.

Agatha keeps perfectly still as Paul moves slowly down the corridor. 'I know I didn't imagine that icy draft. Why will nobody believe me?'

I run my finger along the line. He's word perfect.

He waves his hands in the air as he moves further along.

'You look like a cheap fortune teller,' criticises Mrs Cherry.

Paul tuts. Tries one hand instead.

'Now you look like a preacher.' Mrs Cherry stands up. 'Like this.' She holds her hands up but moves them more slowly as though seeking a particular spot.

He mutters under his breath, then copies her.

'Better.' She sits back down.

Paul carries on. 'It was round about . . . *here*.'

Agatha groans. 'Doctor!' She swings the axe, so it strikes the floor.

We all jump then chuckle as Paul staggers back.

'I've been waiting for you, Doctor.' Agatha strides forwards, swinging the axe over her shoulder again.

'You're not real,' stutters Paul. 'I'm sick. Really sick.'

Agatha slices the axe down. Paul scrambles backwards, his feet skidding from under him. It's all very convincing as he collapses to the ground. Hands shielding his head as he wails. 'No. God, please. No!'

Agatha throws her arms into the air. 'Time for a taste of your own medicine, Doctor!' She brings down her arms in a fierce final blow.

'And curtain!' calls Mrs Cherry. The MADS applaud. 'Right, let's call it a day.'

'That was brilliant,' I say.

Charles pats Paul on the back.

'Jane, give me a hand would you,' calls Agatha.

'Sure.' I leave the script and go to help her.

'Jim was right, the armour's weight disperses when you wear it,' she says as I unbuckle the chest plates. 'Funny I'm usually so shy, but I enjoyed that. I hate giving speeches and things like that, but I find performing as a character is different. I wanted to be a singer, you know, when I was younger.'

'I didn't.'

'Mmm. Opera. But they said my voice wasn't strong enough.'

'That must have hurt.'

She shrugs. A different curtain falling.

'I don't know any opera,' I say. 'Well, not the proper stuff. Only a bit of Gilbert and Sullivan.'

'Do you know *The Yeoman of the Guard*?'

'I don't think so.'

'When I was about thirteen, I was friends with five sisters, and they put on family shows. Their father was a doctor, actually . . . anyway because I was a soprano they asked me to play Colonel

Fairfax. I remember there was a lot of fuss from my mother about my legs being on show even in hose. She made me wear a turquoise cloak to disguise them! Made from one of grannie's pieces. Seeing all these costumes in chests made it all come back. I don't think I was ever happier. I often wonder about those pathways that ran nowhere. Careers that faltered at the first steps. Proposals refused. Don't you?'

'Actually, Agatha. I'm feeling rather tired. I think I'm going to have a lie-down.'

'What about lunch?'

I pick up my script. 'I'm not hungry.'

Her eyes bore into me. 'You must eat, Jane. Take your own advice. It's usually good.'

TWENTY-TWO

THE SWEET SMELL OF FRESHLY BAKED JAM TARTS LURES ME to the still room. Colin's at the flour-speckled table, drawing a motor car on a piece of baking parchment with one of Cook's pencils. A tin of assorted crayons next to him.

'That's very good.' I say, looking over his shoulder.

'I've not finished yet. I'm going to do a dead man, an' all.' He chews the end of the pencil, while he ponders. 'It'll be too hard putting him on the back seat. Going to have him lying on the ground.'

'Nice.' I toss my script onto the table. Go over to the drying rack and prod a jam tart to see if they've cooled enough to try.

'Where did you get the crayons from?' I ask Cook as she gently slaps my fingers.

'They were Jack's. Kitty found them.'

'I thought she wanted her brother gone?'

'She's a softie, really,' replies Cook. 'Her bark's worse than her bite.'

'She certainly likes to growl at me.'

Colin's tongue sticks out slightly as he concentrates on his picture. He's not a bad kid. Just a bit neglected. I wonder what his life is like at home. Kitty mentioned her mam, but is there a father still on the scene? And what kind of a father? Well, it's none of my business.

'So what brings you down here, again?' Cook asks.

'I'm hungry.' My eyes wander to the jam tarts again.

'They're too hot. You'll burn your mouth.'

'How about a sandwich?'

'Go on, then.'

'Thank you.' I kiss her rosy cheek.

'I'll have a butty, an' all,' calls Colin.

'I'll have a butty, an' all – *what*?'

He laughs. 'Please, Mrs Worcester.'

I wander into the larder. 'Can I have some of this roast beef?' I call.

'No, you can't, that's for the Wattses' dinner. I can hardly serve it up with a chunk missing. You can have egg. Fetch me a couple. I'll put a pan on in the kitchen.'

I scan the shelves. Ah, there they are. I scoop up three from a basket, the butter dish – the Wattses are too posh for margarine – and a loaf then follow Cook.

She washes her hands then pours hot water from the kettle into a pan, adds a splash of vinegar and puts it on the electric ring. Then takes the eggs from me and lowers them into the simmering water.

After putting the bread on the table, I take the butter dish and a silver-handled knife over to the range. Kneeling, I open the oven door and hold the dish to the warmth while the eggs begin to rattle in the pan. Remembering doing the same at home, sitting in front of the range, when I was a girl. Two small Staffordshire dogs on the mantle. A wedding present to my parents, just four months before my birth, though my ma always fudged the dates if people asked. It was hard even then to imagine my ma young and in love. The dogs had long gone by the time I'd left home. Pawned along with anything else of worth. I wonder what bridal gifts Agatha will keep, if any.

With Cook distracted I slide the scrunched-up spills and Dr Pearce's diary from my pocket into the oven. I know I'm probably paranoid. The chances of someone working out I'm Jay is highly unlikely, but I'm not taking any chances.

I return the dish to the table and start to slice the loaf with a breadknife.

'Mrs Watts hasn't rehired Ellen, has she? For Christmas, or something?'

She wrinkles her nose. 'I doubt that very much.'

'Why's that?'

Cook bites her lip. 'Well, you weren't working here at the time. Must have been middle of September. Mrs Cherry had persuaded Mrs Watts to host a cast party here for the new season's first show. All the MADS came: Mr Trent, Mr Ramsbury, Reverend Whittle, Miss Caldwell and some other faces I don't know so well. Reporters and photographers too. Oh and Dr Pearce. Champagne and canapes. It went on till well past Midnight.

'Come Sunday morning, Mr Ramsbury can't find his tie pin. Gold and mother of pearl, it was. The box was still on the dressing table.'

I spread the butter evenly. 'And . . .'

'Well, Ellen was the only other person to go into his room.'

'No. I don't believe it. She'd have to be a fool to take that kind of risk, especially when she'd so obviously be in the frame.'

'I agree, but what about Dr Pearce's new Onoto pen?'

'Didn't he lose it at the surgery?'

'Possibly. Though he remembered last having it when everyone came to celebrate Mrs Watts' birthday back in March.' Cook takes the pan off the heat and drains the water away. Flushes the eggs with cold. 'And last Christmas Mrs Cherry couldn't find her silver watch. Though she said it had a loose clasp so she may have lost it elsewhere. Anyway, less than a week after the MADS party, we're told that Ellen has decided to leave. Mrs Watts – or was it Dr Pearce? – said her nain was really very unwell and she needed to look after her full time.'

We take an egg a piece to peel. The sharp shell jabbing under my fingernails.

'So it's unlikely that the Wattses would rehire her.'

'Exactly . . . Yesterday morning, I was up the wall, to be honest. The bread boy was late and I assumed he'd taken one look at the journalists barricading the gates and scarpered. I'd decided I'd have to nip upstairs to my room to telephone the bakery to reorganise the delivery. Patience and Kitty were up and down to the Breakfast Room. I was rushing, so it's all a bit vague in my head. I heard voices – one male, one female – at the servants' entrance. I stopped thinking maybe the bakery had already sent the bread boy back with his tail between his legs. Only I saw it was a man, not a boy. He was talking to Kitty, or so I thought. I didn't pay much attention. When I came off the phone, a few minutes later, Kitty came out of the breakfast room with a used tray. It spooked me a bit. Like having seen a ghost. But I told myself I was overworked and that I must have missed Kitty coming up and past me.'

A knob of butter slides off my knife onto the floor. 'It was *Ellen* you saw at the door.'

'Must have been. You know how dark and gloomy Abney is. And the two girls look much alike from the back. You don't look past the uniform, sometimes. When we had maids aplenty, I was always mistaking one for another.'

I bet that was the reporter. But I want to keep that to myself, for now. 'Did you hear what they were saying?'

'He was complaining. Saying it was brass monkeys out. But Ellen wouldn't let him in. I couldn't hear very clearly. I think she said the old house was safer.'

'Buckley Chapel? You don't remember anything else?'

'There was a smell . . . No, I can't think what it was now. Sorry. Now where's that salt got to?'

'If you smell it again, you might remember.'

'I might. Ah there it is.' She reaches for the cellar.

'You think he was a fence,' I realise, slicing the egg and layering it onto the bread, while Cook does the same. 'You think he's made Ellen come back to steal more things?'

'I hope not. Until we have proof, I think it best we keep this between ourselves.' She grinds salt onto Colin's egg, then passes the cellar to me. 'If Ellen is sneaking in, we need to catch her in the act.'

I sigh deeply. The last thing I need is the distraction of a thieving ex-parlourmaid. Dr Argyle is back on Monday, and I need all my focus on him, not jumping at creaking doors and footsteps in corridors like a character in Madge's play.

Sliding the sandwiches onto a couple of plates we return to the still room.

Colin swipes his up straight away and takes a huge bite. 'Gorgeous,' he declares while chewing. 'Are we having a jam tart for afters?'

'If you have room,' says Cook.

'I always have room.' Crumbs fall onto his picture. I slide it out of the way. He's coloured the motor car in. I stare at it. Something's niggling me.

That's it. The motor car is blue. Not green.

I swallow down my mouthful of egg sandwich. 'Colin. Which motor car did you see the dead man in?'

'He wurnt dead. He were sleeping.'

Cook raises her eyebrows at me. 'Is something wrong, Jane?'

'But the motor car, Colin. Was it a blue one? Like in your picture.'

'Duh! Yes, that's why I dun it blue.'

'Not the Wattses' green Wolseley?'

He looks at me like I'm an idiot. 'Nah, a Morris. It's by the railway bridge.'

'Oh God! It was a different MAD Colin saw, Richard not Paul.'

Dread hits the pit of my stomach. 'What if he had an apoplexy or heart attack at the wheel?' I picture him crawling along the ground, pleading for help. 'I've got to go and look for him.'

Kitty's voice cuts in from the other doorway. 'Look for who?

Blimey, faces on you both. Been sucking on lemons?'

'That man I seen in the motor car might be dead after all,' says Colin glibly.

She gawps at us like we're a few egg butties short of a picnic. 'Bloody hell. Dunt tell me you actually believe him.' She shakes her fist at him. 'What've I told you about making stuff up!'

'I'm not!' He shouts, sideswiping the tin. Crayons scatter everywhere.

I recoil. My heart racing.

'Now. Now. I won't have any of that nonsense in my kitchen. Colin, pick up that mess. And Kitty, you'd better go with Jane.' She pulls open a drawer. 'Here's a torch. And let's pray if Richard is still out there that you find him in time.'

TWENTY-THREE

I EXPLAIN THE MIX-UP AS WE TREK THROUGH THE WOODS, BUT Kitty remains unconvinced.

'Probably had an upset stomach like Mr Trent,' she says, half-heartedly scanning the overgrowth as we near the Morris, its bodywork glistening with ice crystals. 'Reckon he got caught short. Then lay down in the back of his car until he felt better. Bet you he nodded off and when he woke, his car was too cold to start. Not exactly the stuff of murder mysteries.'

'We should check the car first then circle out.' I don't confess I was here earlier; only repeat that Jack and I spotted it abandoned the night before.

I poke around in the back while Kitty scopes out the front.

'Ooh. There's a stain here,' she says, waving the torch light around the footwell. I lean closer while she rubs her hanky on the mark. The residue is clear and greasy. 'Don't get excited. It's not blood. Motor oil, maybe?' She sniffs at it. 'It has a faint sweet smell.'

I copy her. 'Macasser hair oil. Richard uses it. He must have spilt some.'

She rolls her eyes. 'Well I dunt think he was poisoned with it.'

We spend another half an hour or so searching nearby.

'Waste of time. I knew it.' She thrusts the torch at me. 'Bloody Colin . . .'

I try to let her ranting wash over me, but she goes on and on. How he picks his nose and wipes it under the table. How his feet stink, his farts worse. Until I can stand it no more. 'At least your brother's alive!'

Kitty's mouth falls open. 'Jane. I'm sorry. I didn't know.'

I clasp my hands to my face. Exhausted. 'Why would you.'

A corvid caws overhead. Black and white feathers rustle in the branches.

'One for sorrow,' I say quietly. Squeezing my thumb until the anger seeps away, the way I've taught myself. I focus on a fleck of dirt under my nail. The creases and lines on my skin. While silence fills the space around us. Kitty must be full of questions. I would be.

Two for joy . . . My ma always saluted magpies. She was very superstitious. Touching wood. Throwing salt over her shoulder if she spilt any. Not walking under ladders. God knows she'd had more than her fair share of bad luck.

Three for a girl. Four for a boy . . . Mrs Cherry said she was "a late surprise" for her parents. Well, my brother David was an outright shock for my ma.

'We should be glad we didn't find a body. That means that Richard chap must be all right. Reckon he'll turn up at the next rehearsal right as rain.'

I nod.

'I bet you've seen loads of dead people, though.' Kitty flushes.

'Sorry. I meant as a nurse, not your family . . .'

'I know you did.' I've already shared more of my past than I ever meant to. I'm just so tired. My ankle aches from walking, and I'm worn out with the effort of soothing and cajoling – and yes, manipulating.

Kitty witters, trying to cover her gaffe. 'So, were you a VAD like Mrs Watts and Mrs Christie?'

I repeat the lie I told Archie and Dr Argyle, that I've only been nursing for six years, even though the chance of her, of anyone, connecting me to Winwick Asylum is very slim. 'Are you interested in nursing?'

'I'm not clever enough.'

'Rubbish!'

Her face lights up and my heart softens. 'I think you'd make a very good nurse. You're bright, hard-working, and you wouldn't crumble under a matron's steely glare.'

She laughs.

'I could ask Mrs Watts if you could look after Dr Pearce with me.'

'She'd never agree to that.'

'I think she might.'

'Really?'

Her face is full of hope as we approach the hall. The sound of laughter is coming from the terrace. Lanterns have been put out along the lawn's edge.

'That sounds like our Colin. What's he doing now?'

We cut down the stone steps.

Thomas and Colin are pushing a huge ball of snow along the ground.

'Oh, 'ello you two. Everything all right?' the gardener cocks his head.

'Colin's told you, then?'

'About the dead bloke, yeah.' He grins. 'I presume you didn't find one.'

'Course not, Mr Budworth,' says Kitty.

'Duh! The murderer will have moved the body by now,' groans Colin. 'Bet he buried him in the woods, like Dandie.'

'Nah, ground's too hard this time of year,' replies Thomas.

'Oh yeah.' Colin looks disappointed. Then he bursts into a smile. 'You gonna help us build our snowman, sis?'

'That's kid's stuff.'

I made one with David once. We stuck pieces of coal in the head for eyes and added one of Pa's old pipes to the mouth. 'I will.'

Kitty looks at me in astonishment.

'What? It'll be fun,' I say, shrugging my shoulders. 'And it'll warm us up.' I scoop up a gloveful of snow and trundle it over the snow so that it picks up another layer. It's harder work than I remember but it grows quickly in size.

Kitty shakes her head but joins me at my side. The snowball soon needs both of us to push it. We try to steer it closer to Colin and Thomas as it increases in bulk and resistance. Soon the paths we've made snake over the terrace like a labyrinth.

'Right, let's stack them on top of each other,' says Thomas, standing back in admiration. The four of us collapse in fits of giggles as we try to lift one massive snowball onto the other, but eventually we manage it.

'He's gonna be huge!' exclaims Colin. 'A Goliath!'

'Right, head next,' I say, slightly breathless.

'I can manage that,' says Kitty. 'You need to add more snow to the middle to join it properly.'

'I didn't know you were such an expert,' I tease.

She throws a handful of snow at me. It scatters over me like a cloudburst.

Thomas wipes his brow. 'Right, I'll just nip t'the bothy and get that scarecrow box, bet there's stuff we can use to dress Goliath.'

Colin and I collect more snow and pat it onto the snowman's middle until he has a nice round paunch.

Out of the corner of my eye, I see Kitty peel something stuck to the surface of her now head-sized ball.

'Bet this belongs to that reporter that didn't show up for the interview with Colonel Christie,' she says, waving a small rectangular card at me. As she gets nearer, I can see it's a press pass, slightly damp from being under the snow's crust.

The letters are embossed and in black ink.

'Dickie Derbyshire.

Journalist.

Stockport Advertiser.'

Patience's jokes make sense now. Not a dicky bird. Ha! And that comment about Thomas making a good bird scarer. I wriggle my index fingers. 'Fly away, Peter. Fly away, Paul.'

Was it Dickie Derbyshire I heard out on the terrace last night?

Kitty sticks Dickie's press card into her pocket and looks the snowman up and down. 'It needs arms.'

'We could use branches?'

'I know where there's some!' Colin dashes off.

I place my hands under my arm pits to ease my chilled fingers while Kitty moulds the snow into two shoe shapes.

Colin is soon back, dragging his quarry. We help him poke the sticks into each side.

Thomas returns a few minutes later. He drops the box onto the ground and Colin dives in. 'And this is from Cook.' He holds a carrot in front of his nose.

'Ha! Brilliant! Ooh, can we use this an' all?' Colin pulls out a waistcoat.

'Pass it 'ere, lad, them buttons will make good eyes.' Thomas takes out his penknife and snips at the cotton.

After selecting a hat and a cravat, Colin dresses Goliath. 'Now for his face.' He pushes the buttons into position, though it takes a couple of attempts to get them to stick. Then plunges the carrot in.

'And 'ere's some sunflower seeds to make a smile.' Thomas drops them into Colin's open hand.

'He looks very smart,' I say, when he's done. 'A proper gent.'

Colin laughs again. Then goes back to the box.

'Aren't you done, lad?'

'Just checking if there's owt else I can add.'

'That's enough,' says Kitty, pulling him away. 'It's going to be dark very soon and you need to get home.'

Colin's lip starts to wobble.

'We should ask Mr Watts to take a photograph of Goliath,' I say, brightly.

'Oh yes! Can we?'

I nod. 'Let's go inside, and I'll ask for you.'

Colin grabs his satchel from the ground and waves goodbye to the snowman. 'Oh wait! I forgot. Got summat here I can use.' He runs back to Goliath, pulls out a pair of spectacles with thick lenses and pushes them into his head.

'Looks different now, dunt he?'

He does. Something about the glasses is tugging at my memory. 'Where did you get them?'

'Found them. It were all right to take them, wurnt it? 'Cause they're broken.'

'Yes,' I reply. Trying to keep my voice steady. 'Where did you find them?'

'By the blue motor car.' He points back towards Newlands Road.

A memory flashes in my mind's eye. Suddenly I recall having seen a blue Morris recently. I'd forgotten all about it. The one pursuing Mrs Christie and her family. I remember it overtaking me and Dr Pearce as we left Manchester. Could it be the same one?

'Something wrong, Jane?' asks Thomas.

Dicky Bird. 'Thomas, what did that reporter you scared off look like?'

'Can't rightly remember. Ordinary. 'e didn't wear glasses, though. Could have been there for weeks.'

I try to picture the man I'd seen at Harrogate. He was the same age and height as Richard Buxton. What about differences? Dicky had dishevelled hair, whereas Richard has sleeked back hair, but that's easily changed with macassar oil. Dicky was skinny while Richard had a paunch like our snowman. Oh! I remember Paul throwing the cushion at Jack to make him look fatter. There was a cushion in the Morris.

Oh God! I think Richard Buxton and Dickie Derbyshire are the same man!

TWENTY-FOUR

I KNOW THAT DICKIE DERBYSHIRE WAS WORKING ON THE Agatha Christie story for his newspaper – I've even read some of his exclusive articles. Being a local reporter, he has the advantage of knowing all about the Watts family, and the MADS audition flyer gave him the perfect opportunity to go undercover as budding am-dram actor Richard Buxton.

A horn blast makes us all turn. It came from the Abney driveway.

'That'll be Dr Pearce,' says Thomas.

My stomach tightens as I remember sitting next to Richard in Buckley Chapel. But fretting about what I and others said to Dickie Derbyshire and his present whereabouts will have to wait. I cut across the lawn and round to the front door.

Titch bounds down the front steps followed by Madge and Jim.

'Ah, Jane. Perfect timing,' calls Madge, pausing while Jim goes to the taxi.

I pull back my shoulders as I approach. Look her dead in the eye. 'I hope you won't think me presumptuous, Mrs Watts, but I've drawn up a schedule of shifts. You will know having been a VAD yourself that Dr Pearce must be monitored throughout the day and night for any signs of concussion.'

'Naturally.' She orders Titch to sit.

'The schedule is quite demanding, as you'll appreciate with now having two patients to care for. But of course, we *both* want to ensure Dr Pearce and Mrs Christie recover quickly.'

'Absolutely.' She glances at the taxi.

Robert's getting out. There's a bandage around his head. His face is greyer than usual, but his eyes brighten when he spots me.

I push on. 'It will be challenging with just the two of us – I'm afraid usual routines will be disrupted somewhat – but hopefully the preparations for Christmas – and your play – won't be too badly affected. But I'm sure Dr Pearce will be comforted to know he is in our capable hands.'

She swallows as the penny drops. 'Our hands?'

I smile. 'Kitty and I. That really seemed the only solution. With your permission, of course.'

Relief floods over her face. 'I quite agree, Nurse Goodbetter. Well done.'

I couldn't agree more.

The driver retrieves the luggage. Two suitcases and a valet case. How long is Robert planning on staying? I thought it would just be a day or two at most.

Jim pays and Madge holds Titch's scruff as the taxi pulls away.

'I wanted to say again how grateful I am for your hospitality,' says Dr Pearce. 'I pray you won't find me too demanding a patient. I know us doctors have a bad reputation.'

'Nonsense. Couldn't have you home all alone, not so close to

Christmas,' says Madge. 'How is your wife's sister?'

'Much the same,' he replies.

'A difficult time for everyone.'

Keeping up appearances.

Madge beckons me nearer. 'Nurse Goodbetter will help you get settled. We've put you on the first floor. The fire's lit and Cook's made you a nice broth.' She turns to me. 'The right-hand side bedroom, Nurse.'

'Yes, Mrs Watts.'

She and Titch lead the way.

Jim deposits the luggage at the bottom of the staircase. Dr Pearce crooks his elbow.

I pass him the valet case. Pick up the suitcases.

'Now get some rest, Doctor's orders,' calls Madge, pressing the electric servants' bell.

Hopefully she's calling for Kitty.

The guest room is perfect for a man of status. Walnut furniture. A shaving stand on a tripod. An oak 'loo' card table. I keep my eyes deliberately from the four-poster bed.

Dr Pearce puts the valet case down on the birch deck chair, then scans the bookshelves. 'Well, I won't be short of reading material. How are you enjoying *Roger Ackroyd*?'

'I've been too tired to read much more.'

'Perhaps you could read it to me.'

'There's plenty of room for your things,' I say, dropping the suitcases onto the deerskin mat. Keeping my tone cheery, though I don't feel it.

'Would you unpack for me, Jane? I'm not up to it yet.'

I frown. 'They were sure you were fit to be discharged?'

'Yes. Promise.'

'Any headaches? Dizziness?'

'No.'

'Drowsiness? Nausea?'

'I do know the symptoms of concussion. My head's fine – but I am confused . . . by you.'

'Me?'

'You haven't been to see me. Haven't even rung to ask how I was.'

'I wanted to,' I hold his gaze to make the lie more believable. 'But how could I? I've been worried sick.'

He takes my hand. 'Your fingers are freezing. Let me warm them.' He pulls my hand towards his mouth.

A floorboard outside creaks. I snatch my hand away. Turn expecting to see someone in the doorway.

'It's just the groans of an old house.' He sits on the bed which creaks too. 'See.'

I keep a respectable gap between us. 'Do you remember anything about being attacked?'

He shakes his head. 'Ouch. Keep forgetting not to do that.' He dabs his fingers against the bandage.

'Let me take a look.'

'It's fine, honest. I'm just being a baby.'

'I'm your nurse, shouldn't I decide that.'

He grins. 'I like it when you boss me.'

I unwrap the bandage. 'Looks like you took quite a whack. We heard that the police think whoever slugged you was after drugs.'

He shrugs.

'Don't you care?'

'Not particularly. I'm just glad I'm alive.' He clasps my hand. 'Jane. We need to talk. About the future.'

There's another creak from the floorboard. I snatch my hand away.

The door opens.

'Ah, Kitty. Perfect timing. I was just looking at Dr Pearce's head injury. I can show you how to replace the bandage.'

↔

Cook's sitting at the table as I enter the kitchen feeling rather pleased with myself. There's a tea towel draped over something in front of her.

'Is that the last of the jam tarts?' I ask.

'No.' Her tone is unusually sharp.

I look round for my script. Can't see it.

'We've made a snowman!' says Colin, coming in behind me with Thomas and Kitty. 'Wanna see?'

'I'm a bit busy, love. I've got to make some soup for Dr Pearce . . .' She glances at me.

'Aww.'

'Anyroad, it's time you got off home.'

'S'pose. It's all right, we got Mr Wattisface to take a photograph. So even if he melts you can still see Goliath.'

Cook doesn't laugh. Something's definitely wrong. She turns her head to Kitty. 'Mrs Watts says you aren't needed to serve tonight.'

'I'll see Colin to the lodge gates,' says Thomas, his brow furrowing. 'Make sure this Dickie chap's not loitering.'

Cook doesn't even ask what he means. Has Mrs Watts said something to upset her?

'We'll leave you to it, then.'

She gives me such a stare that my stomach churns.

'Actually, I want a word, if you don't mind, Nurse.'

'Of course.' I pull out a chair and sit down.

The others have barely stepped out the door, when Cook whips off the tea towel. Dr Pearce's diary is sat in an enamel dish. 'Well?'

The book's only partly scorched, its edges curled and golden brown. Not done to perfection as I'd planned.

'I want to know what that was doing in my oven, and I don't want any flannel, missy.'

But the words won't come. The kitchen clock's ticking sounds extra loud.

'I know you think I'm an old maid. No idea what goes on in the real world, stuck in my kitchen. But I hear plenty. Family and servants alike are forever dropping in on some pretence.' She rubs her temple. 'Grudges and grievances more often than not, but gossip and rumours too.'

I swallow. I don't like where this is going.

'Often its titbits that don't mean anything on their own. Like Patience fretting because she'd knocked over a pair of binoculars in your room while she was dusting. She brought them to me after, to check. With her eyesight so bad she couldn't tell if the focus was working proper. She didn't notice the RP scratched into the strap, but I did. I knew at once whose they were. Didn't think anything of it at the time. But then she made that comment earlier about him carrying on behind his wife's back. Kitty thought she meant Colonel Christie. But then I remembered about her being so-called mixed up about Ellen. She was right about that. What if she was right about Dr Pearce?'

I squeeze my thumb.

'When Dr Pearce arrived, I thought I'd fetch him a welcoming cup of tea.'

The noise I heard. It was Cook.

Her eyes bore into me. 'I always thought he was especially attentive to Mrs Miller and Mr Watts. Now I know why.'

Tears begin to prick. 'That's not fair. He was being a good doctor. It was only later, that things became . . .'

'Intimate?'

I glare. 'Now you do sound like an old maid.'

She picks up the diary and slowly turns the singed pages. 'I presume this contains some evidence of your meetings. That's why you tried to destroy it.' Her chair scrapes as she stands. 'I'm disappointed in you, Jane.'

I snatch up the diary. The truth is, I'm disappointed in myself too. I pound upstairs clenching my fists and march out of the terrace door.

The cold air hits me like a slap to the face. I thought there was an understanding between me and Cook. An alliance. There are plenty of us about, surplus women. Those with dead sweethearts, fiancés, husbands – and those whose cupid's arrow never pierced. Some, like Cook, have accepted solitude as their fate. Is it so wrong that I have not?

TWENTY-FIVE

I NEED A DRINK. THE GEORGE AND DRAGON IS THE NEAREST pub but I'm worried Paul might be there, so I carry on for the White Hart, using the kitchen torch to light my way.

There must be a way to salvage the situation. Who am I kidding? Madge prides herself on her discretion but still there's no way she'd keep an adulteress in her employ. And I can't begin to let myself imagine Agatha's reaction. No. If Cook tells, I'm out on my ear. My reputation in tatters. Again.

I head into the snug. Even though women are allowed in here I still feel like I'm intruding. But I'm experienced at overcoming awkwardness. I go to the hatch. Flick through Dr Pearce's singed diary while I wait to be served.

'Yes, Miss?' The barman who eventually spots me doesn't look old enough to be serving.

I push the diary into my coat pocket. 'A brandy, please.'

Taking in the rest of the oak-panelled room, I see it's mainly couples in here. A handsome dark-haired man standing by the fireplace catches my eye and strides over.

'I'll get that,' he says, drawing out his wallet. One side of his face is smoother, paler. The scar once deep has faded but still runs ragged from his eye and down his cheek. He gives me a lop-sided smile.

I smile back. 'Thank you.'

'And another half of mild, for me.' He slides his empty glass across the counter. 'Not seen you in here before.'

'It's been a tough day. You're a regular, are you?' I ask.

'Sometimes pop in after work. Not the main bar, though. Too much of a scrum. Besides you get a better class in here, myself excepted.' He grins again. 'You work at the Royal?'

'Yes.' My fingers reach for my cap. I forget it's there sometimes. I unpin it and let my hair down.

'Here's to being off duty.' He clinks his glass to mine. 'Cheers.'

We take our drinks over to one of the tables and sit down.

'What do you do?' I ask out of politeness.

'Got my own roofing firm. Been pricing up a job next door.'

'The church hall roof?'

'That's right.' He sips his ale. 'The vicar's quibbling over the cost. He had the whole lot replaced a couple of years back.'

I sip my brandy. 'Big job, is it?'

'It could become one if he leaves it. I've told him it would be a mistake to put it off. Do it soon as and it'll only take me a couple of days. Still, I can understand the vicar's frustration at having to pay out again. There's a few tiles broken, deliberately so, I reckon. I'll have to replace them, patch up the lining underneath. Anyway, you don't want me blathering on about eaves and ridges.'

I smile. 'It makes a change from doctors wanting to know temperatures and pulse rates. Why deliberately?'

'Maybe deliberately is the wrong word. It's just very unlikely that the tiles would succumb to bad weather so quickly. Could have been lads mucking about up there.' His eyes twinkle as though he's done a few mischievous things in his own youth. 'Standing or walking on them would do the trick, or a hammer of course.'

I picture Colin on top of a slate roof, arms outstretched like a tightrope walker. 'You'd have to have a head for heights.'

'That's why I reckon it's kids. They're fearless.' He takes a swig of ale. 'I'm Gil, by the way.'

I plan to give him the first name to pop into my head. Surprise myself when 'Jane' comes out instead.

'You don't sound like you're from Cheadle.'

'Don't I? Not posh enough?'

He grins. 'Sorry, am I asking too many questions? Oh, and that's another.'

'It's all right.'

The door swings open.

'Well speak of the devil.'

I glance round. It's Reverend Whittle. Damn. I hope he doesn't recognise me.

'I suppose I should say hello. Want another?'

'That's generous but I'd better not. In fact, I really should be going.' I get to my feet and put on my coat. 'I've an early shift at the hospital.'

'Fair enough. I'll be heading home soon myself. Can't be clambering about on roofs half-cut.'

'Not unless you want to end up on my ward.'

He smiles, but this time his eyes don't light up. 'I've done my time with your lot. But next time you're off duty and in need of a drink . . .'

'Sure.' My stomach churns with awkwardness. 'Bye then.'

'Bye, Jane.'

I keep my head turned away from the bar, so the vicar won't recognise me. Maybe it's the brandy or the fact I've already nosed about in the surgery, but knowing he's out of the way, I feel the urge to check out the church hall myself. I cut down the narrow street between the White Hart and St Marys, bats fluttering overhead.

I walk around the outside of the building first, straining up at the mock Tudor cladding. I can't see the roof, so I move on to the entrance. The door isn't locked. Reverend Whittle must be very trusting, or maybe he just forgot to secure it after showing Gil round. Safely inside, I flick on my torch, casting its beam over the noticeboard in the entrance hall. Posters advertising the MADS audition and the cancelled jumble sale are pinned to it along with the regular reminders for choir practice and Mothers' Union meetings.

The main room smells of damp. There's a minstrel's gallery balcony at one end – sticking with the mock Tudor theme, I guess – and a stage at the other complete with red velvet curtain and proscenium arch. Aiming the torchlight high, I see the ceiling near to the stage has bulged and burst. There are bits of plaster debris on the floor where several buckets steadily collect dripping water and melted ice. What a mess. No wonder the MADS had to move out.

Done deliberately. Of course. I see it now. Dickie Derbyshire smashed the roof tiles, forcing the MADS into a new rehearsal venue – and I bet he seeded the perfect alternative. Abney Hall.

↔

I slope upstairs, detour to my room to brush my teeth and hide the diary under my pillow. I grab *Roger Ackroyd*, then pop my head round the guest bedroom door. To my relief, Dr Pearce is fast asleep.

'Ready to swap?' I mouth.

Kitty nods eagerly.

I notice as she stands that she's switched the birch deck chair for something more padded. She picks up a tray from the folded down card table and joins me on the landing.

'How's the patient been?' I whisper.

'Grumpy. I don't think he's much impressed by my nursing. Wouldn't let me change that bandage and he made an awful fuss about the thermometer being cold.'

'He'll soon warm to you,' I quip.

'Not sure about that. Kept asking where you were, an' all, but I told him how I was in charge now. Nowt wrong with his appetite, though.' She casts her eyes to the empty plate. 'Straight after his tea I told him he must lie flat and have quiet until morning, just as you said.'

'Well done.'

'You want something sending up? I could ask Patience to bring up some cocoa and toast.'

'Yes, please. But better make it coffee.'

I opt for the birch deck chair – if I get too comfy, I'll nod off then open my book. I'm soon caught up in the story again.

'Here you are, Nurse,' says Patience, entering the room about ten minutes later. 'Oh, bless him. Kitty said he went out like a light.' She puts the tray down. 'Oh, and I think this is yours.' She passes me my script. 'Cook found it under the kitchen table.'

'Thank you.' Actually, I could leave it for Dr Pearce to read. I put it on the bedside cabinet. Then pick up a triangle of toast and take a big bite. 'Just what I needed.'

She beams.

I kick off my shoes. 'My feet are not my friend today.'

'Tell me about it.' Patience glances at the door. 'Won't do no harm to take the weight off for a couple of minutes.' She plops down into the padded chair, just as I'd hoped. I want to quiz her further about Ellen.

'You'll be glad to get to bed yourself,' I say. 'Still, that's another thing we have in common. Long shifts.'

'It's what I'm used to. Up at five and nearly midnight before I can retire. Glad I don't have to climb up all those stairs to the second floor anymore, though.'

'Must be even later, sometimes.' I take a swig of coffee. 'Like when Mr and Mrs Watts had that party for the MADS here in September. Though I imagine Mrs Cherry rather took over the affair.'

'Right bossy boots.' She purses her lips. 'I don't know how Mrs Watts puts up with her.'

'Neither do I. And I suppose Mr Ramsbury made the most of the refreshments,' I give her a knowing look.

'Sozzled.'

I tut and take another bite of toast. 'No wonder he lost his tie pin. Probably fell off as he was staggering about.'

'Oh, but he insisted he'd left it in his room. As if he could be sure of anything when he was three sheets to the wind. Says it's been stolen as Ellen was the only one who'd been in there, she must have taken it.'

'Could someone else have been in his room?' I ask picking up a second slice.

'One of the MADS? If they did, they kept quiet about it.'

'What about Dr Pearce's fancy pen? There was nothing definite to link that to Ellen, was there?'

She gasps. 'You think one of the MADs took that an' all?'

I chew quickly. 'Who would you suspect?'

Patience sighs. 'Could be any one of them. But if the thief does strike again, let's pray someone catches them red-handed.'

TWENTY-SIX

Saturday 18th December, 1926

I OPEN ONE EYE AND GROAN AS PATIENCE SHAKES MY SHOULDER again. 'Let me sleep.' I've only been in bed since 6.30 a.m. when Kitty took watch over Dr Pearce. Before that, I mangaged to doze on and off in the chair.

'You must get up, Miss. A policeman's here. He wants a word with you. In the council chamber.'

'With me?' My heart thuds hard in my chest as I quickly sit up. 'Whatever about?' I glance at my alarm clock. Nine o'clock.

'He didn't say, Miss. Come to arrest you, I expect.' She narrows her eyes at me.

My heart thumps with fear. Does he know about Winwick? I squeeze my thumb. Or is it because I snuck into the surgery? I can explain that away if I have a moment to think. And the church hall wasn't locked . . .

'Your face!' Patience guffaws. 'I was only pulling your leg, Nurse.'

'Oh, I knew that.'

She's still giggling as she leaves the room.

I drag myself out of bed. Splash my face with water and try to make myself presentable. My hair won't play ball. I run a brush through it and kirby grip it into submission, then go to Agatha's room.

She's taking off her walking shoes.

'You're up early,' I say.

'Jack asked me to take the dogs out. We had a lovely time. Just round the lake. It's too cold to go any further.'

I bet getting her out of the house was his mother's idea, so the policeman and Agatha wouldn't see each other.

'You must miss your own dog.'

'Terribly. Peter's number one in my Order of the Faithful Dogs. I hope he doesn't think I've forgotten him. Oh.' She laughs. 'That sounds like a joke. What did the amnesiac say to the doctor? . . . I forget.'

'Well, I'm sure he hasn't forgotten you. And no doubt Rosalind's giving him extra hugs for you.'

Agatha's eyes go to the photograph next to her bed.

'She looks like you.'

'Do you think? Teddy's more like her father in personality. Very matter of fact.' She seems lost in her thoughts for a moment.

'I'm glad you remember her now.'

Her eyes are steady on me. 'So am I.'

I sense her brightness is a little forced. If I push her to talk more, I feel she'll clam up again. Perhaps Dr Argyle will have more success than me.

Downstairs, the sound of chopsticks being played on the piano gets louder as I approach the council chamber.

Entering the room, I see the back of a uniformed policeman

leaning over the grand's keys. I'm slightly relieved it's not a plain-clothes detective. His helmet reminds me of the pickelhaube. I quash down thoughts about the ineptitude of the helmets worn by soldiers in the trenches and move closer. No stripes. Even better.

'You want to see me, Constable?'

He stops playing and turns with a jolt. He has one of those put upon expressions that makes me think of Bonzo the dog from the cartoon strip.

He steps away from the piano. 'Please, take a seat. The family won't be long.'

My pulse quickens.

As usual there's a plethora of chairs to choose from including one with a leopard skin seat and back. I pick a plain oak one and hope it's not a valuable antique. The rest of the wood-panelled room is crammed with other furniture, decorative objects and an assortment of musical instruments.

Madge is the first to arrive. She smiles at me, but her brow furrows when the constable invites her to sit too. In her own house. Poor Bonzo. He clearly hasn't a clue about social manners, but then why would he? I imagine his main duty is plodding round the village as a deterrent. What if *he* saw me trespassing? My stomach rolls.

At least Madge's friendliness suggest that Cook hasn't said anything to the Wattses about me and Dr Pearce, yet. Perhaps I was a little hasty packing up my few belongings last night? I could go downstairs when Bonzo goes to speak to the staff, but the wiser part tells me to leave Cook be. You don't go poking at a wasps' nest when they've just settled.

I stifle a yawn as Jim and Jack arrive.

'Thank you for agreeing to answer some questions . . .' Bonzo begins. 'As I explained, these are just routine enquiries at present.'

Routine? That's a relief.

'Now, I understand your brother-in-law, Colonel Christie, agreed to an interview with Dickie Derbyshire, an investigative reporter.'

Is that why he's here? I control my facial muscles, to mask my surprise. Have the police also discovered that Dickie and Richard are one and the same?

Madge snorts. 'Muckraker, more like.'

Bonzo's face is unreadable. 'This was arranged for Thursday afternoon?'

'At five p.m.,' Jim replies.

'But your brother-in-law changed his mind?'

'He did.'

'Do you know why he cancelled?'

'No.'

'And Colonel Christie has now returned home, sir?'

'That's correct, Constable.' Jim sounds irked. 'He left Abney yesterday morning.'

'Alone?'

'Yes. My sister-in-law has amnesia following a motor car accident. Under medical advice she will remain here until fully recovered.'

Madge shuffles in her seat. Jack throws her a reassuring smile. 'I see.'

Bonzo glances at me. Checks his notebook and turns his

attention to Jim. 'What was the purpose of this interview, sir, and why was it cancelled at the last minute?'

Jim sighs. 'I suggest you ask my brother-in-law.'

'I already have. By telephone. Colonel Christie said the reporter turned up fifteen minutes late. Military men tend to be sticklers for time, I find. He says Derbyshire was full of excuses and rather harried. And I quote: "I didn't like the look of the chap and had second thoughts about the whole thing."'

'This is the first I've heard of it,' says Jim.

I think he's fibbing. And I sense Bonzo does too.

'What does any of this matter?' asks Madge. She pulls on her collar as though it's too tight.

I want to shout. Get to the flaming point!

'It matters because Mr Derbyshire hasn't been seen since that appointment here on Thursday evening. He told his editor he intended to return to the office to file his story straight after . . . although his claim that the paper was holding the presses for it wasn't true. I do wonder if he was in fact planning on selling his story for syndication to the nationals. Anyway, he never showed. Licking his wounds perhaps after failing to get his big break. Only he was absent without explanation yesterday too – and his editor insists that's out of character.'

'Perhaps this reporter hopped on a train. Could have gone to Sunningdale to try and appease my uncle?' suggests Jack.

'And Colonel Christie has promised to let us know at once if that's the case.'

'I still don't see why this has anything to do with us,' says Madge.

Jack squeezes his mother's hand.

'It may be nothing,' replies Bonzo. 'That is the purpose of general enquiries. Now, I noticed on my walk here that there's an abandoned motor car on Newlands Road near the railway bridge.'

So he does know! My spine stiffens.

'I would hardly describe it as abandoned,' says Madge, exasperated. 'It belongs to one of the actors in my amateur dramatic society. We're rehearsing our latest play here.'

'And how long has it been there?'

'I came across it on Thursday night,' replies Jack. 'Looks like it skidded on some ice.'

A smug smile spreads over Bonzo's face. 'Because I've been told *that* motor car in fact belongs to Mr Derbyshire. His editor gave me the registration plate after reporting him missing to the station sergeant.'

'There must be some mistake.' Madge looks to Jim, her face pale.

'What's the name of this actor, Mrs Watts?'

'Richard.' Her voice is quiet. 'Richard Buxton.'

'Really? Dickie is an abbreviation of Richard, isn't it, and Buxton is in Derbyshire. Almost blatant of him.' Bonzo reaches into his uniform jacket pocket. 'I have a photograph of Dickie Derbyshire here. Would you take a look at it, please.' He passes it to Madge.

She groans in recognition. 'It's the same man.'

Jim's eyes widen. 'You're sure?'

Her head droops. She nods. 'He didn't show for rehearsal yesterday,' she adds quietly.

'When did you last see *Richard*?'

'He left here Thursday teatime. About five o'clock.'

Bonzo lets her answer hang in the air. 'And you didn't have any suspicions that Richard wasn't who he claimed to be?'

'Of course not. I would never have allowed him into my house if I had.'

'I understand your anger, Mrs Watts.'

'Do you?' She casts him a steely glance.

But he is impervious. 'How did this Richard come to join your dramatic society – the MADS, isn't it?'

'We held auditions in the church hall, last Saturday.' She looks up at Bonzo. 'He was very good.'

'Indeed. He was certainly adapt at pulling the wool over your eyes, Mrs Watts.' His tone is not sympathetic. If anything, he sounds rather unconvinced. 'Now there is something else that bothers me about this abandoned vehicle . . . but we'll come to that in a moment.' He turns to Jack. 'What time did you see the motor car, Mr Watts?'

'I'm not sure. Half past seven?'

'And can anyone corroborate that?'

'I . . . err . . . well,' he stutters.

'I can.'

Madge's eyes widen at me.

I try to keep my own voice steady. 'I was close by when Mr Watts received a telephone call from a friend who had been taken unwell. Naturally I offered my assistance. We spotted the Morris on our way out of the estate and stopped briefly.'

'Hmm. I see.'

'It was a bitterly cold night,' says Jack. 'I assume having left his motor car, Mr Derbyshire returned home. I imagine he lives locally?'

Bonzo skirts the question. 'Mr Derbyshire's landlady hasn't seen him since Thursday morning.'

'Perhaps he owes her rent,' surmises Jack. 'From the state of his motor car, I would say Mr Derbyshire was rather strapped for cash.'

Bonzo does not reply. Instead, he refocuses on Madge. I think he sees her as the weak link. 'Your sister's motor car was found abandoned after an accident, was it not? Two forces on the case and it takes them the best part of a fortnight to find her! Even though she'd posted a letter to her husband's brother saying she was off to a Yorkshire spa for a few days' rest. Southerners!'

She stretches her collar away from her throat again.

I want to point out that Agatha likely wrote that letter before she left Sunningdale, but the sooner this ordeal is over the better.

Bonzo flicks back through his notebook. 'Your sister's motor car was found at Newlands Corner. Quite the coincidence.'

'There must be plenty of places called Newlands,' stutters Madge.

'Indeed, but how many with crashed, abandoned vehicles?'

'These ambitious reporters like their stunts,' cuts in Jim. 'I fancy this Dickie thought he could get a story out of leaving his motor car there.'

He could be right. I remember what Kitty said about the reporter who faked Mrs Christie's shoe print.

'Of course, some of those same journalists have reported that

Mrs Christie's disappearance was all a publicity stunt for her new book.'

Madge gasps. 'Nonsense. Absolute nonsense.'

Jim stands. 'As you can appreciate, Constable, it has come as a shock to us all to learn we have been deceived by this Dickie/Richard scoundrel; it seems he was intent on causing my family further embarrassment for the sake of his own career. However, I can assure you we know nothing of his present whereabouts. And to be frank, I couldn't care less. So, if that's all?'

'Not quite. Could you please tell me who was present here at Abney Hall on Thursday afternoon? One of your guests may be able to shine some light on Mr Derbyshire's whereabouts.'

Jim breathes heavily through his nose, rather like a bull. 'Madge?'

'The four of us. My sister and her husband.' Hand at her collar again. 'Let me see. Dr Pearce and Dr Argyle were here part of the day. It really is quite difficult to be sure who was here when. Then the MADS. Mrs Delia Cherry. She's my friend and the director and producer of my play.'

Bonzo scribbles away.

'Charles Trent, a close friend of the family.'

'He works for S & J's,' adds Jim.

'He's an actor too?' asks Bonzo.

'That's right. Paul Ramsbury and Iris Caldwell. Oh and Reverend Stephen Whittle called over with some old clothing. You'll know him, of course.'

'Indeed. Well, I think it would be wise to speak to them all. Get their impression of *Richard*. Do you think you could persuade them to come to the house later this afternoon? Shall we say half past four?'

'I . . . I suppose I could suggest another rehearsal.' She doesn't sound keen.

'Excellent. In the meantime, I'd like to speak to any staff on duty.'

'Must you?'

'Is there any reason I shouldn't, Mrs Watts?'

She shakes her head.

'Now, if I could have the names of your servants and their duties . . .'

'Jane, would you go downstairs and see who is available?' says Jim.

'Of course, sir.'

After their interrogation, the family will want to discuss what on earth just happened. But will they tell Agatha?

TWENTY-SEVEN

'YOU ARE PATIENCE DODDS, CORRECT?' ASKS BONZO.

'I am, sir. I mean, Constable.' She looks rather awkward sat on one of the family's best chairs. She took some persuading to sit down. Insisted that I stay while she answered Bonzo's questions.

'And you've been at Abney Hall for some years, Miss Dodds?'

I nod encouragingly at her.

'That's right, s . . . Constable. I'm very happy working here.'

'Good. Now, Miss Dodds, I want to ask you about Thursday.'

'I'll do my best, Constable.' She seems pleased she got it right this time.

'Can you tell me what happened that day?'

Her brow becomes even more wrinkled with concentration. 'Well, I would have done the fires first thing. In the old days there'd have been chamber pots too, only course we have indoor facilities now. Mind you, bathrooms take a lot more effort. Can't give them a quick swill! The other maid, Kitty, does them. Then we help with breakfast and afterwards do the bedrooms. Dusting. The window ledges. And we have to vacuum or sweep the floors an' all.'

'Very good. Now what can you tell me about the movements of your guests.'

She looks horrified. 'Nothing at all, sir. Constable. Wouldn't be my place to.'

'Your mistress mentioned you helped the gardener,' he checks his notebook, 'Mr Budworth, to bring in the Christmas tree.'

'I don't rightly remember. My memory's not what it was.'

'I see. Don't worry, I can check with Mr Budworth.'

Patience flushes. 'I'm not saying Mrs Watts isn't correct.'

'Of course not,' I soothe.

'Now, in the afternoon, Cook . . .' he glances down again, 'Mrs Worcester. She was preparing afternoon tea for Colonel Christie. Who'd arranged an interview here at five p.m.'

'That's what we were told, Constable. Cook did a lovely spread.'

'But the interview was cancelled. Do you know why?'

Her eyes widen in offence. 'No, sir. Constable. I know my place.' She crosses her arms.

'On Thursday afternoon, the MADS came here to rehearse Mrs Watts's new play. They used Buckley, the old chapel. You went to open it up, is that correct?'

She glances at me.

I nod my head. 'You're not in any trouble, Patience.'

'I did, Constable. I laid a new fire. It can be perishing in there.'

'I see. Do you recall a dark-haired man? Richard Buxton?'

'The new chap?'

'That's right. Did you happen to see who he was talking to? Overhear anything that sticks in your memory?'

That look of offence again. 'I did not, Constable.'

He sighs. 'I think that will be all. Thank you, Miss Dodds.'

Patience looks relieved.

'Would you send Miss Johnson . . . err Kitty, to come in next.' Bonzo drills the end of his pen into his notebook.

'Perhaps I should stay too,' I offer. I imagine it's easier interviewing hardened criminals than tight-lipped servants. He looks more hangdog than ever.

'Thank you.'

Kitty flounces in. Flops onto the chair facing me and Bonzo before he can invite her to sit.

He flicks over a page in his notebook. 'You are a parlourmaid, too?'

She nods her head. Looks bored with the whole thing already.

'How long have you worked here?'

'Five weeks. What's this all about? Patience was in a right state.'

'It's nothing to worry about, Miss Johnson. I'm merely making enquiries.'

'Go on then.'

I suck my lips together, so I won't laugh.

'Thursday. There was a rehearsal taking place in Buckley, the old chapel. You were there.'

'For a bit. The vicar turned up with some boxes of clothes for Mrs Watts. To be used for costumes. I'nt that right, Nurse.'

'It is. There was a box for the MADS and another for scarecrows.'

'There was a gentleman there. One of the actors.'

She shrugs. 'Which one?'

'Richard Buxton. Dark haired. Glasses.'

'S'pose.'

'Did you notice who was talking to him? Overhear anything curious?'

She pulls a face. 'I sticks to my duties. I don't go round earwigging.'

'Mmm. What time did the MADS leave?'

She blows out hot air. 'I dunno. Before five o'clock, cause Patience and I had to set up the afternoon tea in the terrace room.' She glances at me. Wondering what I might or might not have said about her running down to the lodge gates to have it out with the reporters gathered there.

'But the interview was cancelled,' says Bonzo.

She shrugs, uninterested.

'Have you seen Richard Buxton since?'

She thinks. 'No.'

Bonzo wrinkles his brow. 'Thank you, Miss Johnson.'

Kitty leaves.

'Reckon I'll get anything out of the cook or the gardener?'

'Honestly? No. Staff pride themselves on their discretion – not that I think they have anything to tell you, anyway.'

Bonzo huffs. 'What about you, Nurse? You're not staff, exactly, are you?'

'No. But I know that a loose tongue soon leads to a bad reference. I value my position here as much as the servants.'

He closes his notebook. 'Bet it's a different matter when you're all together in the servants' hall. If you should hear something useful, I'd appreciate it if you'd let me know.'

'I'll see you out,' I say, getting up.

He snorts. Follows me to the front door. The ground is thick with fresh snow.

'Goodbetter. Unusual name,' says Bonzo.

'Not in my family.' I give him my best placid smile.

'Ha. Anglicised, I presume?'

I flush. 'My mother's family were from Germany. It was Goodbeiter originally.'

'Ah, I thought so. Understandable her changing it. Well, goodbye, Nurse.'

'Goodbye.' And good riddance.

I pause by the stuffed lion. 'Don't suppose you've seen a stranger sneaking about?' Its glass eyes are as vacant as ever. 'Not telling? And I thought we were friends!' I give its nose a violent tweak.

Cook's room is at the far end of the cross corridor. I knock and go in. She's sitting in her armchair studying a recipe book. There's a round table laid with a white cloth, bread, butter and a china tureen in front of the fire which crackles invitingly. But Cook's expression tells me I'm not welcome. That and her silence.

I cock my head towards the plain oak chair near the table. 'May I?'

She shrugs. 'You'll please yourself, anyway.'

About to drag the chair closer, I decide its wiser to leave it where it is. Appear docile.

'Constable's gone. He's decided he doesn't need to speak to you and Thomas.'

'Right.'

I squeeze my thumb. 'I want to thank you for not telling the Wattses about me and Dr Pearce.'

She tuts. 'Soft soap won't work on me. Any road, I didn't do it for you. They've enough worries without me adding to them and now this copper pestering them. Still, suppose we should all be grateful it wasn't a detective, or worse still that Chief Constable, or whatever his title is, acquaintance of Mr Watts who kept promising they were "taking Mrs Christie's disappearance very seriously". Sharp as a marble, the lot of them. They'd still be looking for her now if it wasn't for that banjo player recognising her.'

A loose strand of hair dangles annoyingly in front of my eye. I tuck it back under my cap. 'I thought it was the hotel maid?'

'Either way, it wasn't the police.' She points to the china tureen. 'You may as well finish them.'

I lift the lid. Leftover sausages. I pick one out. 'Well, I wouldn't underestimate this one; he struck me as very determined.'

I repeat the little that Bonzo told us between bites.

'Reckon Colin caught this Dickie chap napping in his motor car,' says Cook. 'No wonder, juggling working for *The Advertiser*, learning lines for the play and rehearsals on top. Plus the extra pressure of having to change your appearance; pretending to be someone you're not. Still at least he's not dead!'

His appearance! 'Cook, remember that bloke you heard talking to Ellen at the door. The smell you couldn't place . . . was it coconut?'

Her eyes widen. 'That were it! I should have known.'

'It was macassar oil; Dickie was using it on his hair when he was being Richard – and there was some spilt on the floor of his motor car too.'

You mean Ellen was helping him? Oh, silly girl. You should go and see her, Jane. Tell her to have nothing more to do with him. She and her nain, Mrs Griffths, live at the bottom end of Cromer Road. Number Four, I think.'

Griffiths. Why does that ring a bell? Oh, when we were in the boathouse Robert said he was going to call on a Mrs Griffiths.

'Would you let Kitty know I'll switch places with her again at one o'clock?'

'I will. And, Jane, come straight back and tell me what the little minx has to say for herself.'

'Oh! There you are, Nurse,' says Madge, frowning as I exit Cook's room. 'I'd like a word.' She steps aside so Jim can pass.

He has the suit of armour strapped to the sack trolley. 'Just taking Sir Arthur over to Buckley.'

Madge indicates for me to sit on one of the twin velvet-covered pews which line the wall. The fancy men and women in lace collars in the portraits all around seem to peer down on us, like they're eavesdropping as she perches next to me.

'Mr Watts and I think it best if Agatha is not told about the constable's visit earlier. It would only worry her – especially this business about a missing reporter. I hope we can count on your discretion.'

'Of course.'

'Good.' Madge absently runs her finger over the upholstery brass studs. 'I also wanted . . . to say thank you properly, for helping Jack the other night. He's told me about Paul.' She trails her fingers back again. 'The MADS – *I* – would appreciate your discretion.'

'Of course.' I smile. 'I gather this is not the first incident.'

She presses her finger against one of the studs hard. 'Afterwards, Paul always swears it won't happen again. I even think he means it. He stays sober a few days, sometimes weeks, even months. Then convinced he no longer has a problem he decides there's no harm in having just one.'

'But of course, it's never just one.'

'No. And the trigger's just as unpredictable. A drink to celebrate success is just as likely as one to drown his sorrows. There's always some excuse.'

I shuffle slightly. 'Will you have to replace Paul in the play as well as Richard?'

'That's up to Mrs Cherry.'

A carousel indeed.

TWENTY-EIGHT

I CHECK MY FOB WATCH. AGATHA WILL BE HAVING A LATE breakfast with her family. If I skip mine, there should just be time to pay Ellen a visit. Though my stomach does not like the idea. Sadly I don't own a fur coat like Iris, so as ever I'll have to make do with my rather worn wool one. As I follow the driveway, I spy Colin at the water's edge. He's got a spotted handkerchief around his neck.

'You be careful,' I shout.

'Pirates aren't careful,' he shouts back.

'They are if they want hot drinks and biscuits in the kitchen later.'

He grins. 'Aye, aye, Captain!'

I catch a snowflake on my hand and look up. The sky looks ominously heavy. I think we're in for another good few inches.

That boy is out in all weathers. Not scared of the dark either. Hang on. I twist round. If anyone is likely to have seen Dickie in the grounds, it's Colin. May even have seen him with Ellen.

'Aww. You're not going to tell me off again, are you?' he complains once I catch him up. 'I wasn't going on the ice. Promise.'

'No. I was thinking . . . Pirates are always on lookout, aren't they? Up in the crow's nest, and all that.'

'Mmm.'

'And they'd know where all the good hideouts are, too. Like the greenhouse.'

'Hah. Greenhouse is no good. It's made of glass. Everyone would see you.'

'Not necessarily. No one saw you take that mink stole.'

He gulps. 'I only borrowed it.'

'Oh. I know. Don't worry, I won't say anything to your sister. Or Thomas, the gardener.' I let that sink in. 'I think someone else has been hiding at Abney though. A man. Thought you might have seen him. Going to Buckley Chapel maybe?'

He blinks rapidly. 'No.'

'But you've seen someone?'

He stares at the ground. 'Not a stranger. They work here.'

'A man?'

He shakes his head. He's gone all green-looking. 'A maid.'

'But not your Kitty. When did you see her?'

His eyes remain downcast. He twists his foot nervously in the mud. 'On Thursday night. I told our Kitty, but she said I was making it up. But I wasn't. I saw her go into the house – I thought she must be a ghost only she didn't walk through the wall. She opened the door so she must have been real and . . . and . . .' He clams up again.

'Go on, Colin.'

'You won't believe me.'

'I promise I will. Go on . . .'

His eyes widen. 'She had *blood* all down her.'

I tilt my head. 'All down her? Or on her apron?'

He looks up. 'Her apron. You seen her an' all?' His face pinks.

'Her name's Ellen. And I've seen the apron too. You're sure she went into the house?'

'She had keys.'

'If you see her again, or the man, come to the house and ask for me. Straight away. But Colin, don't go anywhere near them.'

⟷

Number Four Cromer Road is a bit more unkempt than the rest but is otherwise identical to the other two-up, two-down terraces.

I rap the knocker and rub my hands together as I wait.

I'm about to give up until, 'It's not locked,' a woman with a slight Welsh accent calls. 'Just turn the handle.'

I do so. A woman – Ellen's nain, I assume – looks up at me from a wicker invalid chair.

Her face illuminates. 'A nurse. Do come in before we lose all the heat.'

'Thank you.' It's as cold inside the house as out. 'I'm Jane Goodbetter.'

Mrs Griffiths slowly spins round. 'Shall we go into the parlour. I don't get many guests.'

I follow her into the room.

'Don't stand on ceremony, love.' She points to an armchair beside an unlit fire. 'Now what can I do for you?'

'Is Ellen in?'

She twitches. 'She's not. What's this about?'

'Oh, nothing to worry about, Mrs Griffiths. I just wanted to update her about Dr Pearce.'

She places a hand on her bosom. 'Such a nice man. Calls in

on me now and again, to see how I'm getting on. Got our Ellen a little job in his surgery. Yes. A very nice man.' She gestures to the skuttle which has not much more than dust in it. 'I'm sorry I can't offer you a cup of tea, nurse, but we're waiting on a coal delivery. I could fetch you a glass of water if you like?'

'No, please don't go to any trouble, Mrs Griffiths.'

'You come from the surgery, have you? I'm sure our Ellen's mentioned you.'

'No. I'm currently working for the Wattses.'

Her face drops. 'I see.'

Suddenly she's not so chatty.

'The Wattses have invited Dr Pearce to convalesce with them,' I explain. 'I think it very unlikely that he'll be back at his practice until after Christmas. I wanted Ellen to know.'

'I'll pass on your message.'

'Actually,' I lick my lips, 'could I have that glass of water after all?'

She hesitates. 'Of course.'

I wait a moment then follow her into the kitchen. 'Dr Pearce speaks very highly of your Ellen,' I say. 'Such a help at the surgery.'

Mrs Griffiths pours water from a jug into a glass for me. 'I'm glad she's appreciated at last.'

I nod. 'Cook told me what went on. So unfair.'

'It was,' she agrees. 'It makes me so cross knowing those two "gentlemen" are having a very merry Christmas up at Abney.'

Two?

'What does Ellen think happened to Mr Ramsbury's tie pin?'

'That Mr Trent took it, of course.'

Ah so that's the two gentlemen.

'She remembers seeing the tie pin in Mr Ramsbury's room?'

'Oh, yes. On his dressing table. She even admitted admiring it. Only she swore to them – and me – that she never took it.'

'I assume there was a thorough search for it?'

'Mr Ramsbury insisted on it. As Ellen had been the only staff in his room, he had poor Patience on her hands and knees looking under the bed and down the back of the drawers. Then, later, when it still hadn't been found, he said Ellen must have stolen it and that she should be dismissed at once. The old Mr and Mrs Watts would never have agreed to that, not without evidence, but I suppose these young ones wanted to stamp their authority on the place.' She snorts.

'And how does Ellen know Mr Trent is the thief, Mrs Griffiths?'

'She doesn't for sure, but stuff only seems to go missing when the house is busy with guests – and Mr Trent is among them. Ellen reeled off a list of things . . . a fancy silver watch, Dr Pearce's fancy pen was one, an expensive travelling clock. She reckons most visitors don't like to make a fuss. Think it's bad manners. And folk like that can afford to buy a replacement or claim off the insurance. In a house like that, already crammed full of stuff, must be hard for owners to keep track of what's where, and the Wattses were old. But the servants notice. At least our Ellen did.'

'But she didn't share her theory when Mr Ramsbury accused her of taking the tie pin?'

'What good would it have done? He'd have denied it – and who's going to believe a young parlourmaid over an old friend of the family?'

I take a drink of water, pushing away my own remembrances. 'But if someone could prove it – a journalist. Then it would be a very different matter. Is that what Dickie Derbyshire told Ellen he'd do?'

'I don't know that name.'

'No? Think carefully, Mrs Griffiths. Because I'm not the only one asking questions about him. We've had the police at the hall this morning. He's been reported missing. No one's seen him since Thursday evening – when he was with your Ellen.'

She rubs her hands together, anxiously. 'You know it all, then?'

'Not quite, Mrs Griffiths. Perhaps you could help me fill in the gaps.'

She sighs. 'You know what it's like in a small village, everyone knowing everyone's business. So, I suppose it wasn't hard for this Dickie chap to learn that our Ellen worked at Abney Hall until recently. He wanted someone with inside information about the Watts family – and she must have seemed ideal. Course, our Ellen got excited at him being a reporter. She said she'd give him information about the family, the house, whatever he needed – if he could prove the thief is Mr Trent.

'They met up there a couple of times. Trying to work out a plan. Then on Thursday morning, I caught Ellen rifling through my kitchen cupboards. She put some things in a bag and went back up to the hall.'

'What did she take?'

'Just a tin of coffee – well not even half a tin, really. Oh, and some of my senna powder.'

A laxative. Charles's upset stomach! Richard must have put

senna in his coffee. But why? As some kind of payback?

'Where's Ellen now?'

'At Abney. Dickie had wired to say to meet him at noon. He had proof.'

I look at the wall clock. It's ten past. If I hurry, I might catch them.

'Where exactly was she meeting him, Mrs Griffiths?'

She sucks her lips together in thought.

'The old house?' I suggest. 'Buckley?'

'Not old . . . boat. The Boathouse.'

TWENTY-NINE

I'M HOT, SWEATY AND OUT OF BREATH WHEN I REACH THE boathouse. I take out my torch and switch it on, then snatch open the boathouse door. Hold my breath as I scan the beam wide.

'Who's there?' cries a voice. Panicked.

'*Colin?*' I shine the light towards the voice.

'It wasn't me,' he sobs. Tears stream down his freckled cheeks.

'What wasn't?'

He gasps for air as he points to the slipway that runs down into the water.

I swallow. Panning the torch to the right, light cascades over the sloping ground. There's something there next to the old rowing boat. Try to make sense of it. Not something. *Someone.* On their back. Partially submerged.

I shine the light on to the face.

Oh God. It's Ellen.

I've seen dead people before. Some go easy. Some don't. As a nurse, I should be hardened to it but I'm not.

'Stay there, Colin.' A pointless order. He's rigid with shock.

'She's . . . she's dead. Isn't she?'

I ease myself forwards down the wet slipway, then crouch.

For a second Ellen's face is superimposed by matron's. I shake my head to banish the memory.

I press my fingers to her carotid artery, the skin is cold and blueish, but to my surprise and relief there's a very faint pulse.

'She's alive, just.' My voice trembles as adrenalin pumps into my blood. Still on my knees, I plunge my arms into the filthy, icy water. The cold shocking.

Hook Ellen under both arms. Heave.

But she's too limp.

Can't keep hold.

Grit my teeth. Try again.

My muscles strain as Colin's sobbing loudens.

And again.

My arms numb. Fingers burn.

The lake. It won't give her up.

So cold. Please, God. I've got to get her out.

Tears sting. Again.

Suddenly the balance tips. I sense the lake loosen its grip. Weakening.

Yes . . . Yes!

I tighten my hold. Still got her. I can do this.

I lurch back onto the slipway. Ellen's wet body pinning me down. 'Colin . . . fetch Thomas. Tell him Ellen's badly hurt. Wait . . .' I wheeze. Inhale. 'Bang on the servants' door. Tell Cook to meet us at Thomas's cottage. We'll need several hot water bottles – but filled with *warm* water. Have you got that?'

He wipes his snotty nose and nods.

'Good lad.' The door clatters behind him.

I drag myself from under Ellen and peel off her drenched coat and dress. Take my own coat off and use it as a blanket. I brush a long strand of hair from her face. Bloody lucky her head didn't go completely under.

'You're going to be all right,' I repeat over and over. Don't know if she can hear me. Hope it's true. Tears start to flow.

It seems an age before the door opens again. Thomas moves swiftly. Scooping up Ellen as though she's as light as a pile of crisp autumn leaves. I rub my chilled hands together as we follow the line of the walled garden, then cut up the path to Gardener's Cottage. A bit of a misnomer as it's a big house, symmetrical looking with two chimneys in the middle.

The front door is open ready for us.

'Up here,' calls Cook.

Thomas adjusts his grasp on Ellen and starts up the stairs.

I follow, hoping he doesn't take a misstep.

We enter the back bedroom. The bed's made. The curtain's drawn.

Colin clings to Cook. His wet face pressed into her bosom.

My nursing instincts kick in. I pull back the blankets so Thomas can lie Ellen on the mattress.

'You were smart to suggest bringing 'er 'ere, Mrs Worcester.'

I look gratefully to her. 'Oh. We'll need pyjamas or a nightie for her.'

Cook points to the dresser. 'Got some. Best I could find in a rush. I fear they'll be too big for the poor mite.'

'They'll be fine.' I pick them up. The material warm and soft.

'Come on, Colin. Let's give the ladies some space.' Thomas

shuffles them both onto the landing.

With some difficulty Cook and I manage to get the flannelette pyjamas over Ellen's clammy white skin. No cuts. No bruising. If she swallowed any of the lake water, she'll be at risk of infection. I need my thermometer.

Next, I check by pressing my hand against each of the rubber hot water bottles to make sure they're not too hot and place them at her chest, neck and groin. Then cover her with the blankets.

'I just hope we found her in time.'

Cook presses her hands together as in prayer. Then pops her head round the door. 'You can come back in now.'

'Do . . . do you know who she is?' Colin gulps, hovering in the doorway next to Thomas.

'Her name's Ellen,' I say.

'Wurnt she a parlourmaid? Like our Kitty?'

'That's right, love.'

He looks guiltily at me. 'She's the one I seen on Thursday evening. I know you said not to go near her if I saw her again, but she went into the boathouse, and I was using it as my pirate den. I thought she'd tell our Kitty and I'd be in trouble for lighting fires.'

'Did you see anyone else go in?'

He shakes his head. Eyes wild. 'The police will think I hurt her! Don't let them take me away. I don't want to be locked up.' He spins round.

'Woah there, lad,' says Thomas, clasping his arm. 'Now why would the police do that? You're the one that saved the lass.'

He shakes his head violently. 'They won't think that. They'll . . . blame me. They did last time.'

'Last time?' My stomach flips. Remembering how Kitty called him a delinquent. Could I have misjudged him?

'The . . . old woman . . . who lives across the street . . . called them.'

'Easy now. Take your time,' I soothe.

'She said my ball had smashed her window. She was bawling at the copper. At me. At our Kitty. Saying I wurnt right in the head.'

I smile reassuringly. 'That must have been very frightening.'

'It were. But our Kitty stuck up for me. Swore it wurnt me 'cause I'd been at home with her all day. The woman got even crosser then. Said we were both filthy liars. Couldn't prove it, though.'

'Did you get your ball back?'

He shakes his head not realising I've caught him out. 'Got a walloping from our Kitty an' all. She said if I were ever in trouble with the coppers again, she'd tell 'em to lock me up.'

I gaze at Colin's desperate face. To me he's a scared boy, but what will the police see? A tearaway. I've become accustomed to being with people like the Wattses for so long that I've almost forgotten how it is for people like me and Colin. If you've got money and status, you're ahead of the game. You're automatically trusted. Respected.

'It was an accident. The ground's all wet and slippery in that boathouse. Ellen must have lost her footing and fallen into the freezing cold water.' I look to Thomas and Cook. 'There's no need for the police to be told, is there?' Will they back me?

'Best we keep this between ourselves for now,' agrees Cook. 'The last thing we all need is a load of uniformed clodhoppers traipsing everywhere.'

'Aye,' says Thomas.

'Good.' I smile at Colin. He looks so young.

'I'll move into the bothy, till Ellen's recovered,' says Thomas. 'But who'll look after the lass?'

I frown. 'I really don't think I can. I have Mrs Christie and Dr Pearce to take care of already.'

Cook checks her watch. 'Well, I can stay a little while, but there's a stew in the oven that needs taking out.'

'We can do that, can't we,' Thomas says to Colin. 'Get a nice cup of tea while we're there.'

Colin nods.

'Someone should go to Ellen's nain's too. Explain what's happened,' adds Cook. 'She lives at Four Cromer Road.'

'I'll add it to my list.'

Tears start to well again. 'You're a good man, Thomas.'

'Hey, stop that. 'ere.' He pulls a mucky hanky out from his sleeve and hands it to me. 'Go on, 'ave a good blow.'

'The state of that!' scolds Cook. 'Here, take mine.' She reaches into her apron.

Her hanky's smeared with sticky jam.

'You're all right.' I grin, wiping my face on my sleeve. 'Who'll stay with Colin while you go into the village, though?'

'Don't worry, love. We'll work summat out,' says Thomas.

I take a deep breath. 'I'll walk over to the house with you both.' Reach out for my coat.

'You can't put that back on,' says Cook.

She's right.

'Come downstairs,' says Thomas. 'I'll dig out Alice's Sunday best coat. I've been meaning to do summat with it.'

'If you're sure?'

I wait in the living room with Colin while Thomas rummages under the stairs.

Thomas's wife died a few years back, but a woman's touch is evident in the decoration. Floral curtains. A porcelain snake charmer on the mantlepiece. A ceramic Dutch girl next to the wireless and the lace tablecloth underneath. Everything is very neat and tidy. There's lots of houseplants too, naturally. I wander to the bookshelf. Mainly gardening tomes but there's a copy of Agatha's *The Man in The Brown Suit* and a couple of Dickens novels. *Oliver Twist* and *A Christmas Carol.* It always irks me that we call grumpy, tight-fisted people a Scrooge even though he's redeemed at the end. Goes to show it's harder to lose a bad reputation that a good one.

'Try it on, then, lass,' he says a couple of minutes later, holding out a smart plum coloured wool coat. 'Let's see 'ow it fits.'

I oblige. 'Spot on,' I say. 'Thank you, Thomas.'

We set off for the house. I need someone to be with Colin and someone to be with Dr Pearce. Oh! Of course. The solution's obvious. But if I'm going to make it work, I'll need Agatha's assistance.

After Thomas and Colin go down to the kitchen, I search the ground floor. I find Agatha in the library.

'Jane. What's the matter? You look awful.' She puts down her notebook. 'Have you been crying?'

'I'm all right.'

'No. You're not. Now what's happened? Has someone upset you?'

'You've your own worries . . .'

'Yes, and I'm learning that if I'm to overcome them, I have to talk about them. Now sit down.'

'It's Dr Pearce,' I say quietly. 'It's been troubling me. What you said about him liking me. I didn't want to believe it at first. But when I think about it, he did visit Abney a lot while I was looking after your mother and Mr Watts. More than I'd consider normal, and I suppose I became glad of his company. I never dreamed he'd misinterpret our friendship as anything more.'

'You didn't know his wife had left him?'

I drag my chair closer. 'No. I swear.'

'And now Punkie's invited him here to recuperate. She said you'd suggested sharing shifts with that new parlourmaid.'

I nod. 'Kitty. I thought if I only had to be at his bedside when he was sleeping, I could manage. But now he wants to talk about "our future". Insists we're meant to be together. I've been such a fool.'

'Nonsense!' Agatha leans forwards. 'You mustn't blame yourself. Men, especially those of a certain age get these fancies. I remember one time I'd been at a house party, when this soldier attached himself to me like a limpet. Wanted to partner me at tennis, croquet. Constantly trying to engage me in conversation until I really had to be quite rude to him. When I was leaving the hostess said he'd give me a lift in his motor car to the station so I could get the train back to London. No doubt he'd persuaded her I'd like the idea. Fortunately, it would only be a short drive and then I'd be rid of him. I got aboard. Grateful to be alone at last.

'Then, as the train was pulling away from the platform, he

suddenly yanked open the door and bounded into my carriage. It was awful. He glared at me in this uncomfortable manner and declared he was madly in love with me. That he'd known from the moment he'd seen me coming down to dinner. That I was the "one woman in the world for him".

'I politely rejected his advances, but he continued to protest his love, oblivious to my discomfort.'

'That's just how it is with Dr Pearce. It's making me feel quite unwell.'

'I can see that. Well, it's quite clear what you must do. You must stay away from him.'

'You make it sound so simple.'

'Because it is. We just need to think of someone who can take your place.'

'Everyone in the house is busy. Jim with his business. Jack with his studies. Your sister with the play, you have your sessions with Dr Argyle, and there's all the Christmas preparations on top.'

'There must be someone.'

'Well . . . Dr Pearce isn't showing any signs of concussion. He doesn't really need a nurse. I think he just needs company.' I pretend to think for a moment. 'Kitty has a brother, he's about twelve. Very chatty. Full of spirit. I always think a young person is ideal company for an older person.'

She ponders my suggestion. 'Let me speak to Madge. If I can convince her, you can tell Kitty to bring him here. Now. Do you feel better?'

'Much, thank you.'

THIRTY

I GO UPSTAIRS, BUOYED BY THE THOUGHT THAT AGATHA WILL hopefully persuade her sister about Colin. I nip into my room to collect a thermometer and Dr Pearce's binoculars.

At the door to the guest bedroom, I beckon Kitty into the corridor.

'Sorry I'm late,' I whisper. 'Will you help me with another patient?'

'Mrs Christie?'

I shake my head. Pass over the thermometer. 'Cook will explain. You're to meet her at Gardener's Cottage.'

Kitty raises her eyebrows. 'Very cloak and dagger.'

'Thank God,' says Dr Pearce, putting down my script, as I go in properly. 'Come and sit here.' He pats the bed. 'I've been desperate to see you.'

'I was here all night,' I reply, putting the binoculars on the window ledge.

'Were you? I must have slept for hours.'

'You work too hard. It will do you good to have a few days' rest.'

'I'm not tired now.' He grins at me. 'Now, do as I say and come here.'

'Then perhaps it's time you moved into a chair.' I need to distract him. 'There's something I didn't tell you, yesterday. I . . . I went to the surgery.'

He sits up straighter. 'Oh?'

'I . . . I found a key and went into your office. I didn't want your wife finding your personal diary and discovering we'd been . . .'

'Oh Jane. There was no need to worry about that.'

'So I gather. Because she isn't at home, is she? Hasn't been for two months.'

'I kept meaning to tell you . . . but I didn't because I knew just how you'd react. The way you always do when I try to talk about us properly. You look just like that. Like a rabbit caught in a trap.'

I turn away. 'Because that's how you make me feel, Robert.'

There's a knock on the door.

Patience walks in with a tray. 'I've brought some lunch for you both.'

I quickly compose myself. 'Thank you.'

'That smells good,' Dr Pearce says, as she puts it on the card table.

'It's beef stew, Doctor.'

'My favourite.'

'Ha, you said that last night about Cook's chicken broth.'

He laughs too. 'Now what's the latest gossip from the kitchen? That young lass tells me nothing.'

'Quite right too,' I interrupt, in case Patience should blurt something about Thomas being in the kitchen instead of Cook. I thrust a bowl and spoon at him. 'You want to be concentrating on getting well, not tittle tattle.'

'A bit of banter is just the thing to raise my spirits,' he responds, before taking a mouthful. 'Delicious.'

'I'll ring when we've finished with our dishes,' I cut in.

'Yes, Nurse. Make sure you eat it all up, Dr Pearce. Your patients need you fit and well.'

I cross to the window. 'It's stifling in here. Let's get some fresh air circulating . . . That's better.' I pick up my bowl and tuck in.

About twenty minutes later there's a tap at the door.

'Mrs Christie,' says Dr Pearce. 'What a pleasant surprise. And who is this?'

Colin's mouth falls open.

Agatha nudges him. 'I was just telling Colin here, that a friend of mine was staying with us who might appreciate some company. I was just explaining that you've had an accident and have to stay in bed. Say hello to Dr Pearce, Colin.'

Colin goes rigid. 'He's a doctor?'

'Mmm. I thought I mentioned that?' She pushes him forwards. 'Sorry, it's my memory.'

Colin continues to gawp. He's clearly still anxious after his ordeal in the boathouse.

'We thought Colin would be company for you,' continues Agatha, looking rather perplexed by his sudden reticence. 'He's quite the chatterbox.'

Colin's eyes flash to me.

'Won't you sit down, Colin,' I say, getting up so he can take my place.

He slides over to the birch deck chair. His gaze fixed again on Dr Pearce. 'Mrs Christie said someone whacked you on the head.'

He gushes. 'You were knocked out.'

'That's right. But I'm on the mend now.'

'Do you really have to stay in bed?' he asks, his eyes flicking to me again.

'Yes. Or I'll be in trouble with Nurse Goodbetter. She can be rather bossy.'

'She is,' agrees Colin, seriously.

'I like that young people are plain speaking,' says Agatha, laughing. 'Don't you? My own daughter is very direct.'

'How old is she?' asks Colin.

'Seven. You might meet her when she comes to stay for Christmas.'

'It's only a week away,' he says, excited. He turns his head to Dr Pearce. 'I'm hoping for a fishing rod. Do you like fishing?'

'I did when I was your age. Then one morning I was sitting by the riverbank when this big bird came swooping down and plucked this whopping big fish out of the water right by me. And after that I became an ornithologist.'

'A what?'

'Let's leave them to it,' Agatha says, with a wink.

⟷

Agatha says she's going to rest. So, I leave her and take the tray down to the kitchen.

Cook pours me a glass of water. 'The last thing we want is you collapsing from dehydration. Kitty's with Ellen. So, you can sit down and tell me how you came to find her in the boathouse.'

I take a swig and fill her in on all that Mrs Griffiths told me. Ellen's suspicions about Charles Trent. Dickie Derbyshire promising to clear her name in return for information about the Watts family. How she'd taken her nain's senna powder up to Abney.

'Then this morning a telegram came for Ellen telling her to meet Dickie at the boathouse – and, well, you know the rest.'

Cook gives a long whistle. 'I wonder what proof Dickie found.'

'It would have to be the tie pin itself, wouldn't it? After Colonel Christie cancelled his interview, Dickie must have gone somewhere. Perhaps he went to see Charles Trent. Thinking that Ellen's thief story was better than no story.' I drain the last of the water. 'I'm hoping she might be awake now. Then I can ask her.'

Back at Gardener's Cottage, I ease open the spare room door. Kitty is sitting next to the bed.

'Any change?'

'She's been murmuring, but I can't make out what she's trying to say.'

I move closer. Ellen's skin colouring is normal. 'How's her temperature?'

'Rising steadily. It's up to 96.5.'

'Almost back to normal. Excellent.' I test it again to be sure, and nod. I place my hand on one of the water bottles.

'I've put fresh warm water in,' adds Kitty.

'Thank you.'

She lets out her breath audibly. 'I still can't believe our Colin found her. I suppose we should be glad for his running about the place for once.' She twists her fingers together. 'How was it you found them both?'

'It's a long story.'

'Should be a good one then.'

I explain how Ellen's been trying to prove she's not a thief. How she received a note this morning telling her to go to the boathouse. That Colin had been playing pirates close by, and so on.

'Do you remember your Colin saying he saw a blood-soaked maid? Well, he wasn't making it up. It was Ellen he saw. The MADS found a sanguineous apron—'

'A *what*?'

'A bloody apron . . . in the costumes yesterday afternoon and Patience identified it as one she'd lent to her.'

Kitty curses under her breath. Looks down at Ellen. 'So where did all the blood come from?'

'Not from Ellen. When Cook and I changed her into those pyjamas I was alert for any sign of a cut – but there wasn't one.'

'Dickie's blood then? You said they'd had an argument – and he hasn't been seen since. They could have had another argument, only this time it turned violent. You've got to take a proper look at the boathouse, Jane.'

'And what about Ellen?'

'I can stay with her.' She grins wickedly. 'If she wakes, I'll interrogate her.'

'But I'm supposed to take over from you so you can get back to your duties.'

She shrugs. 'Patience can take up the slack for once.'

↔

Tri-pointed bird footprints pepper the snowy path down to the boathouse. Dr Pearce is always good at identifying them. I can make out which are webbed and which aren't, but that's about it.

I glance back at the hall. I bet Robert's in his element, telling Colin how to tell a coot from a moorhen.

Leaving the boathouse door open for more light, as it's starting to go dark, I take a deep breath and re-enter the building. I turn Dickie's torch on again and highlight Colin's campfire. I've brought an old hessian sack with me. I drop the discarded apple cores into it. The stone fire circle is next; I lob the cobbles out into the long grass then use an old burnt stick to make the ash less obvious.

Satisfied, I go to the water's edge. If this was a scene in one of Agatha's books, I would find something incriminating, but all I can discern are footprints. Ellen's presumably, mine, Thomas's and Colin's, in a confused, overlaid pattern. There could be another set among them, but I can't be sure. I sniff the air, for the distinctive scent of macassar but all I can smell is the slightly pungent lake water.

I look at the spot where we found Ellen. If she was here with Dickie, I can't find any evidence. Kitty was right. The only way to find out is to ask her.

Giving up, I close the boathouse door and retrace my steps. As I reach the driveway, I see headlights coming up the road. As it nears, I see it's a Ford Model T van with the name 'Fitups' painted on the side. It parks up by the hall's entrance, between Mrs Cherry's red Packhard and Iris's green Crossley. Charles Trent gets out of the passenger side.

Are all the MADS here?

The driver's door opens but it's not Jim's brother, Humphrey, as I expected. I do a double take. It's the roofer from the White Hart.

Gil goes to the back of the van and opens the doors.

I stroll over. Fighting the urge to ask him if Dickie Derbyshire paid him a visit on Thursday night.

'Morning, Jane,' calls Charles, tipping the brim of his bowler.

Gil pops his head out. He looks surprised then pleased.

I'm already warm from walking, but I feel another sudden flush of heat.

Charles arches an eyebrow. 'You can manage to get the flats out without me, can't you? We'll put them in the boys' room.' He saunters up the steps. 'Shan't be long.'

'I've heard that before,' Gil calls after him.

I rest my hand on my hip. 'What are you doing here? I thought you were a roofer?'

'I am. Want me to prove it?' He points. 'I can wax lyrical on the difference between those grotesques and gargoyles if you like.'

'Is that why you're here? To do some repairs?'

He shakes his head. 'I volunteer with the Manchester Amateur Dram—'

'MADS.'

The side of his mouth dimples with amusement. 'Oh, you've heard of it? I wasn't sure with you not being from round here. I put together sets for them. Not working at the hospital today?'

'No,' I say. Caught on the hop.

The dimple reappears. 'Only I did read in *The Advertiser* that the Wattses has hired a private nurse to look after Agatha Christie while she's recuperating here.'

I squeeze my thumb.

'Understandable you wouldn't tell a stranger your real role,'

Gil continues. 'Makes me sick how everyone's been speculating about Mrs Christie. Folk should mind their own bloody business.'

'I'd better go in.'

'Sure.' His expression hardens. 'I've plenty to do myself.'

Walking along the long corridor, I hear excitable voices coming from the drawing room. I halt and am about to press my ear to the door just as it opens.

Mrs Cherry looks down at my muddy galoshes. 'Been into the village again? And don't fob me off. You passed my window yesterday and this morning. I have a good view of passersby from my armchair.'

I should have known she was a busy body. 'I like to go—'

'Birdwatching? Yes, Madge mentioned that about you. Forgotten your binoculars?'

'I gave them back to Dr Pearce.'

'Oh yes. He enjoys birdwatching too, doesn't he?'

My heart thuds.

'No, I don't miss much. Funny, I hear you've roped some boy into looking after Dr Pearce, instead of you. I thought nurses were normally desperate for an opportunity to mop their doctor's brow, or is that only in hospitals?'

'Ah, Jane.' Jim strides over. 'You'd better come in, seeing as this concerns you too.'

He ushers me inside then closes the door behind us.

THIRTY-ONE

THE FURNITURE HAS BEEN ARRANGED IN A SQUARE. TWO settees. Mrs Cherry with Iris and Madge, opposite them Paul, Charles and Reverend Whittle. The perpendicular lines are formed by two pairs of armchairs. Jack sits next to Jim. I unbutton my new coat and sit in one of the other two. It feels just like the denouement in *The Mysterious Affair at Styles* when Hercule Poirot gathers all the suspects together. Only it's Bonzo sitting in the centre of us all.

Iris snaps shut her compact while everyone else returns their teacups to their saucers.

'Now are you finally going to tell us what this is all about, Constable?' demands the vicar.

'Quite,' adds Mrs Cherry, seemingly cross at being just as in the dark as everyone else. She looks to her friend. 'I thought we were having a rehearsal not an inquisition.'

I suddenly realise that outside of the Watts family I'm the only one who knows the real purpose of this gathering.

'We're just waiting on one more person,' says Madge.

I help myself to tea, black, feeling strangely unsettled.

As the clock strikes half past the door opens again. My cup

rattles against the saucer in surprise.

'Dr Argyle. Do come in,' says Jim. 'Thank you, Patience.'

'How is Mrs Christie?' He looks over Mr Watts's shoulder. 'She isn't here?'

'No. We want to shield her from any further worry. She knows nothing of this . . .'

Dr Argyle pours himself a tea and sits next to me. 'Most wise. Her nerves are quite fraught.'

'Mr Watts,' prompts Bonzo, opening his notebook.

Jim looks rather awkward. 'Ah. Yes.' He stands. Tries to take in every face. 'As you know, the rehearsals for *When I Grow Rich* were recently moved here due to a hole in the church hall roof.'

Reverend Whittle shuffles in his seat.

'And very grateful we are for having you host us,' reiterates Mrs Cherry, patting Madge's knee.

'Let the man speak,' says Paul.

'. . . And as with all productions there have been the usual stresses around casting.'

'Is this about Richard?' asks Iris.

'Must be,' replies Charles. 'He's the only one of us not here – and he missed yesterday's rehearsal.'

Paul stares at Dr Argyle. 'Are you his replacement?'

'I beg your pardon?'

'Dr Argyle is treating Mrs Christie after her ordeal,' says Mrs Cherry.

'Shush!' Jim frowns.

Her eyes widen. I don't think anyone has ever shut her up before.

Dr Argyle takes another sip of tea. He seems completely bemused as to why he's been summoned. I know I am.

'As I was trying to say . . . Unfortunately, it has come to my wife and I's attention that one of us is not who they claim to be.'

I know he means Richard Buxton, but my heart still skips a beat. My eyes flick to Dr Argyle again, but his eyes remain on Jim.

Jim gives a little cough. 'It has become apparent that Richard Buxton is in fact an undercover reporter . . .'

'My goodness,' says Reverend Whittle.

'His real name is Dickie Derbyshire.'

Blank faces. Iris looks like she's trying to work out the answer to a crossword puzzle clue.

'From *The Advertiser*?' asks Mrs Cherry.

All eyes turn to her.

'You know him?' asks Bonzo. His eyes brightening.

'Well, not really. I think he's rung me once or twice for a quote about one of my shows. Quite the act he's been putting on! Perhaps I should have given him a bigger role.'

'Delia!' scolds Madge.

'Actually, Mrs Watts,' says Reverend Whittle. 'I must admit, I did think he looked rather familiar when you introduced us. But you said he was a clerk which confused me. I suppose it's possible I've given him some snippets of church news in the past.'

Bonzo's pencil is going like Billy-o across the page.

'Dickie . . . Dickie,' repeats Charles. 'Oh, yes. Ha! Skinny fellow. Don't you remember, Madge, darling? He was here for the MADS party in September. Said to you he made me think of the stoats and weasels when they break into Toad Hall! Rather out of place.'

Her brow wrinkles.

'You must remember . . . he was admiring that painting of Cromwell, and you offered to show him his christening robes.'

'That was him?'

Did Madge and Charles really not recognise the reporter sooner? Or could it be that Dickie Derbyshire wasn't as undercover as he – or I – presumed. And what of the other MADS? A good actor can easily feign surprise and confusion.

'Wanted the inside scoop on Agatha, I imagine,' continues Mrs Cherry. 'Of course I pride myself on being discretion itself. I'm certain nothing I said to him made it into one of his articles.'

Jim clears his throat. 'I think we can assume an exposé on Mrs Christie's illness and treatment was the reason for Dickie Derbyshire's deception . . . initially. But things became rather complicated when by chance Colonel Christie offered him an exclusive interview on Thursday evening.'

'Bet he couldn't believe his luck,' says Charles, with a whistle. 'Could sell a story like that to the nationals. Nice little earner.'

'Yes, it would explain him dropping out from rehearsals,' says Iris.

Now Bonzo clears his throat and stands. 'After leaving Abney after rehearsal on Thursday, it seems Dickie Derbyshire took the back road in order to make his appointment with Colonel Christie. A mishap with his motor car meant he had to continue on foot and was late for his interview. Colonel Christie was irate at his tardiness and sent him packing. This was at approximately five twenty.

'That was the last time Dickie Derbyshire was seen by anyone.

His employers reported him missing on Friday afternoon.'

Everyone looks to each other, but no one utters a word.

Jim clasps his hands together. 'Naturally, since the constable's visit this morning, I have done a little investigating of my own. I telephoned Mr Derbyshire's editor at his home to express how disgusted I am by his reporter's behaviour. I stressed that *The Stockport Advertiser* currently enjoys significant advertising revenue from S & J Watts.'

'Hear. Hear,' calls Reverend Whittle. 'I shall cancel the vicarage's regular order, and I implore you all to do the same.'

'Thank you, Vicar. Anyway, after a fulsome apology, the editor confided that Mr Derbyshire had pitched him a number of potential other stories relating to Abney Hall. 'The first was a background piece about Mrs Christie's new doctor.' He nods at Dr Argyle. 'He also thought there might be – and I quote – "a decent story in this church hall roof business".'

Reverend Whittle jumps up. 'What a load of rubbish.'

I'm tempted to speak out. To say I know the roof damage was caused by Dickie but I hold my tongue. Curious if there will be more admissions before I dare add my own.

'And, more ambiguously, he had a couple of leads to follow up involving stories about members of the MADS,' finishes Jim.

Mrs Cherry is calmer. 'I certainly have no skeletons in my cupboard. The very idea!'

'You mean there could be an . . . an exposé in the papers about any one of us?' squeaks Iris.

'What's the matter? I thought you believed that all publicity was good publicity,' teases Charles.

Agatha Christie's disappearance has turned her from a little-known author into a household name. A story by Dickie Derbyshire would give Iris's career a similar boost, so what has she got to hide?

'I wish I knew where that little worm is now,' adds Paul, his gaze on Jack. 'Because I'd quite like to squish Dickie Derbyshire under my heel.'

Bonzo's eyebrows rise. 'Perhaps I could start by asking you a few questions. It's Mr Ramsbury, isn't it?'

Paul grunts.

'Actually, would you mind if I went first,' says Reverend Whittle. 'I still have my sermon to write. I've decided to cancel the vicarage's order. It's disgusting how this chap is exposing a private affair to all and sundry. In fact, it would make a fitting theme for Sunday's sermon.'

Madge pales.

'I would rather you didn't discuss an active investigation with your congregation,' says Bonzo.

'Ah, yes. Certainly.'

'This shouldn't take long, Reverend.' He looks to Jim. 'Is there somewhere . . .'

'You can use my study,' says Jim. 'This way.'

The three go out.

'I could do with a smoke,' says Charles.

'I'll come with you,' says Iris.

Everyone seems keen to get out of the room. It won't be so easy to get out from under Bonzo's steely gaze.

'Well, if we all have to stay to be interrogated one by one,

I hope you will at least feed us, Madge,' declares Mrs Cherry.

'Oh. Well. Yes. Of course, Delia. I'll speak to Cook straight away.'

Poor Cook.

'Good.' Mrs Cherry scoops up her carpet bag. 'You don't mind if I use your room to freshen up?'

Madge smiles.

Mrs Cherry goes out into the corridor. Her voice rises again. 'Gil. Just the man!'

Her tone of unexpected pleasure is over-the-top, as ever.

'Now, Delia, I'll tell you the same as I told Reverend Whittle. I'm happy to fix the hole in the church hall roof. Once this snow clears, I'll do a temporary fix so rehearsals can move back there.'

'You are wonderful. Actually, it was a different matter I wanted to speak to you about.'

Jack stands. 'Her voice is like a gramophone. The only way to reduce the volume is to close the door.'

'I'll do it,' I say.

But he gets up with me, anyway.

We step out into the corridor. I tug the door shut behind us and head towards the cross corridor.

'I'm not going to like this, am I?' Gil's resting another flat against the wall. His eyes catch mine for a moment then focus on Mrs Cherry, whose back is to me.

'You were such a darling stepping in last minute when we were doing Cinderella.'

'Oh no, I wasn't,' he deadpans.

She laughs. Slaps his arm as Jack and I pass them. 'Oh, yes

you were. Now, you know I wouldn't ask if we weren't absolutely stuck.'

I glance round, wanting to catch his reaction.

'Last time you said that, it was me that got stuck – in the back end of a pantomime horse. A matinee and three evening performances. I've never sweated so much in all my life – and my back.' He rubs his lower lumbar.

The drawing room door opens again and Paul comes out. 'Wait up, Jack.'

I pause too.

The servants bell rings in the distance.

'You'd be upright this time – very upright,' continues Mrs Cherry. 'It's only a small role. A solicitor. You'd learn the lines in no time. I've a script here, somewhere.' She delves into her bag.

Gil groans. 'You're going to keep asking until you wear me down again, aren't you . . . Fine. Now do you want to take a look at these flats?'

'Of course.' She hands him the script.

They head back towards the boys' room.

Paul has caught us up. He jabs Jack in the chest. 'Did you tell the police I was at the George and Dragon Thursday night?'

'No.'

'Carry on, Nursie. This doesn't concern you.' He tries to jab Jack again.

I brush his hand aside.

He totters slightly. 'Well, make sure you don't.'

Paul staggers away.

Why does he want to keep his being at the pub secret? The

servant bell is still ringing making my head throb. Made worse as the terrace door thuds. Probably heading to the George and Dragon now. Not that he'll get very far.

Jack rolls his eyes. 'Better go after the idiot.'

Outside, the ground is so thick with it that I sink down to my ankles with every step. Colin's snowman has gained an extra layer of snow making it misshapen.

We follow his deep footsteps across the terrace lawn towards the wood.

'He's giving up,' says Jack, 'look.' His footsteps turn off towards the old chapel.

'Thank God.'

When we get to Buckley, the door is wide open. There's an unexpected but all too familiar odour in the air as we enter. Sharp and metallic undercut with other bodily odours. The smell of death. Blood.

I clasp a hand to my mouth.

A dark-haired man is spreadeagled face down on the floor. Sir Arthur's poleaxe embedded in his neck. Only this weapon is all too real.

'Oh God. It's just like when the doctor is attacked in the play,' says Jack.

'Is he dead?' stutters Paul.

A ridiculous question. The axe has severed the cervical vertebrae and all the vital arteries causing a massive haemorrhage. He'll have bled out in minutes.

'I'm afraid so.'

'Oh God. I think I'm going to be sick.' Paul starts to retch.

My nursing instincts kick in. 'Take him outside. Then fetch the constable.'

Jack takes Paul's arm. 'Come on, pal.'

I move closer. Though the body is face down, I recognise the build and crumpled suit. I carefully lean over and tilt his face to be sure.

'Dickie Derbyshire.'

His skin is waxy. His eyes dull and sunken.

He hasn't been dead long.

There's something in his right hand. I peer closer. The stub of a candle. By his shoes a puddle of melted wax.

'Here comes a candle to light you to bed,' I sing grimly. 'And here comes a chopper to chop off your—'

THIRTY-TWO

MADGE CLASPS HER HUSBAND'S HAND AS BONZO DRAPES a blanket over Dickie's body.

'Dr Argyle, please telephone the station and tell the desk sergeant we have a suspicious death. Likely foul play. I will stay with the body until a detective inspector arrives. With this damn snow it could be some time before he reaches us from Stockport.'

'Use the one in my study,' says Jim. 'We want to keep this quiet for now. We don't want to cause a panic.'

'Understood.' Dr Argyle leaves.

'I suppose the inspector will wish to speak to everyone when he gets here,' Jim asks Bonzo.

'Yes, sir.'

'Not Agatha,' pleads Madge. 'She's still very unwell.'

'That will be for the inspector to consider,' continues Bonzo, pushing back the peak of his helmet. 'Though I expect he will want to know Mrs Christie's movements the same as everyone's. In the meantime, I wish to double check that I have all your guests' names.' He opens his notebook and reads them out.

Madge nods at each. 'Gil Clark is here too. He puts together scenery for the MADS. Oh, and we have Dr Pearce staying with us, though he's confined to his bed.'

Bonzo jerks his chin with interest. 'Nasty business. I went round when the attack was called in. And the same staff working as yesterday?'

'Yes – plus Kitty Johnson's young brother is here. He's acting as a companion to Dr Pearce.'

'Not Colin?' He laughs. 'Right little scallywag.'

Madge shoots a confused look at me.

'You may both return to the house now, while I take an initial statement from your son and Nurse Goodbetter. But please ask that everyone remain at Abney Hall until the inspector has questioned them. Even if that means staying overnight.'

'Of course, Constable.'

The MADS won't like that. They haven't so much as a toothbrush with them.

Madge and Jim leave.

Bonzo frowns. 'I had feared this case would end with the discovery of Mr Derbyshire's body. I must admit I theorised that he met his demise on Thursday evening, not this morning. He must have been hiding out here. Hoping for another exclusive. Got in through an unsecure window, no doubt.'

'There is one. Thomas, our gardener, cleared up the broken glass. We were going to get Mr Clark to board it up.'

'Show me.'

We look at the empty windowpane from inside and out. It's big enough and low enough for someone to gain access.

'Could be footsteps in the mud under this snow. There's

certainly plenty to and from this building, pawprints too,' adds Bonzo.

'My father and I walk our dogs regularly around the grounds. Villagers too, sometimes, we've locked the lodge gates, but you can cross the fields if you know your way about.'

'Hmm. Likely one set belongs to his attacker. Damned difficult to know which.' He sighs. 'Did his attacker come in this way too, or did Mr Derbyshire let them in?'

His helmet is speckled with snowflakes. His nose and chin pink from the cold.

'You may go back to the house, Mr Watts. I will speak to you after Nurse Goodbetter has given me her statement.'

Jack nods.

Bonzo and I go inside and sit on one of the pews.

He reopens his notebook. 'Tell me again how you both came to find the body.'

'Mr Ramsbury was rather upset,' I begin. 'He went out to get some fresh air. Jack and I were concerned and followed him.'

'And Mr Ramsbury will confirm that, will he? When I take his statement.'

'It's the truth.'

'And then . . .'

'The door was open. I went in, followed by Jack. I knew at once something was wrong. The smell . . .'

He clears his throat. Not wanting to linger on delicate matters. I would have expected a policeman to be hardened to death. I wonder what he did in the war. Then realise he was probably too young to fight. 'I could see that Mr Derbyshire was dead.

Jack took Paul outside and we returned to the house and found you.'

'This is not your first post here at Abney Hall, is that correct?'

'Yes, I nursed Mr Watts's mother-in-law and father until their passing.'

'You are employed privately by the Watts family.'

'Yes.'

'I see. How did you come to work here?'

'I answered an advertisement in the local newspaper.'

'The *Stockport Advertiser*?'

'Actually, I think it was the *Manchester Evening News*.'

'You have been a nurse for how long?'

I hesitate. Alarm bells ringing. 'Since 1908.'

'You were a VAD?' His voice is friendly enough. But those alarm bells are still ringing.

'No. I never worked in the war hospitals.'

'Never met Dickie Derbyshire before Wednesday?'

'Definitely not.'

'Nothing to connect the two of you?'

'Not that I am aware of – only that I am caring for Mrs Christie.'

'Well, thank you, Nurse Goodbetter. You may go.'

Patience is scrubbing the porch tiles. She drops the brush into her bucket and runs a hand over her damp grey streaked hair. Her face is sweaty with effort. I wince with guilt. Kitty should be the one on her hands and knees.

'Like Pauldens in here with all the comings and goings,' she says crossly. 'And that blooming dog. Look at the state.

Wouldn't leave me alone. Jumping all over me.' She tuts. 'And all these extra people traipsing in and out of the house.'

'I'm afraid they're going to be here a bit longer yet.'

'You must be sick of them, an' all.'

'One or two,' I whisper.

'If it would help, I'd be happy to sit with Ellen awhile.'

'Kitty and I are managing for now, but thank you for the offer.' I feel bad for turning her down, but she's too scatty to be relied upon.

Patience looks disappointed. She starts scrubbing again. Still more mucky pawprints to deal with. I tip toe along the edge. It feels ridiculous, seeing Patience toiling, but I really am wiped out.

I go to the study and tell Jack I'm back.

Then go down the corridor to check on Agatha, patting the lion's head like a talisman as I pass.

I open the library door. Dr Argyle is running a finger smoothly across Agatha's forehead. Her expression is blank. Is she in a trance?

'You are resting. You are rested. You will be strong again. Happy again.'

Agatha's eyes flash open. She beams at Dr Argyle.

'There. You feel better?'

'Yes. Much. Thank you, Doctor.'

'I will tell your sister that you made a significant breakthrough today. Enjoy Christmas with your family, Mrs Christie. Then in the new year I suggest you take a holiday. Where you can fully relax. Somewhere hot. When you return you can continue your therapy.' He writes something in his notebook, tears out the page and passes it to her. 'As your intention is to live in London, I recommend you contact a colleague of mine who has a practice on Harley Street.'

'That sounds ideal, Dr Argyle.'

'Shall I send your sister in after I've spoken with her?'

'Yes, please.'

'What was it like?' I ask, once he's left the room. 'Being hypnotised?'

'It was good. Well, a bit uncomfortable at first. Those eyes of his are so piercing. I couldn't help but hold his gaze. Then a strange feeling of calm flooded over me and now I can see it all so clearly, Jane. How I came to be so lost.'

'You've got your memory back?'

'No, not all of it. There are still gaps. No, I meant how I came to be emotionally lost. As we go through life the person we are changes. Who you are in here,' she presses her hand to her bosom, 'well it can get a bit forgotten. Most of the time we see ourselves in relation to others. Daughter. Wife. Mother. Sister. Perhaps our job. Nurse. Author.'

I nod.

'This year, two key parts of my identity were taken from me. My mother died and then Archie told me he no longer loved me. I tried desperately to hold on to those roles. I couldn't save my mother, couldn't even save her home.

'So when Archie came to Ashfield to ask for a divorce, I was desperate to save our marriage. To remain his wife. He tried to convince me I would be happier without him. I could travel. Concentrate on my writing. But he was never really concerned about my happiness, only his own.'

'Oh, Agatha. I'm so sorry.'

'I begged him to stay for Rosalind's sake. And he said he'd try. But it was no good. As I told Dr Argyle, Archie couldn't stand to be near me.'

There's a tap on the door.

Madge comes in. Titch at her side.

The spaniel rushing towards us. Buries her nose into my apron. I gently push her head away.

'Hello, girl,' says Agatha, patting her brown head.

'We're dining in the breakfast room. I thought you'd prefer that with the house being so busy.' Madge strokes her sister's cheek. 'I was wrong to allow Delia to hold the rehearsals here. You're supposed to have complete rest and . . . and . . .' A sob catches in her throat.

'Oh. Punkie. Please don't get upset. I'm the one who has disrupted everything, not you. I never intended to cause you so much worry and trouble. It all just spiralled.'

'Dr Argyle seems pleased with your progress,' Madge adds. Her voice full of hope. 'Has your memory returned?'

'Enough for me to face what happened that Friday night.'

'You and Archie had rowed, that morning . . .'

Agatha looks sheepish. 'We both said some terrible things. He stormed out. I waited for him to come home – but as the hours passed, I knew he'd gone to be with her instead. Something inside my mind fractured. I was miserable. Desperate. A lot of that Friday evening and the day after are still hazy. But it's clear that I took my car. Drove aimlessly. Until I found myself at the cottage – Hurtmore. To do what, I don't know. I just know I wanted them to feel the pain that I did.

'In a novel, the wronged woman would march up to the door and shoot the adulterous couple. But I couldn't even get out of my car.

'Suddenly, all I wanted was to get as far away from them as possible. Their happiness. Away from my grief. My heartbreak. Myself. I had all these thoughts in my head. Everything swirling.

'I let go of the steering wheel and let the car run down the hill towards the quarry. But it veered and struck a hedge. That must have been when I struck my head.' Her fingers go to the now faint bruise.

Madge throws her arms around her sister. 'I'm just so glad you didn't go over the edge.'

So am I.

I slide out of my seat and leave them to talk in private.

People may continue to question what really happened during Agatha's missing days, if her memory loss was real, but I am convinced. I hope now she can move on with her life and find the happiness she truly deserves.

THIRTY-THREE

Sunday 19th December, 1926

MY UNDER-EYES ARE BLACK. MY SKIN IS DRY. FRANKLY, I LOOK and feel a mess. But at least I have fresh clothes and my toiletries, unlike everyone else who was forced to spend the night. Poor Bonzo didn't even have a proper bed. He had to camp down in the old chapel.

I go to Dr Pearce's room first. He is in his dressing gown, gazing out of the window. His bed isn't made. Probably used to his wife doing it.

'Run out of people to fob off on me?' he asks.

'You are not my patient,' I snap. 'Agatha is.'

'And you've made it abundantly clear you don't want me here.'

'I don't.'

He breathes in heavily. 'Then as soon as this damn snow clears, I'll go home.'

Halle-bloody-lujah.

Up to the second floor next, to find Colin. There's no opulence to the old servants' rooms although they're still generous in size. The simple window design suggests the architects felt curlicues and the like would be wasted on the working inhabitants of Abney – no doubt saved its owner a bob or two. There are no patterned turkey carpets nor four poster beds. Instead, it's floorboards and sturdy iron bedsteads. Plain and practical. Good enough.

Colin is tucked up in bed. My temper subsides. He looks so peaceful.

'Hey, sleepyhead. Rise and shine.' I used to say the same to David each morning.

Colin yawns and ruffles his hair which is stuck up like porcupine quills.

'I'm going to see how Ellen is. I thought you'd like to come with me. I'll wait on the landing for you. And make sure you wrap up.'

A few minutes later, his hair isn't much better, but at least he's dressed. Dr Pearce's binoculars around his neck.

'Dr Pearce says you like bird spotting too.'

'I do.'

He nods approvingly. 'Yesterday I saw a robin. An eri . . . *erithacus rubecula*,' Colin says. 'I've been practising saying that. It's Latin. Oh and a *pica pica*. That one's easier.'

I think he's testing me. I grin. 'Did you salute it for luck?'

I raise my hand to the side of my head.

He laughs and copies me. 'There's a stuffed one downstairs. Dr Pearce said he'd show it to me.'

'That's kind of him,' I reply. 'We might see some different corvids on the way to Thomas's cottage.'

Everywhere is so white outside that it hurts my eyes. Even just walking as far as Thomas's cottage is exhausting, the snow's icy crust crunching under our feet. Colin pretends to be a rabbit, hopping so he can leave bigger prints.

The door isn't locked. But I pull the snip across once we're inside.

Patience startles as we enter the back bedroom. 'You made me jump out of my skin.'

Colin chuckles.

'Shush. Sorry. Where's Kitty?'

'We swapped places. She thought Mrs Watts might ask questions if she wasn't at breakfast. I'd done my main duties. I'll get something to eat later. Kitty left some coffee, but it's probably cold by now.'

'Well, you can go back now and have your breakfast.'

She looks anxiously at Ellen.

'She'll be fine. Off you go.'

'If you're sure, Nurse.' She looks uncertainly at Colin. 'I was getting a bit uncomfortable in that chair.' She rubs her hip as she gets up.

Then comes right up to me and whispers in my ear. 'I can't believe they've found that missing reporter dead in the old chapel. It's like something you'd read about in the *News of the World*! Terrible isn't it.

I think she's secretly thrilled.

She steps back. 'Told you I sensed evil here at Abney, ever since them MADS started coming, didn't I. Oh. Nurse. I wanted to ask. Have you worked out who the real thief is yet?'

'Thief?' repeats Colin, eyebrows rising.

'Shush. Cover your ears.'

He does. 'I can still hear,' he says with a grin.

'I didn't mean literally. Actually, stay like that.' I face Patience. 'Ellen thought the thief was Mr Trent. She and Dickie Derbyshire have been trying to find proof.'

'Not Mr Charles, surely? Well. I never. And him always so nicely turned out. Got a good job. Fancy motor car. What reason does he have to be stealing trinkets?'

'Well Dr Pearce's pen and Mr Ramsbury's tie pin are hardly that. And I imagine Mrs Cherry's silver watch was valuable too. Though it might just be the challenge he enjoys, or perhaps he just can't help himself. Doctors say stealing is a compulsion in some people.'

She shakes her head. 'Well, I don't know about that. All I know is it's wicked.'

Patience leaves. Colin plops himself into her chair.

Ellen looks peaceful. Too peaceful. I give her a gentle shake. 'Ellen, love. Wake up.'

She starts to stir.

I shake a little firmer.

She moans. But to my relief her eyes open. I help her to sit up. 'Good morning.'

'Nurse Goodbetter? Where am I?' Her eyes are glassy. She looks round the room. Spots Colin.

'I found you. In the boathouse,' he says. 'You were in the water.'

'Was I?'

He nods. 'I thought you were dead an' all, but you were just dead cold.' He grins. 'I'm glad you're better now.'

I pour some of the coffee into the cup, it's warmer than I expect. I lift it to her lips. 'Here. Take a sip.'

She pushes it away. Pulls a face. 'I already said I don't like coffee. Isn't there any tea?'

I take the cup away. 'I can make you some. In a minute. Do you know where you are, Ellen?'

'Mmm. Mr Budworth's cottage. That new parlourmaid said.'

'Kitty. That's right. And do you know why you're here?'

She puts her hand to her temple. 'I was supposed to meet Dickie . . .'

'He was helping you. He had proof Charles Trent is the thief. Was Dr Pearce helping you too?'

Her head sways. 'Where is he?'

'Don't worry. You're safe here. Try to stay awake, Ellen.'

But it's no good. She slips back into unconsciousness. Frustrated, I take a quick swig of the coffee.

'Can I have some?' asks Colin.

'You're too young. Besides, it's bitter. You wouldn't like it.' I must admit I'd rather a cup of tea myself. 'Do you mind staying with Ellen a while?'

'Protect her, you mean?'

'If you like. Don't let anyone in. Well, unless it's me or your sister.'

'Or Mr Budworth.'

'Well yes, it is his house.'

He nods solemnly.

Looks like I'm the last to come down to breakfast. I look round the dining-room table. Reverend Whittle, Dr Argyle, Iris, Mrs Cherry. No Paul.

Charles looks like he's getting second helpings. Making up for having starved himself all day Friday.

Gil leans over his shoulder. 'Jeez. Can you get any more on that plate?'

I stand behind him. 'You've got sawdust on your hair.'

He ruffles his hand through his mop. 'Better than dandruff.'

'Careful, you'll get it in the scrambled eggs,' I joke.

I hope there's more than scraps left. At Winwick the catering staff made sure there was no favouritism. Good food was seen as a vital part of the patients' recovery, and the regularity of meals gave each day structure and boosted everyone's morale. It was just as important for staff, long hours, often on your feet, meant mealtimes provided sustenance and a chance to relax and catch up with each other.

'Dr Pearce. How marvellous to see you up and about,' calls Mrs Cherry.

My heart sinks. I can feel him like a shadow, as he joins the short queue for food.

'Beats a bit of soggy toast, this lot doesn't it,' says Gil. 'And you should see my bed too. Like something out of a fairytale. Four posters and a canopy!'

I can sense Dr Pearce's eyes on me. On Gil. I pick up a plate and try to shake off my unease.

Mrs Cherry scrapes back her chair. Yesterday's trouser suit now rather creased as she strides over.

'Now we can't have you standing in line after your terrible ordeal.' She picks up a plate and thrusts it at me. 'Where are your manners. You should get Dr Pearce his breakfast.'

I imagine smashing the plate over her head.

'He can have this one,' says Gil, intercepting.

Mrs Cherry beams at him. Then hooks her arm around the doctor's and leads him to the table. 'Do you think the police will want you to look at the body too?'

'Body?' he asks, sitting to her left.

'Hasn't Nurse told you? How remiss.'

I ignore her and concentrate on what I want to eat.

'Paul found Dickie Derbyshire splayed out on the old chapel floor with an axe in his neck,' says Charles.

Dr Pearce slides a hand over his own nape. Pales.

'You probably met him at our cast party here,' Charles continues. 'Back in September. Reporter. Skinny. Scruffy dark hair.'

'Not that I recall.'

'He's been spying on us all. Here at Abney Hall under false pretences. Told Delia his name was Richard Buxton when he auditioned for the MADS.'

Mrs Cherry's eyes gleam. 'Clearly there's a lunatic on the loose. Quite likely a drug addict. Escaped from Cheadle Royal, I expect. That's where the police should be making enquiries, not here.'

'Asylums are very secure, Mrs Cherry,' Dr Pearce replies. 'Breakouts are extremely rare.'

'But they do happen. I read about such a case in yesterday's *Advertiser*. This particular asylum was being turned into a war hospital. I have the story here if you want to see.'

'Actually . . .' says Dr Argyle.

Bile burns in my throat.

THIRTY-FOUR

THE DOOR OPENS AND MRS CHERRY CLASPS HER HAND TO her bosom. 'Paul, darling. Come. Sit. Sit.' She pats the chair to her right.

I release my breath as Dr Argyle gets up. 'I think I'll take a walk in the grounds.'

He goes out.

'How are you feeling?' asks Charles, following Paul to the table and sitting next to Iris.

'Doped up. That stuff Dr Argyle gave me had me out for the count.' Paul reaches for the coffee pot.

'I'm glad I didn't find the body,' says Mrs Cherry.

'All that blood,' says Iris.

'Oh, that wouldn't bother me,' Mrs Cherry continues. 'No, I meant because whoever discovers a victim is often the police's main suspect.'

'True,' replies Iris. 'And worse still, Paul was also the last person to see Dickie Derbyshire alive.'

We all stare at him.

'Were you?' I ask.

Paul narrows his eyes at Iris.

'He met Richard on Thursday night. At the George and Dragon,' she explains, folding her arms.

'But I didn't know who he really was. Did I? He just wanted to make up for nearly scalding me during the rehearsal. That's all.'

'And you never turn down a drink,' snipes Iris.

I shoot her a look to hush. 'Go on . . .'

He leans back. 'Dickie was finishing his second pint when I arrived. He could knock the stuff back. Suppose that should have been a clue that he was a reporter, that and all the questions. But I swear I didn't have the faintest.'

Mrs Cherry nudges Dr Pearce and raises her eyebrows in a distrusting manner.

'What did he want to know about?' I ask.

'Anything and everything. How I got into acting. How I knew you all. What I thought of you. He was a good listener . . . and I suppose I was glad to vent. Yeah, I know. He was trying to sniff out a story.'

'And you gave him one,' says Charles. His tone disappointed.

'Not at first. But after a couple of drinks, Richard – I mean Dickie – said he'd noticed the awkwardness between Iris and me. "Why was that?"'

'And?' I prompt.

'Some of you already know, but Iris and I are cousins. Our mothers were sisters. Iris's mother died when she was a young girl.'

Iris looks worried where this is all going.

'My mother was the black sheep, just like Great Uncle Hector. She likes a drink even more than I do.

'Anyway. Last summer, I was starring in *The Admiral Crichton.*

Iris came to watch. Didn't you?'

She cocks her head, nonchalantly.

'I introduced her to the rest of the MADS afterwards. It was press night so there were photographers and journalists around too. Maybe Dickie Derbyshire was among them. I didn't notice.'

Iris shrugs.

'He could have been,' adds Mrs Cherry.

'Two evenings later, before curtain-up, Charles strolls over to me with that day's *Advertiser.* Jabs his finger at a picture of me and Iris backstage and berates me for not being clear who she was. Goes on about how S & J's are working on some fresh designs. Geometric patterns. The kind of prestige work that could only be done by Caldwell's. Problem is, they have orders secured for months, if not years, in advance. Charles couldn't get a toe in the door, never mind a foot. But with Iris's help, the door would swing wide open.

'Now I'm no convent novice. I told Charles I had to be the one doing the deal. I knew he'd want a profit margin big enough so he could cream some off the top. Well, I thought it was only fair that I get a cut too.'

Iris snorts.

'And Charles was happy with that arrangement?' I ask.

'What choice did he have? I was upfront with you, wasn't I?'

She turns her head away.

'Listen. I'm telling the truth. I told Iris that Charles and I would get her an audition if she persuaded her father to let me pitch on behalf of S & J's. I just left out the fact that Charles and I would be making a bit on the side from the deal.'

Paul addresses Mrs Cherry. 'I worried you'd take some persuading, Delia. But you thought Iris would make a lovely Cinderella.'

'Well, no offence,' replies Mrs Cherry, 'but it's a role that only requires a nice personality and a pretty face.'

Iris sneers. 'Charming.'

'Why do I get the feeling there wasn't a fairytale ending to this arrangement?' I ask.

He scoffs. 'The deal was a good one. The goods were delivered on time and sold quickly. There was a decent profit for S & J's with enough margin for Charles to cream a little off the top for us both. The new design was flying off the shelves. Firms across the country were placing big orders with us and we were quickly running out of stock. Charles reassured them that a new delivery was imminent and began taking orders in advance at inflated prices. I went back to Caldwell's, tripling the size of our next order. Only, I admit it . . . I got greedy. When it was time to pay up, I said I wanted to renegotiate the price. I thought I had Mr Caldwell over a barrel.'

'Nobody gets the upper hand with my father,' says Iris.

'So I discovered. Mr Caldwell told me he'd rather burn the cloth than let S & J's have it. And he meant it. He was livid. Meanwhile S & J's customers are demanding their fabric or their money back. Charles and I were going to have to tell the Watts brothers what we'd done.'

'But Charles still works for S & J's,' I say. 'And you obviously remain on good terms with Mr and Mrs Watts.'

'Because they know nothing about it.'

The fog clears. 'You told Iris.'

Paul nods. 'Charles convinced me there was no other option. I said I'd made a genuine mistake and got my figures wrong. I don't think Iris believed me, but the last thing she wanted was a scandal surrounding her family and the Wattses.'

He turns to Iris. 'Your father may be pig-headed, but he'll do anything to keep you happy. Luckily for Charles and me, that meant handing over the printed fabric to S & J's at the original price. Course Charles and I didn't get our cut and Mr Caldwell will never deal with him or S & J's again. Quite a nice story for Dickie Derbyshire. Probably would have made Monday's edition if you hadn't murdered him before he got a chance to write it up.'

'Me?' exclaims Charles. 'You think I stuck an axe in the man to stop him putting some titbit in the paper? I doubt his editor would have printed it. For one, who cares about some rag trade deal that nearly fell through, and two, as Jim said yesterday, that paper gets a lot of advertising revenue from S & J Watts.' He picks up a slice of toast and waves it. 'They know which side their bread is buttered.'

'Miss Caldwell, Mr Ramsbury telephoned you later that evening and asked if you would pick him up from the pub. That's correct, isn't it?'

She blinks at me. 'Err. Well, yes. I didn't want to.'

'And you rang Abney Hall and asked Jack Watts to help because you knew Mr Ramsbury would be inebriated.'

'You know I did, because you came along too.'

'I did. What I'd like to know, Miss Caldwell, is how *you* got to the George and Dragon.'

THIRTY-FIVE

'THE GEORGE AND DRAGON IS SOME DISTANCE FROM your father's home. Is it not?' I ask.

Reverend Whittle dabs his mouth with a napkin. 'I don't see that it matters, but I gave Iris a lift.'

Oh. I wasn't expecting that. 'So, you were with Miss Caldwell when Mr Ramsbury telephoned?'

He looks to Iris.

'Yes,' she answers.

'Why was that, Vicar?'

He folds the napkin carefully and places it on the table still looking at Iris, seemingly seeking a sign that he should continue.

Iris tucks her blonde hair behind her ear. 'You may as well explain, Reverend. People will hear soon enough. And the police are bound to want to know too.'

No doubt.

'Now for the second act!' says Gil, stabbing at a crisp rasher of bacon on his plate. Dr Pearce glares at him from over his tea cup.

'If you're quite sure, dear.' Reverend Whittle turns a reluctant face to me. 'Miss Caldwell came to me a couple of weeks ago for some advice. Confided that she was in a relationship with a young man, but that her father wouldn't approve of him. When I brought the boxes of donated clothing to Abney on Thursday, there was a discussion about eloping. I feared that was what Miss Caldwell and her beau were planning. So I went round that evening to try and talk her out of it. Only I was too late. She confessed that she and Mr Trent have already married.'

Paul's eyes flash. 'What!'

Oh! I suspected Iris liked Charles, but married! I honestly didn't think he was the type. I hope Jack won't be too disappointed.

'Well aren't you a pair of dark horses,' says Mrs Cherry.

I bet she's already wondering how she can use their romance to boost ticket sales.

Iris sits up straighter. 'I knew my father would never have agreed to my marrying Charles. So, we did it in secret. We caught a train to Scotland on Monday while my father was on trade fair business in Castle Bromwich.'

'They don't read the bans up there,' adds Charles taking his wife's hand, 'and you don't need parental permission even if you're under twenty-one like Iris.'

Reverend Whittle shakes his head disapprovingly.

'My father was due home on Thursday. Charles and I were going to tell him our news. Only Charles was unwell and had to stay at Abney. So I went home alone. Not that it made any difference. You see my father wired to say he was stuck in Birmingham. Still is. All the trains are off because of the snow. And then Reverend Whittle turned up.'

'Did either of you see Dickie Derbyshire when you arrived at the George and Dragon?' I ask.

'I did not,' replies the vicar.

'No,' says Iris. 'But I know where he was planning to go later.'

Gil widens his eyes at me.

I rub my temple, trying to keep up with all these admissions. 'You do?'

'Oh yes. To Delia's cottage.' She sits back with satisfaction.

Mrs Cherry laughs nervously. 'Wherever did you get that idea?'

'From your lips,' continues Iris. 'When we were all getting in our motor cars, I heard you invite Richard to pop over and go through his lines. Everybody knows how you like to take newcomers under your wing. Well, the young male ones.'

'Ha.' Her cheeks flush. 'That was just a casual offer. I certainly didn't pin him down to a date and time.'

'Look at Delia's face,' whispers Gil in my ear. 'Clearly a porky.'

Porky pie. Is that an idiom? Dickie would have known. There are lots of sayings for lies. Tall tales, bending the truth, spinning a yarn. A whopper. Oh, someone said that recently! Who was it?

'Won't be five minutes, Gil,' I say. 'Got to see a man about a dog.'

I dash out of the room and down to the kitchen.

Patience is at the table having a brew. Feet up on one of the chairs. She jumps, almost spilling her tea. Quickly swings them off. I sit down.

'You said something to me the other day,' I say rapidly. 'Wednesday, it would have been.'

'I can't remember what I said five minutes ago, half the time. But I'll do my best. Important, is it?'

'I'm not sure, yet. It wasn't long after we'd arrived from

Harrogate. Mrs Cherry dropped in, unannounced.'

'Oh, yes. She's always doing that.'

'Mrs Watts asked you to set up Buckley so they could rehearse the play in there.'

She nods. 'Thought I'd never get that fire going. Place hadn't been used in weeks, likely longer.'

'You told me you heard Mrs Cherry on the telephone.'

'Did I? Well hard not to. Gob like a foghorn.'

I laugh. 'You said something like, it wasn't a little white lie. It was a whopper.'

'Ha. That's right.'

'Patience, what was it that Mrs Cherry said?'

She puts down her cup. 'Am I in bother for eavesdropping?'

'No. You couldn't help it, could you?'

She rolls her eyes. 'Hardly.'

'Well?'

'She said: "The others mustn't know who you really are. Just act as though we've never met," and then the person on the other end of the line must have said something funny, because she laughed and then she said, "As I said, you scratch my back and I'll scratch yours."'

I fling my arms around Patience.

'Oh!' She exclaims. 'It was important then?'

'It was.'

I race back up the stairs to Mr Watts' study.

'Sir, I'm sorry to interrupt.'

'What is it, Nurse?'

'Thought you'd want to know. I've just learnt that Mrs Cherry knew Richard Buxton was Dickie Derbyshire all along. That she said to act as though they didn't already know each other.'

'That is quite an accusation. You are certain?'

'Patience overheard her on the telephone to him. She said, "you scratch my back and I'll scratch yours".' I grimace.

'Where is Mrs Cherry now?'

'Still in the dining room, sir.'

'Would you keep trying to get through to the police, doctor?'

'Of course, sir.'

Jim marches across the corridor straight into the room.

'Delia. Is it true?'

The room falls silent. Reverend Whittle's poached egg drops off his fork onto his plate.

Mrs Cherry folds her arms over her bust. 'Is what true, Jim?'

'That you knew all along that Richard Buxton was Dickie Derbyshire.'

Her eyes flash to me with pure hatred. 'What lies have you been telling, Nurse?'

'I see from your face that it is true,' growls Jim. 'You brought a reporter into *my* house.'

She lifts her chin. 'I did it for Madge.'

He splutters. 'You mean she knew too?'

My jaw drops.

'No, of course not. I meant that I did it so her play would be a success. I knew how hard she took it when they cancelled *The Claimant*. I thought this was the perfect opportunity to get some decent coverage for *When I Grow Rich*. Maybe even get the attention of a West End producer.'

'I don't think many impresarios read *The Stockport Advertiser*, Delia.'

'No, but Dickie assured me he could get the nationals interested.' She makes a rainbow with her hand. 'A behind the scenes feature. Of course, to really tempt them, I had to get Agatha involved in the rehearsals. That's why I suggested she act as prompt.'

'You were willing to expose my family's private business with all and sundry for a bit of publicity!'

'I had nothing to do with his death, though. I swear. You've got to believe me.' Mrs Cherry looks frantically round the room.

'Not nice being in the dock, so to speak, is it?' says Paul.

Suddenly an idea seems to seize her. She grabs Dr Pearce's wrist. 'The drug fiend. The one who attacked you! He must have murdered Dickie.'

Dr Pearce pales. 'I'm afraid that's impossible, Delia.'

I've never seen her like this. She has lost all control.

'It must be. Please! Tell them.'

Dr Pearce shakes his head. 'I wasn't attacked by a drug fiend. I was attacked by Dickie Derbyshire.'

A gasp goes round the room.

Mrs Cherry releases her grip. She seems to shrink in front of me. She slumps onto the table.

Dr Pearce stands. 'I'll fetch a sedative. I have some in my doctor's bag upstairs.'

'Not before you've explained yourself,' Jim says.

Dr Pearce sighs. 'When I left here on Thursday, I walked home along Newlands Road. As I reached the railway bridge, I noticed a motor car parked up. A blue Morris. Rather bashed about. The driver was asleep. He was an unkempt looking fellow with a strange slick of grease in his hair. I tapped on the window. Said: "This is private property. What are you doing here?"

'He wound down the window. Flashed a press card at me. "Got an appointment with Colonel Christie. Who are you? Friend of the family?" Then he clocked my doctor's bag. His face lit up like a Christmas tree. He jumps out of the car all excited. "You were at the Hydro Hotel. Dr Pearce, that's it, isn't it? Been to see Mrs Christie, have you? Or was it her nurse you were visiting?" He gives me this sly grin. Said: "I bet she gets your temperature rising." I saw red and socked him.'

I cover my face. 'Oh God.'

'That was doubly idiotic because though he was a weedy looking thing, Dickie Derbyshire had the advantage of youth. He shoved me to the ground. I snatched at his shoes and ankles, trying to bring him down too, and, well, it's all a bit unclear after that.' He touches the back of his head. 'I must have caught it on the edge of his car door.

'When I came round, I was lying in the back of his motor car. There was no sign of Dickie Derbyshire. He must have panicked. Perhaps he thought I was dead. I don't know. I'd bled like a stuck pig. Well, you know how head injuries can be.

'My doctor's bag was still by the Morris . . . I cleaned myself up best I could with some bandages. I thought I was all right, but I must have collapsed when I went into my consulting room. The change in temperature, I expect.

'I shall tell the police, of course. Humiliating though it is. I'd better get dressed.'

He goes out.

'Well, I never,' says Mrs Cherry.

My mind swirls as I try to absorb everything. Flaming hell. It must have been Dr Pearce that Colin saw, not Dickie. That's why he was acting a bit strangely when Agatha brought him in. He must have recognised him. What was it he said again? 'Someone whacked you on the head. You were knocked out.'

And then I remember what Colin said this morning. How he was looking for a pica pica. That Dr Pearce had promised to show him the stuffed one downstairs.

Everyone's conversation is just background buzz as an image of Dr Pearce's diary flashes in my mind. All the birds he jotted down. I can't remember them all now. Nuthatch? Woodpecker? Jay, of course. But there's one that I'm absolutely sure of.

Magpie.

I've seen the one downstairs that Dr Pearce said he'd show Colin. At its nest. Something shiny in its beak. The thief.

Bloody hell. What if 'magpie' was code too?

THIRTY-SIX

I RUSH OUT OF THE ROOM AND UP THE STAIRS TO HIS ROOM. 'I've worked out you've been meeting Ellen,' I blurt.

He calmly unclips his doctor's bag. 'What on earth do you mean?'

'I've got your diary, Robert. I remembered how you like to compare people to birds. I'm the jay. At Harrogate, you said Mrs Christie was like a tawny owl. Ellen's the magpie. Isn't she? You nicknamed her that, because you know about the thefts at Abney.'

'I can explain.' He puts his bag on the bed and sits.

'Go on then.' I pull up a chair.

'Ellen came to see me after Mr and Mrs Watts let her go. She insisted she hadn't taken my pen. That it was someone else at the house.'

'You believed her?'

'I wanted to. She seems a good girl. Dotes on her nain. On the other hand, I knew money was tight. I could see Ellen being tempted by shiny, pretty things. And when I mentioned, anonymously, an interesting case to Dr Argyle, he said sometimes stealing is a compulsion. Kleptomania.'

'You gave her a job.'

'Yes. Just a few hours cleaning now and again. That's most of the appointments you saw in my diary. I told myself it was altruism. With no wage coming in, I knew Mrs Griffiths and Ellen would soon be in dire straits. But I must also admit I was curious. I thought if stealing was a compulsion, things would soon go missing at the surgery.'

'And did they?'

'No.'

I breathe out heavily. 'Did you know Dickie Derbyshire was trying to help her prove her innocence?'

He holds my gaze. 'Not until Thursday night. After Dickie attacked me, and I woke in the back of his motor car, I really didn't feel well. I'd mopped the blood up a bit with bandages, as I told you, but it hadn't stemmed the flow. I was a bit frightened, to be honest. Thought I'd best return to Abney. Get proper medical attention from you.

'I hadn't gone very far when I saw Ellen coming towards me. She was in her old uniform. At that point, I was suddenly really woozy. I must have swayed. Ellen caught me and realised I was bleeding. She took off her apron and held it to the wound.'

So that explains the blood-soaked maid Colin saw. The blood wasn't Dickie's, it was Dr Pearce's.

'I was a bit out of it, so she didn't tell me all the details. Just said they were going to use Dickie's silver cigarette case as bait to trap the real thief.'

I remember how as Richard, Dickie kept offering everyone a cigarette. Now I know why.

Dr Pearce takes a bottle of Mellotal out of his doctor bag, and

I follow him in a daze back to the dining room. I hover by the sideboard while he fills a glass with water and mixes the powder into it.

'Here you are, Delia.'

She swallows it down.

I start filling a plate.

Gil comes over to me. 'You look like you've lost a shilling and found sixpence.'

'I'm going to take the constable some breakfast. He must have had a rough night of it.' I think it's time I told him what I know. I put another plate over the top of the bacon and scrambled eggs.

'Let me carry that,' says Gil taking the plate from me. 'Better take these too.' He picks up a knife and fork.

He doesn't say to keep me safe, but I know that's what he means. The killer might not have an axe anymore but there's lots of ways to murder, and Abney has more weapons than most homes. I'm not sure cutlery offers much of a defence.

Gil and I go out of the terrace door and down the steps.

We're only a little way across the patio when someone calls for us to wait. We turn to see Jim Watts.

He catches us up. 'You taking that to the constable?'

I nod.

'I've just got off the phone. The detective inspector is still stuck in Stockport. The roads are impassable. I'd better let the constable know.'

With each step we sink into the deep snow. I clamp the plates tightly together. I'm not sure how hot it's going to be when we get there.

The door to the old chapel is wedged open just enough for someone to squeeze inside. The snow stopping it from being widened any further despite Gil's best efforts.

'Constable,' I call, stepping inside. 'We brought you some breakfast.'

Three pews have been pushed together as a makeshift bed against one wall. His helmet sat on a grey blanket.

There's a slight aroma of coffee in the air.

'He must be in the kitchen.'

I hand the plates to Gil and pull open the door.

Bonzo is lying lifeless on the floor. His face contorted. His left hand at his throat. There's an empty coupe in the other.

I stumble back into Gil, who drops the plates. China shatters. Scrambled egg goes everywhere.

'Is he . . .'

'Yes.' I steady myself. Tread carefully over the broken crockery and bacon. Crouch over the constable's body. Not sure what I should be looking for. 'I think he was poisoned.'

'I'll fetch Dr Argyle,' says Jim. His face white.

'He went for a walk around the grounds,' I reply. 'Dr Pearce is in the dining room, but I think it best he stays in the warm while he's been unwell.'

And out of my way.

'I'll ring the police station again. They'll have to try harder to get a senior officer to us now.' He hurries out.

'Strychnine?' I ponder. I remember Agatha's words. 'There's a clue to the killer there.'

Dr Argyle sends Gil and I back to the house while he examines Bonzo's body. Mr Watts asks us not to say anything to the others for now.

'Bloody hell,' says Gil as we leave the chapel. 'That's two dead men now.'

'It's like some horrid nightmare . . . first Dickie felled by poleaxe and now a poisoning.'

'In the champagne,' says Gil. 'I noticed the coupe.'

'It's the same methods the killer uses in *When I Grow Rich*. Someone's using the script as a murderer's manual.'

We go back into the dining room without another word. Both lost in our thoughts.

Iris and Charles are sat together chatting happily one side of the table. Mrs Cherry and Dr Pearce are on the other. She's leaning heavily on his shoulder. The sedative's clearly taken effect.

'I must look a mess,' she drawls.

'Frightful,' spits Paul, who stands by one of the bookcases.

'I want to see. Where's my carpet bag?'

'You can use my compact, Delia.' Iris reaches under her chair and scoops up her clutch bag and opens it. Frowns. 'Oh. It's not here.'

'Let me look, darling.'

She passes the bag to Charles.

He checks inside. 'Perhaps you left it in your bedroom.'

'I suppose I must have.'

Mrs Cherry tips suddenly and almost slides off her seat. 'I know I have my carpet bag here somewhere. A ha! She pops back up again. 'Ta dah!' She waves it like a flag. Starts rifling through, pulling out all sorts. A large purse. A script. A newspaper. She holds a round metal compact aloft. She snaps it open and peers into the glass. Then moans.

Charles picks up the newspaper. 'Is that the article you were talking about earlier?'

My stomach flips.

'What? Oh, yes,' she wafts an arm. Uninterested.

'Listen to this . . . "ASYLUM TRAGEDY LINK TO CHRISTIE DOCTOR – exclusive. The doctor now treating author Agatha Christie at her sister's Cheadle estate was once embroiled in a shocking killing. Dr Callum Argyle was appointed as part of a team overseeing the commissioning of Winwick Asylum as the Lord Derby War Hospital.

'All asylum patients were set to be evacuated in 1915. But tragedy struck the day before a block of imbecile boys was set to be transferred.

'One inmate, aged fifteen, was discovered trying to escape with the help of a ward nurse." There's a photograph from the inquest.' He peers closer then looks up at me.

I put my hand to my face. Ashamed.

'My God. That's you, isn't it, Jane?'

Charles turns the newspaper round, but Mrs Cherry suddenly revived snatches it from him. 'Let me see. It is! I mean, you're older now, but people don't change that much in ten years . . . Wait, there's more on the inside. I didn't get that far before.' She turns the page.

I want her to stop. But there's no point wasting even breath.

'Nurse Jane Morrow, who was on duty during the fracas, was

called to give evidence at the inquest, but she insisted she had no recollection of the events despite the fact it was later discovered she was in fact related to the boy who tried to escape.'

'Bloody hell! You've been asking us all these questions when all along you've been lying about who you are. Goodbetter isn't even your real name!' she scoffs.

There's no denying it. Not when it's all there in black and white. I just have to try and explain . . . 'Goodbetter is my mother's maiden name – well, Goodbeiter. I anglicised and adopted it after the inquest. No one was going to hire a nurse whose name had been all over the papers.'

'And who would blame them,' jabs Mrs Cherry.

'Let her speak,' says Gil.

I look gratefully at him. But even he looks unsure of me now.

'I saw how people reacted to me afterwards. How they judged me. The whispering. Crossing the street when I approached. The reporters begging me to tell all.'

Gil's face softens a little. Maybe I can make them understand? 'When I refused, they went scurrying like rats to former friends and neighbours. Desperately trying to dig up more dirt. Could it be that madness ran in the family? Did they think it would be better if I was locked away in an asylum too.'

'And do you remember what happened?'

I turn in surprise at the new voice.

Agatha's. She's been listening all along.

'Well, do you, Jane?'

I close my eyes. 'I will never forget.'

'Would you all mind leaving us alone,' says Agatha. 'I suggest you go to the boys' room and practise your lines.'

They trail out. Their eyes on me until the last moment.

Agatha pulls out a couple of chairs and places them by the window.

And then she waits.

All this time I've been desperate to keep my story a secret. Terrified someone would find it out. Now I realise what I feared most is actually what I need most. A chance to explain. A chance to admit my wrongs.

So, I begin.

'There were eighteen years between me and my brother. He was a late surprise for my ma, especially as my pa had died four months before David was born. Ma and I knew early on that David was different. He didn't want to play. Struggled with his letters. And when he was frustrated, he'd flare up. Ma took him to see a doctor in Manchester. She came home in floods of tears. He'd said David was developmentally abnormal and mentally deficient.' I snatch a breath. 'Ma and I did our best to raise him, taking in laundry, but then when David was eight, Ma got sick. Cancer. After she passed, I tried to convince the authorities that I could manage on my own. But they said he needed special care. He'd live with about sixty "imbecile" boys in a newly built block attached to Winwick Asylum.'

'Oh, Jane. I'm so sorry.'

'I was all alone. I needed to find a job. Somewhere to live. The solution seemed obvious. I applied for a job as a nurse there.' I take a deep breath. 'Morrow was a common enough name, and no one noticed the family resemblance. When you're a nurse it's rare for someone to see past the uniform.

'I had to go through the usual training, but eventually I was able to ask to be assigned to the boys' block. David was thrilled to see me. But a lot of the boys are demonstrative, trying to hug you or hold your hand. I told David we were playing a new game. He couldn't call me "Jane" anymore, only "Nurse". He always took rules very seriously, and he never slipped up. I was able to watch him grow into a young man. He was settled at Winwick and I was too.

'But seven years later, in 1915, our world was turned upside down. Matron called me into her office and told me the asylum was going to be turned into a war hospital. That all the patients were to be sent to other asylums. Some to Lancaster, some much further away. Staff were likely to stay at Winwick.'

She takes my hand. 'Go on.'

'Then Dr Argyle came on a precursory visit to plan the takeover. I pleaded with him to at least let the boys stay, but he said the decision for complete evacuation had already been made. There could be no exceptions.' I squeeze my thumb.

'I couldn't sleep for worrying what would become of David. He thrived on routine. I knew being moved to a new place would terrify him, especially when I couldn't go with him.

'It was on my mind all the time. I couldn't concentrate on my work and had been reprimanded several times. One more mistake and I'd lose my job. I had to act and quick.

'There seemed only one option. I had to leave with David. Nothing dramatic. No smashing a window and climbing over fences. I simply took one of the male orderly's white jackets from the laundry. Went to the ward. Told David to go into the toilet and put it on. Said we were going for a walk. One I knew would take us away from Winwick forever.

'Only when David came out, another boy noticed my brother was wearing the uniform. He started shouting. "That's not yours! That's not yours!"

'I tried to calm him, but he was too wound up. He was snatching at David's sleeve. Trying to get him to take off the jacket.

'David pushed him. He stumbled back.

'The boy shouted for matron.

'I panicked. This was my only chance to rescue David. I grabbed his hand. Told him to run.

'But David went rigid. He said, "My friend. I hurt my friend."

'I said his friend was fine. Tugged on his arm. Made him run.

'Only now matron was in the doorway. Blocking our exit. The younger boys were crying.

'"What's going on, nurse?" she demanded. "Why all the commotion?"

'I told her to let us pass. But as I tried to push round Matron, she wrenched David from me, pushed me aside and screamed. 'Help!'

'I pleaded for her to let my brother go.

'She looked at me aghast.

'Two older boys started a chant. "Let him go. Let him go."

'Soon they were all chanting.

'"Stop that noise!" shouted Matron. "Stop!" She tightened her grip on David.

'David's friend ran towards her.

'She shouted for him to get back. But he didn't.

'He screamed. "Let him go!"

And when she didn't, he raised up his arm and brought it down hard on her head.

'Matron just sort of . . . slid to the floor. Her skull thudded against the ground.'

I put my face in my hands. 'She was dead.'

Neither of us speak for a minute.

'And afterwards, Jane. What happened to David?'

'He was sent to Lancaster Asylum. I wrote asking to see him, but they refused. He needed time to adjust . . . Three weeks later, David and another two boys took ill with influenza. I only found out when they wrote to tell me he'd died.' A coldness fills my chest as it does every time I think of that letter. 'I should have been with him.'

I crumple in on myself. Agatha wraps her arms around me.

THIRTY-SEVEN

'FEELING BETTER?' ASKS AGATHA. SHE OFFERS ME A GLASS OF water. 'It's like a weight's been lifted, isn't it?'

'Yes. I hate to admit it, but Dr Argyle was right. Bottling everything up is not good. Though I'm not letting him hypnotise me,' I add with a smile.

'And with honesty in mind, I hope at least you will tell me what on earth has been going on these last few days. At first, I thought it was everyone talking about me behind my back, but it's not just that. Is it?'

'Perhaps you should ask your sister.'

'I'm asking you.'

I take a deep breath, and I tell her everything.

By the time I've finished, she just gapes at me.

'Two murders! Here at Abney!'

'We were trying to shield you from it all. You haven't been well.'

'So you let me carry on wandering around not knowing there's a killer on the loose. And that's not the worst of it!'

'It's not?'

'Of course not! It's the fact no one asked me to work out who the murderer is! I write detective novels, for goodness' sake!'

I almost point out that they're made up, but think better of it.

Agatha paces back and to. 'Well, there are lots of potential solutions to who the killer is – or killers.'

'There are?'

'Yes. Take Charles, for example. He may only have been faking his upset stomach. Perhaps Dickie saw him steal his cigarette case and he knew he'd have to kill him to stop his reputation being ruined. Or perhaps the upset stomach was genuine, and Charles came back from one of his trips to the lavatory and saw Dickie searching his room. Only Dickie didn't realise. He lures him to the old chapel – on the pretence of a confession – probably tried to blackmail him into silence. And then whacks him with the axe.'

'I suppose that would work. But I still can't see Charles stealing his own wife's compact. I'm not convinced he is the thief.'

'He might not be. He might just have wanted his own back on Dickie for putting senna in his coffee – he would have remembered he was the one to give him the drink.'

'And killed him with an axe in retribution? No, Agatha. That is too far-fetched.'

'I suppose. So perhaps Iris is the thief. She hides her own compact as a bluff – so she isn't suspected. She stole Dickie's cigarette case. Then later, when she came back to Abney, she snuck into Charles's room to see how he was feeling. She catches Dickie searching the room looking for the cigarette case. Panics that when he doesn't find it, he'll realise somebody else is the thief. Iris doesn't want Charles and her father finding out she's a thief. She tells Dickie she has some evidence. Tells him she'll bring it to him at the old chapel – and kills him.'

'So, now you don't think the killer is Charles?'

'No. Though, in one of my books, once someone's been ruled out, I like to twist it so they're back in the frame.'

'You're giving me a headache.'

'What if the thefts are a red herring? Dickie found out a secret about one of us. Charles and Paul could be a secret couple. Charles marries Iris for her money and is planning to kill her . . . Or what if Mrs Cherry had murdered the major.' She pales. 'Oh. Punkie! She could have disguised herself as a maid – as Ellen – and killed Dickie because he kept writing stories about me.'

'Agatha! Stop. You're really not helping. I can't think.'

I exhale deeply. 'Don't real life murders tend to be simple? I think the murderer is the thief – and one of the MADS. Because Paul's tie pin was stolen at the cast party and now Iris's Cartier compact. What a shame neither of us was there. We might have seen something suspicious. Wait . . . I've an idea. What about your sister's press cuttings book? Won't there be newspaper articles from that night in it? Dickie was there – I bet there was a photographer too.'

'Even if there wasn't, I bet Jim took some.'

'Of course. Is it still in the boys' room?'

'I think so.'

We race down the corridor.

'Here it is,' says Agatha, picking it up from one of the chairs.

We drop to our knees, and she starts flicking through the pages until she finds what we're looking for. A press cutting from *The Advertiser*.

'MADS CELEBRATE NEW SEASON by Dickie Derbyshire.

'Members of the Manchester Amateur Dramatic Society marked curtain up on their latest show with a fabulous cast party hosted at Abney Hall on Friday night.'

There's nothing of any interest in the article itself, but the accompanying photograph is a posed one in the drawing room. The MADS – Mrs Cherry, Charles, Iris and Paul. Reverend Whittle, Dr Pearce, Madge and Jim and his father.

I study the picture closely. 'I think Mr Ramsbury's wearing the tie clip,' I say.

Agatha leans in. 'I agree.'

I turn the page. There are several more candid photographs. These ones taken by Jim, I presume.

Iris and Charles together, her hand on his arm. Patience and Ellen by the drinks table. Dr Pearce talking to old Mr Watts. Ah, a close up of Paul and Mrs Cherry chatting. Both holding champagne coupes. The tie clip is much clearer in this image. I show it to Agatha.

'So, he was definitely wearing it at the party,' she says.

'Yes. And Ellen admitted she saw and admired the tie clip in Mr Ramsbury's room. But when Mr Ramsbury awoke, he found the box was empty.'

'The thief must have snuck into his room while he was sleeping. Risky but possible. Of course, they could have slipped a sedative in his drink to ensure he wasn't accidently roused.'

'Course, Mr Ramsbury is well known as a hard drinker. I'm not sure he would have needed any help going to sleep,' I add.

'You know what we need to do next,' says Agatha. 'We need to examine the scene of the crime.'

⟷

We've thrown on a couple of old men's overcoats from one of the chests and made our way to the old chapel. I knock on the church-like wooden door, still clutching Madge's press cuttings book, and enter.

'Thomas?'

'Jane.' He whips off his cap. 'Mrs Christie.'

'We thought we'd take over for a bit,' I say. 'So you can nip to the loo and get a hot drink. Would you check on Ellen, please. I left Colin with her. But I think it best someone else watch over her, given there's been another death.'

'Course, love.'

We examine Dickie's body first.

'The cold will make it harder to determine time of death,' says Agatha. 'You said the constable thought he was killed sometime yesterday. That doesn't help narrow down the list of suspects, does it.'

'We need to go over Dickie's movements. We know he was here on Wednesday, pretending to be Richard Buxton at rehearsals – making a show of offering round his cigarettes so that Charles Trent would see the case and be tempted to steal it. Dickie notes that Charles is a coffee drinker.

'Thursday morning, Ellen is seen in the hall by Patience and Cook. Cook saw Ellen talking to a man at the servants' entrance and mistook her for Kitty. I think we can assume that man was Dickie. She heard Ellen say meeting at the old house was safer. But she could have said boathouse. We know that's where Ellen was meeting Dickie yesterday when she ended up in the water.'

'Then Archie holds his press conference – which went badly.' Agatha smiles to herself. 'Dickie must have been there, because he offered him an exclusive interview.'

'At 5 p.m.' I nod. 'Dickie goes to his car and disguises himself as Richard Buxton using macassar oil, glasses and a cushion.

'I was late to rehearsal, but when I got to the old chapel Dickie was passing out drinks from a tray. He must have stirred the senna powder Ellen took from her nain's into Charles's coffee to upset his stomach. Then he repeated his generosity with his cigarettes.

'After rehearsal he drives his car out of the lodge gates, goes into Cheadle village and takes the back road. But he hits a patch of ice and has to abandon his car by the railway bridge. He's too early for the interview and likely tired from trying to be two people – writing news articles, learning lines. He closes his eyes for a few moments rest – only for Dr Pearce to stumble upon him. They get into a tussle. Dickie is now going to be late. He goes off. Dr Pearce is bleeding, feeling woozy and lies down in the back of the car. Where Colin sees him and thinks he's dead.'

'Archie is annoyed that Dickie is late and cancels the interview. Then what?' asks Agatha.

'He goes to the George and Dragon where he's arranged to meet Paul Ramsbury, just earlier than planned. Tries to get another story for the paper – and learns about the S&J/Caldwells deal.

'He might have gone on to practice lines with Mrs Cherry. But I think he was back here at seven-thirty because I overheard a man and a woman talking out on the terrace. He said something like "I told you it would work." The bait had been taken. And she said something about being careful not to be seen. I think Ellen let him into the hall so he could search Charles's room.'

'But they didn't find it – because Charles isn't the thief. So what then?'

'They need a new plan. Dickie can't go back to being Richard because he fears his cover's blown. We know he didn't go back to work or his flat. I think he decided to hide out. Either in the hall or here in the old chapel. That's our gap up to his body being found by Paul Ramsbury on Saturday.'

Agatha drapes the blanket back over Dickie Derbyshire and we move on to the kitchen.

I focus on the coupe in the constable's hand. Something's niggling me about that glass.

'There's a scene in your sister's play,' I say, 'where Alice is poisoned during the toast.'

'Strychnine in the Champagne. I remember. But look at the jaw. Strychnine causes *risus sardonicus.* Spasm of the facial muscles so they form a painful grimace and frothing at the mouth. That's not the case here.'

'So the glass might have been deliberately put there, like the candle in Dickie's hand, as a theatrical touch. To forge a link to your sister's play. The killer wants to point the finger of suspicion at the MADS. That seems to suggest it's not one of them, unless it's a double bluff.'

My eyes flick round the kitchen. The lid's been left off the Tivoli biscuits. Empty. Bonzo must have polished them off. No sign of a Champagne bottle.

I think of Reverend Whittle and his taste for sherry. My preference for brandy. Frown. 'And I can't picture Bonzo drinking Champagne. Especially two-day old flat Champagne.'

'And not while he was on duty,' agrees Agatha.

'No. He wasn't the type. Not even if he was cold. But when Gil and I were here earlier I smelt coffee. Only Richard used the last of Mrs Griffith's coffee during Thursday's rehearsal when he spiked Charles's drink with senna. Someone must have brought a fresh tin over since then. Ellen?'

I take out the pair of ladies evening gloves we also borrowed from the costume's chest. Put them on and open the cupboard.

'I was right.' I hold the tin under my arm and ease off the lid with the end of a teaspoon.

Agatha takes a cup from the side, and I shake the brown powder into it. 'It smells like ordinary ground coffee,' she says.

'Bonzo said it took strength to wield the axe. But if Dickie was sedated it would have been much easier to slice the axe through the back of his neck.'

'There'd be lots of blood spray either way,' says Agatha. 'What? Sorry, but it's true.'

We peer at the coffee. It's impossible to tell if a sedative has been crushed and added to it just by looking at it.

'A lab would be able to tell,' says Agatha. 'The . . . zwikker test would detect barbiturates.'

'Agatha, what happened to the Mellotal Dr Pearce gave you? Did you throw it away?'

'No. I presumed you did. Oh! You mean the killer has been in my room and took it. How awful!'

I stare at the coffee. 'Oh God. That's why Ellen's been so sleepy. There was coffee by her bedside. Left by the killer . . .'

'Who, Jane? Who?'

THIRTY-EIGHT

'PATIENCE? YOU'RE SURE?' AGATHA LOOKS BEMUSED.

'Absolutely. She's the thief and the murderer. I'm sure of it. But there isn't time to explain.'

We run from the chapel to Thomas's cottage. My ankle throbbing again.

We're both breathless as I throw open the door. Ellen is coming down the stairs. She's holding Colin's binoculars.

I swear under my breath with relief. 'You didn't drink the coffee?'

'I told you it was 'orrible. Colin was mithering about trying it after you'd gone, so I tipped it out of the window. I thought you were him, actually. Come back for his field glasses. He was going on about wanting to see some stuffed bird in the hall.' She shrugs. 'I told him to find Patience. She'll show him where the magpie is.'

My heart thuds. 'Agatha, stay with Ellen. I'm going after Colin.'

I dash downstairs and out onto Newlands Road and into the hall via the side entrance.

I can hear Colin chatting happily somewhere on the cross corridor. My heart eases a little. As I turn onto it, I see he's standing with Patience facing one of the taxidermy cases.

'Dr Pearce says magpies like to steal things. Anything shiny they take back to their nest.'

'Is that right? I didn't realise they had such pretty feathers. I thought they were just black and white.'

I inch nearer.

'They are iri . . . iridescent,' he replies proudly. 'You can see purple and blue and green.'

'Come here, Colin.' I try to keep my voice light but I can hear it shake slightly with anxiety.

'I haven't done owt wrong. I was just looking.'

'I know.'

'Oh, hello, Nurse,' says Patience, smiling.

For a moment I wonder if I can be wrong. How can this seemingly gentle old parlourmaid be a killer. But all the evidence tells me it has to be her.

'Colin.' My voice is sharper than I mean it to be.

Something in Patience's expression changes for just a second. Fear? No, something more predatory.

She hooks her arm through Colin's. 'Tell me more about magpies. I didn't realise they were so fascinating.'

'Let him go.'

His eyes widen. That is fear. He knows something is wrong. Just not what. I can see he's not sure who to trust.

'That's not the only magpie at Abney Hall,' I say.

His shoulders relax. 'Isn't it?'

'No. There's a bigger one. Want me to show you?'

Patience's arm remains locked.

'You were right about magpies being thieves. Only the thief at Abney Hall isn't a bird – it's Patience.'

His eyes shoot to her face. Her softness falls away and I see the real Patience. Cold and cruel.

Colin tries to pull free.

She squeezes his arm tighter.

'I thought Kitty was unfair when she complained about you. Said your scattiness was a cover for your laziness. But she was telling the truth. You've been pretending to be confused when actually, you're really clever. You play a role better than any of the MADS.

'You're stronger than I would have credited too. All those years of manual labour. Strong enough to help Thomas bring in the Christmas tree. To swing an axe as though it was a feather duster. Though you took no chances there – you drugged Dickie with Mellodal in his coffee first.'

Colin yanks his arm, trying to pull free.

'Keep still, Colin. Patience doesn't want to hurt you.'

She tilts her head to one side like a bird. She's a starling. Willing to kill to get what she wants.

'Parlourmaids are a lot like nurses,' I say. 'No one really takes notice of us. You can go where you like. Always seemingly occupied with one chore or another. Who would question you taking a tin of coffee down to the old chapel? They'd run out, maybe Mrs Watts even asked you to take it. I haven't had chance to ask her yet. Only you knew Dickie was there, didn't you? That's something else Kitty told me that I didn't heed at the time. You were both meant to set up the afternoon tea for Colonel Christie's interview with Dickie Derbyshire, but she said you were more interested in earwigging. That's when you saw the reporter and realised he was pretending to be Richard Buxton. You already knew Ellen's comings and goings. Did they tell you their plan to trap the thief or did you work it out?'

For a moment I think she won't answer. But she can't resist telling her story. Having someone listen to her cleverness.

She looks smug. 'They told me. Fools. They thought they could trust me. They never suspected that I was the thief. When they didn't find the cigarette case in Mr Trent's room, I told them I'd help look for it. That they should both stay away from Abney. I'd already started letting slip that I'd seen Ellen here. Planted that apron in the costume chest to make sure she'd look guilty – not me. She had to look after her nain anyway, so it made sense for her to go home. But Dickie was working on other stories, so he wanted to stay in the old chapel. The net was tightening. I had no choice but to get rid of them.'

'You sent a telegram to Ellen to lure her to the boathouse. You wanted it to look like Dickie killed her. Only your plan failed – I found her just in time. You offered to look after her so you could finish the job – this morning you went to the cottage with coffee for her. Only she didn't drink it.

'Dickie wasn't so lucky. You decided to kill him next – but you needed to point the finger of suspicion elsewhere again. You'd seen Mrs Watts's script when I left it in the kitchen – and you'd seen Sir Arthur. If you could recreate the murder scene the police would think one of the MADs was the killer.

'When the constable came looking for him on Saturday, you

realised you'd have to kill the reporter without him in the frame for the attack on Ellen. The kind, helpful old maid turns up with a new tin of coffee. Even offers to make it for him.'

'You have no proof.'

'No, but I've a good idea where I'll find it. When I came back into the hall after Mr Ramsbury found Dickie's body, you were scrubbing the porch tiles. Titch was all over you – because she could smell his blood on you. You had your skirts tucked up while you worked, they were wet from your cleaning. I didn't notice any blood. But I did notice you ran a hand over your head. You always wear that old-fashioned mob cap but you can't have been wearing it then or I wouldn't have noticed the grey steaks in your hair. When you swung that axe there would have been blood spray. You could wipe your face, but not that mob cap. You had to hide it. And I think you used the same place I did when I wanted to hide some newspaper spills from Mrs Christie. I think you dropped it in the suit of armour's visor.'

Her pupils dilate. She's worried. I know I'm right.

I suddenly point up the corridor. 'Colin! *Pica pica.*'

Patience turns.

I throw my hand into a salute then jerk my elbow.

Colin copies. Jabs his into her stomach.

Patience moans and clutches her middle. 'You little delinquent! You'll pay for that!'

'Run!'

He sprints down the corridor shouting for help.

Patience is on his heels. Fury giving her speed I wouldn't expect.

But I am faster. I lunge at her back. Bringing her down. Just as they taught me at the asylum.

↔

I'm sitting on the front steps with Titch, massaging her long ears. A shadow falls over me. Agatha holds out a cup and saucer. 'I didn't think you'd want coffee.'

I smile and take the tea. 'Not for a while.'

She sits beside me. 'You know, I think you've earnt entry to a very select group – the Faithful Old Dogs.'

'The what?'

'It's a bit like a Band of Brothers. Those who have shown loyalty to me. My wire-haired terrier, Peter, is the most important member. My secretary, Carlo, and now you.'

'Thank you. Though I'm not sure about the old bit.'

She laughs.

I've explained everything to Mr and Mrs Watts. About Patience and David. It's been a lot for them to take in, but they're the resilient type. I can feel that machinations are already in progress. They found all the older stolen items in a small brown suitcase under Patience's bed along with Dickie's cigarette case and Iris's compact. The mob cap was exactly where I said it would be, in the bottom of Sir Arthur along with a pair of gloves.

They acted fast after that. A phone call to Cheadle Royal and another to the police station. Though we're still waiting on that inspector.

Dr Argyle has offered to personally transport Patience to the hospital as soon as the weather eases. He says her case sounds a most fascinating one.

'How is Ellen?' I ask.

'She's fine. Dr Pearce is looking after her.'

'Good. And Colin's definitely all right too?'

'He's in his element. Telling everyone how he helped trap the murderous thief and driving Kitty crackers.'

'Please, no. One loopy parlourmaid is quite enough.'

'There's one part I still don't understand,' says Agatha. 'How did you know Patience was the thief?'

'It was something Ellen's nain said to me. She said after the tie clip went missing Mr Ramsbury had Patience on her hands and knees looking for it. When she didn't find it, he accused Ellen of stealing it.

'In your books, the detective always questions a statement of fact.'

Agatha nods, her eyes twinkling. 'Go on, Jane.'

'The morning after the party, when Mr Ramsbury made Patience look for the tie clip everyone assumed it had already been stolen at that point. But what if that wasn't true!

'He was definitely wearing the tie clip at the party – we saw that in the photograph in your sister's newspaper cuttings. We also know that Mr Ramsbury was drunk. He goes back to his room, stumbling about, no doubt. The tie clip is still on his tie. He takes it off, something he does almost without thinking, and puts it back in its box. Only he's clumsy and it actually falls onto the floor.

'The next morning, he makes Patience look for it. She finds it and slips it into her apron pocket.

'When Ellen was accused, Patience just let her take the blame.

She couldn't confess she had the tie clip, because it wasn't the first time she'd taken things that didn't belong to her. Dr Pearce's pen. Mrs Cherry's watch. An expensive travelling clock. Miss Caldwell's compact. Patience stole them all – other things too, no doubt. She was building up a little nest egg.'

'Oh you are clever!' says Agatha, grinning at me. 'Have you ever considered writing detective novels?'

I laugh. 'I think I'll leave that to you!'

EPILOGUE

Three weeks later

THE AUDIENCE APPLAUDS AS THE MADS TAKE THEIR BOWS. I've got a seat on the back row. I nearly didn't come at all, but in the end, I was persuaded. I turn to Colin.

'Did you enjoy it?'

'It were brilliant. Especially the murder.'

There's a tap on my shoulder. Gil.

'I thought it was you, Jane. Came to admire my flats, did you?'

'Some might say the backdrops were the best part,' I reply with a grin.

'But not the most wooden.'

'Ha. Dr Pearce did his best. I mean he has the experience to play Dr Tremayne if not the talent.'

The cast are starting to file into the auditorium. Though that sounds a bit grand for a church hall. Mrs Cherry goes over to meet Dr Pearce. Kisses him on the mouth.

'Urgh,' says Colin.

'Shush. I think they make a lovely couple.'

Charles and Iris are greeted by an older man who has a look of

Miss Caldwell. Looks like Mr Trent has been welcomed into the fold after all. His charm doesn't usually fail. I just hope the maids have sussed his wandering hands – though perhaps he's stopped all that now he's married. Probably not.

There's a smattering of applause. Mrs Watts is last to come into the room. She looks as pleased as Punch. Agatha and Rosalind give her a hug.

She and Mr Watts put on a magnificent performance at the inquest into Dickie and the constable's death. Told the coroner that their faithful servant, Patience, had been troubled with her memory for some time and that she was prone to making mistakes. When she had taken a tin of coffee as requested down to the old chapel as requested by Mrs Watts, she had taken a bowl of sugar too. Only somehow in her confused state Patience had filled the bowl with sleeping powder not sugar.

Even though the Watts are much respected in Cheadle, I still feared the coroner wouldn't buy their version of events. It was a relief when his verdict agreed both men had accidentally drunk the fatal combination resulting in their accidental deaths. The last thing we all want is for the scandal of a double murder splashed across the newspapers!

'Did you have a nice Christmas?' Gil asks.

'My stomach still hasn't recovered. Cook put on a magnificent feast. Oyster soup, turbot, roast turkey and all the trimmings. Sirloin of beef. Christmas pudding, trifle and mince pies!' I had mine down in the kitchen with Mrs W, Thomas, Kitty and Ellen.

'Just as Christmas should be. Though the company's what matters.'

'It is.' I look down the aisles to where Agatha stands next to her little girl, Rosalind.

She spots me looking and waves.

'How is Mrs Christie?' asks Gil.

'Why don't you ask her yourself? She's coming over.'

Agatha beams as she weaves her way to us.

'Not talking about me, I hope?' she says. A twinkle in her eye.

'I was chatting up, Jane, actually,' says Gil. 'But how are you?'

'I'm a little tired of being asked that question – but I'm much better thank you. Thanks to Jane and Dr Argyle.'

'You've been continuing your therapy sessions in London?' I ask.

'Yes. I like my new doctor – he's recommended I take a holiday. Rosalind and I will be making a trip to the Canary Islands next month.'

'Oh, that sounds lovely. Make sure you send me a postcard!'

Agatha nods. 'And what about you, Jane? What are you up to?'

'Me? Oh, I'm working at Cheadle Royal.'

'You've told that lie before,' says Gil, taking my hand.

I laugh. 'Don't you believe me?'

THE END

AUTHOR'S NOTE

I READ MY FIRST AGATHA CHRISTIE WHEN I WAS ELEVEN YEARS old and was instantly hooked. I went on to read as many of her brilliant books as I could, becoming a devotee of Hercule Poirot.

I also especially enjoyed watching the TV adaptations of the Miss Marple novels starring Joan Hickson with my grandmas, and loved the Peter Ustinov Poirot film adaptations too. As a grown-up I have returned to Agatha's books several times and I have been fortunate to see many of her stage plays too. I am undoubtedly a fan!

I knew a little of Agatha's disappearance in 1926, but I was surprised to learn that after she was found at the Hydro Hotel in Harrogate, she went to stay at her sister's house – near Manchester and Stockport!

The press at the time followed the Watts and Christies back to Abney Hall, Cheadle, where Agatha was examined by two doctors and her amnesia confirmed.

What happened during those wintry days in the run up to Christmas, I wondered.

Here was a gap in history that I thought I might like to reimagine . . .

⟷

Margaret 'Madge' Frary Watts was the older sister of Agatha Christie. She lived with her husband James 'Jim' Watts and their son James 'Jack' Watts at the beautiful Abney Hall.

Madge was a writer like her sister – having written short stories before her marriage, some of which were published in the weekly British magazine *Vanity Fair*. She also wrote a small number of plays, her debut *The Claimant* produced at The Queen's Theatre in London's West End. Another of her scripts was called *Oranges and Lemons* – which the invented *When I Grow Rich* plays homage to. Madge was apparently a member of the Manchester Amateur Dramatics despite my best efforts I have yet to identify which local group this was – the members of *The Secret of Abney Hall's* MADS are entirely fictious.

St Mary's Church in Cheadle is real but my church hall/theatre is invented, as is Reverend Whittle. Likewise, Nurse Jane Goodbetter, and the two doctors who treat Agatha during her seclusion at Abney Hall, though they are inspired by the real medical practitioners who helped her recover.

Winwick Hospital/Asylum, near Warrington, opened in 1901 and cared for many patients including young boys. In May 1915 it was taken over by the War Office and became the Lord Derby War Hospital.

Abney Hall is no longer a family home. The house and contents were sold off in 1958 following Jack Watts's death. It was used as council offices and later restored and used as private offices.

It is not generally open to the public, however the beautiful grounds can be enjoyed, forming the Abney Hall Park.

ACKNOWLEDGEMENTS

AS A WRITER WITH APHANTASIA – NO MIND'S EYE – I FIND it hugely helpful to be able to visit the real-life locations in my books. I owe a huge thank you to the current custodians of Abney Hall, Bruntwood. Thank you especially to Ben Mort, Nina White and Demi Fletcher who responded to my enquiry regarding a potential visit and welcomed me with virtual open arms!

Thank you in particular to Darren Pye who showed me around the inside of the hall and answered my follow-up questions. Abney Hall really is a maze inside, and I was thrilled and somewhat overwhelmed to be shown her many, many rooms and corridors.

I also paid a visit to the former Hydro Hotel in Harrogate, now The Old Swan Hotel, for afternoon tea with my lovely friend Jenny Czerwonka (who has illustrated the covers of my children's books titles). Thank you to the staff on the day who provided us with a delicious menu even though I'd accidentally booked the wrong month!

One of my favourite parts of writing a book is the research.

As well as reading as many biographies about Agatha Christie, her autobiography, novels and pseudonymous books, I also used microfilm facilities at Lancashire Archives, Preston, to study news coverage of her disappearance. Thank you to the staff for assisting me with access to copies of national and local titles.

I also used the Abney Hall newspaper cuttings folders, copies of photographs, plan of the ground floor and auction catalogue from the sale of the house, provided as part of Stockport Libraries local history provision at the brilliant Stockroom and Cheadle Library.

Public libraries are a godsend to authors! I have paid several visits to Eccleston Library, St Helens, to work on this book and Skelmersdale Library to make use of their free access to the British Newspaper Archive.

I am indebted to the staff at Manchester Central Library for allowing me access to the Abney Hall visitor book, inventory and valuation catalogue for Waring and Gillow Ltd for insurance purposes, including interior photographs. As well as online access to census materials relating to the Watts family.

Thank you to Jess Smith, Senior Curator, Creative Arts Archive at John Rylands Research Institute and Library, for guidance on the Basil Dean archive and the staff who assisted my visit (on the wrong day – are you sensing a theme here!) to view the incredible cuttings files relating to *The Claimant.* I was also especially thrilled to see a handwritten letter from Madge Watts to the play's producer Basil Dean inviting him to pay a visit to Abney Hall in 1937.

I am also grateful to Warrington Libraries for access to a

reference copy of *A Place of Safety* by Kenneth Lewis, which chronicles the history of Winwick Hospital/Lord Derby War Hospital. I also found the County Asylums blog and Winwick Hospital Remembered website very helpful.

Thank you to Andrew Frazer at Cheadle Civic Society for assistance with my research and sharing photographs and other materials with me relating to Abney Hall. And to Trevor Evers at Cheadle Civic Society for encouragement and support, and for telling me all about the society's Agatha Christie A Year of Celebration events which I have loved attending.

Thanks also to the British Library, London, for access to a copy of an original copy of the Claimant script held as part of the Lord Chamberlain's plays collection in London, and the staff at Boston Spa who processed my reader's pass.

The Secret of Abney Hall began life as a final project for my MA Creative Writing: Writing and Publishing Fiction at the University of Chester. Thanks to my tutors Dr Ashley Chantler, Dr Peter Blair and Prof Alan Wall for your support and advice. Also to my fellow students for feedback on early chapters – Neil Barlow, Becky Kelly, Isabelle Mason, Emma Skyte, Lee Stevenson and especially my crit partner James Moston.

I would also like to thank Louise Jones for beta reading an early draft and Liz Milne for feedback on early chapters.

A huge thank you to Hazel Holmes, publisher at Fox and Ink Books, for embracing my book and to the whole team there for supporting our crazy plan to try and have *The Secret of Abney Hall* out in time for the 100th anniversary of Agatha's disappearance. I couldn't have got over the finish line without you all. I am especially grateful to Jasmine Dove for her edits right up against the clock. Thank you to Becky Chilcott for typesetting and cover art direction, and freelance designer and illustrator David Wardle for perfecting it. It is gorgeous! Thank you also to Nicki Marshall for proofreading, and Janet Aspey, publicist.

Thank you to Bounce Marketing, especially Louise Corcoran, and all the booksellers, librarians, journalists and bloggers for your ongoing support. Thanks especially to Simply Books, Bramhall, for arranging signed pre-orders of this book.

Hugs to all my family, friends and colleagues who have cheerleaded my books and spurred me on. Your support makes all the difference. Shout out to the Southport Library team who have made me so welcome since I joined them!

Finally, a MASSIVE thanks to my marvellous mum, who has spent SO many hours reading drafts, pointing out typos, missing words, continuity errors, discussing knotty plot issues and always pushing me to email Hazel, finish the next chapter, and to write the next book. I love you!

ABOUT THE AUTHOR

SUSAN BROWNRIGG IS A LANCASHIRE LASS WHO LOVES sharing northern stories. A journalism graduate, she worked for over ten years as a reporter and sub-editor for a series of local newspapers. Susan then switched careers to heritage and wildlife education at a number of visitor attractions, including as a Learning Manager at a museum. She was recently awarded an MA with distinction in Creative Writing by the University of Chester.

When not writing, Susan works part-time as a library assistant. She has published five novels for children including The Gracie Fairshaw Mysteries series which are set in historic Blackpool. *The Secret of Abney Hall* is her debut novel for adults.

Find out more at susanbrownrigg.com

HAVE YOU EVER WONDERED HOW BOOKS ARE MADE?

Fox & Ink Books (formerly UCLan Publishing) is an award-winning independent publisher. Based at the University of Lancashire, this Preston-based publisher teaches MA Publishing students how to become industry professionals using the content and resources from its business; students are included at every stage of the publishing process and credited for the work that they contribute.

The business doesn't just help publishing students though. Fox & Ink Books has supported the employability and real-life work skills for the University's Illustration, Acting, Translation, Animation, Photography, Film & TV students and many more. This is the beauty of books and stories; they fuel many other creative industries! The MA Publishing students are able to get involved from day one with the business and they acquire a behind-the-scenes experience of what it is like to work for a such a reputable independent.

The MA course was awarded a Times Higher Award (2018) for Innovation in the Arts, and the business was awarded Best Newcomer at the Independent Publishing Guild (2019) for the ethos of teaching publishing using a commercial publishing house. As the business continues to grow, so too does the student experience upon entering this dynamic master's course.